SEAN BLACK

LOCKDOWN

Complete and Unabridged

CHARNWOOD
Leicester

First published in Great Britain in 2009 by
Bantam Press
an imprint of
Transworld Publishers, London

First Charnwood Edition
published 2010
by arrangement with
Transworld Publishers
The Random House Group Ltd., London

British Library CIP Data

Black, Sean.
Lockdown.
1. Bodyguards- -New York (State)- -New York- -
Fiction. 2. Suspense fiction.
3. Large type books.
I. Title
823.9′2–dc22

ISBN 978–1–44480–384–6

X000 000 0384374

Published by
F. A. Thorpe (Publishing)
Anstey, Leicestershire

Set by Words & Graphics Ltd.
Anstey, Leicestershire
Printed and bound in Great Britain by
T. J. International Ltd., Padstow, Cornwall

This book is printed on acid-free paper

For Jim and Lorna, whose faith never wavered, and in memory of my grandfather, George Robertson, who sacrificed so much for his country at such a young age.

Prologue

Nobody guards the dead. Once that occurred to Cody, the plan had come together in no time. Drive to the cemetery, dig her up, sling the coffin into the back of the truck, and disappear into the night. Easy. Apart from one tiny hitch.

'Man, this ground is like concrete.'

Cody glanced over at his companion, the moonlight splitting his face in two. 'Quit bitching.'

Usually he liked to work alone. But moving a body was a two-man job. No way round it.

'I ain't bitching. I'm making an observation.'

'Well, observations ain't gonna get this done.'

'Neither's digging. We're gonna need dynamite to get this old witch out of the ground.'

Don was right. They'd picked the worst time of the year. November on the Eastern Seaboard. A bitter winter with the wind coming off a slate grey Atlantic. Freezing the living, as well as the dead.

Spring would have been better. The nights would still have been long, but the ground would have been softer. Thing was, though, they didn't have a choice. Not as far as Cody was concerned.

The way he saw it, the clock was ticking. Every day lives were being lost. Hundreds, maybe even thousands. No one really knew for sure. And these deaths weren't peaceful. Not like the one this woman had experienced: slipping gradually away, the fiery edge of pain dulled by drugs, her loved ones around her to say goodbye.

No, these deaths were torturous and lonely. A final spit in the face to cap a miserable existence.

The anger he felt thinking about it rose up in him. He punched down hard on the lip of the blade with the heel of his right boot, and finally found some purchase. Frosted grass gave way to frozen top soil. He stamped down again. The blade dug in another inch. His breath clouded in the freezing night air as he sucked in oxygen and repeated the process.

A full hour later, Don was the first to hit something solid that wasn't earth. The two men were exhausted, but the clatter of metal meeting wood spurred them on.

Thirty minutes after that they were loading the remains into the back of the truck. Cody made a show of dusting off his gloves as Don pulled down the rear door of the box truck they'd jacked a few hours earlier from a quiet street in Queens.

Don opened the cab door and started to climb in. Halfway up, he stopped and turned back to Cody. 'Well, we did it,' he said.

Cody smirked. 'Are you for real, brother? That was the easy part.'

1

Ryan Lock peered through the floor-to-ceiling windows which fronted the reception area of the Meditech building. Outside, freezing rain was sweeping down Sixth Avenue in sheets, jamming the dozen or so animal rights protestors into a tight knot on the sidewalk opposite.

'Who the hell stages a demonstration on Christmas Eve?' the receptionist asked.

'You mean apart from turkeys?' Lock said, hunching his jacket up around his shoulders, pushing through the revolving doors and stepping out into the near-Arctic weather.

Three months as head of security for America's largest pharmaceutical and biotechnology company had left Lock with little patience for the animal rights people, no matter how earnest their cause.

A fresh gust of wind stung his face. He pulled up the collar of his jacket and scanned the protestors. Front and centre was Gray Stokes, the protestors' de facto leader. In his early fifties, with a vegan's bony frame, Stokes stood with his customary smug expression, a loudhailer in one hand, his other hand resting on the handle of a wheelchair.

In the chair sat Stokes' daughter Janice, a pretty brunette in her mid-twenties, her left leg rendered useless by a rare form of progressive,

3

terminal multiple sclerosis. The placard she held in two red-gloved hands had four words etched on it in thick black capital letters: NOT IN MY NAME.

Lock watched as Stokes raised his loudhailer and began to harangue the half-dozen uniformed cops who were there to ensure good order. Closest to Stokes, one of the city's finest, a portly sergeant by the name of Caffrey, made a show of eating a Big Mac, punctuating each bite with stage-whisper yum-yum noises.

Lock registered Stokes' reaction with interest.

'Hey, pig, you ever wonder what goes into those things?' Stokes yelled at Caffrey. 'Maybe the ALF left some of Grandma in with the rest of the meat back at Mickey D's.'

Anyone who had picked up a copy of the New York Post or flicked on to a news channel during the past six weeks would have gotten the reference. The manager of a Times Square fast food joint had found the disinterred body of seventy-two-year-old Eleanor Van Straten, matriarch of the Meditech corporation, on the sidewalk outside his establishment.

The link between Mrs Van Straten's unscheduled appearance so soon after her funeral and the animal rights movement had been a no-brainer. The next day Lock had been invited to head up the Van Stratens' close protection team.

Lock watched Caffrey slipping the last of his burger back into its Styrofoam container and turned his attention back to Stokes.

'So how come, if God didn't want us to eat

4

cows, he made them out of meat?' Caffrey taunted.

The comeback prompted a few snickers from the other cops, and Stokes to step out from behind the barrier and off the sidewalk.

'That's right, buddy, you keep coming,' Caffrey yelled. 'You can cool your heels in Rikers for a few hours. Plenty of animals there for you to hang with.'

Lock watched as Stokes eye-balled Caffrey, calculating his next move. The protestors saw arrest as a badge of honour. Lock saw it as a good way to get the company on the news for all the wrong reasons. Speed-walking towards the barrier, Lock's right hand dropped to the Sig 9mm tucked into his holster. The gesture didn't go unnoticed by the protestors. Meekly, Stokes stepped back behind the barrier.

Lock checked his watch again. Zero eight fifty. If he was running to schedule, Nicholas Van Straten, Eleanor's widower, and the company's new CEO, would be here shortly. Lock's hand went up to his collar and he pressed down the talk button of his radio. 'All mobile units from Lock.'

Lock's earpiece crackled with static, then cleared.

A moment later, the voice of Lock's second-in-command, Ty Johnson, came back, calm and in control. 'Go ahead, Ryan.'

'You got an ETA for me?'

'Be with you in about two. What kind of reception we got?'

'Usual sidewalk static.'

'Principal wants to come in the front.'

'I'll make sure we're clear.'

Lock crossed back to Caffrey, who'd by this time beat a diplomatic retreat to his cruiser. He tapped on the glass and took a moment to enjoy Caffrey's irritated expression as he cracked the window and the cold air rushed in.

'We're bringing him in the front.'

Caffrey rolled his eyes. 'Ain't it bad enough that I have half a dozen officers tied down here every freakin' morning?'

'Half a billion bucks and a direct line to the mayor, not to mention the US Constitution, says he can walk in the main entrance of his own office if he so desires,' Lock said, turning on his heel before Caffrey had a chance to respond.

Caffrey shrugged a *big deal* to Lock's back and rolled the window back up as four blocks away three blacked-out GMC Yukons fitted with B-7 grade armour and run-flats muscled their way through the morning gridlock, heavy with menace.

2

Inside the lead Yukon, Ty Johnson checked his weapon, then the position of the other two vehicles in the side mirror. All good.

Ty gave the signal for his driver to move over into the left-hand median and occupy a lane of oncoming traffic, which was momentarily stopped at a light. Blocking the junction allowed the other two SUVs to move up seamlessly on the inside, so Ty's vehicle was now at the rear and he could have a clear view when the passengers got out.

Ty popped his head out the window and glanced behind. About half a block back, which in this traffic equated to a good twenty seconds, an up-armoured, fire engine red Hummer rolled along.

Inside the Hummer was the CA, or counter-attack team, led by Vic Brand, a former colonel in the US Marines. Ty knew that Lock had resisted their appointment. Normally a CA team was the preserve of the military in ultra-high threat environments, and Lock had felt it was overkill. However, Stafford Van Straten, heir apparent to the family empire and perpetual thorn in Lock's side, had confused a stint in the Reserve Officer Training Corps when he was at Dartmouth with actual security expertise, and insisted on recruiting them, somehow convincing his father

7

they'd be a useful addition to his security detail.

Lock had no time for Stafford; neither did Ty. And they had even less time for Brand, a man who delighted in regaling the younger men in the CA team with his exploits in Iraq, many of which, Lock had told Ty, were fictitious. Ty, having checked with a few of his former Marine buddies, wasn't so sure.

The close protection world was full of guys like Brand, serial fantasists who confused talking the talk with walking the walk. To Ty, a good bodyguard was like Lock, the archetypal grey man who blended into the background, emerging only when a threat arose.

The way Ty saw it, Brand blended like Marilyn Manson at a Jonas Brothers gig.

Lock watched as the protestors on the street were cleared fifty feet further back by the cops. If one of them made a rush, Lock would have Nicholas Van Straten in the boardroom with his decaf latte and a copy of the *Wall Street Journal* before they made it to the front door.

The front passenger door of the rear vehicle opened first. Lock looked on as Ty made his way round to open the front passenger side of the middle Yukon for the designated bodyguard. As the rest of the personal escort section deployed, spreading out so that they had eyes on a full three hundred and sixty degrees, the clamour from the activists rose in volume.

'Murderer!'

'Hey, Van Straten, how many animals you plan on killing today?'

The bodyguard, a lean six foot two Mid-westerner by the name of Croft, opened Nicholas Van Straten's door, and he stepped out. For a man who got death threats the way most people received junk mail, he looked remarkably composed. His four-man personal escort section had already made a closed box formation around him, ready to move him into the building. But Van Straten clearly had other ideas.

Taking a right turn behind the Yukon, he began to walk towards the source of the obscenities emanating from across the way. Lock could feel a surge of adrenalin starting to build as Van Straten embarked on this unscheduled walkabout.

'Where the hell's Stafford?' Nicholas Van Straten asked one of his aides, who appeared to be having difficulty keeping pace as his boss made a beeline for the protestors.

'I've no idea, sir.'

'He was supposed to be here,' Van Straten said, with an air of disappointment that didn't stretch as far as surprise. Evidently, he was used to his son letting him down.

Lock watched as Van Straten confronted Stokes at the barrier. Anxiously, he keyed his mike. 'Where the hell's he going?'

A second passed before Ty's response came back. 'To meet his public?'

The four-man PES stayed tight around Van Straten. Croft glanced over at Lock as if to say, 'What the hell do I do now?'

9

Lock could only offer a shrug in return. This didn't feature anywhere in the playbook, and he didn't like it.

'Sir, if you wouldn't mind . . . ' Croft's request trailed off.

'If I wouldn't mind what?'

Van Straten seemed to be enjoying the panic emanating from the men around him.

A few yards back the red Hummer was drawing up. Lock could see one of Brand's men in the front seat raising a gun, an M-16, by way of deterrent. Sighing, Lock keyed his radio again, waiting a beat to make sure that the start of his transmission wouldn't be cut. 'Brand from Lock. Tell that moron sitting in front of you to put the showstopper away. In case he hadn't noticed, we're in Midtown, not Mosul. If I see it again, he's gonna find it doing double duty as a butt plug.'

Lock breathed a sigh of relief as he saw the M-16 popping back below the dash.

'What's your boss doing? Get him inside that freakin' building before we have a riot on our hands.' Caffrey had ambled his way across the street and was talking to Lock.

Static in Lock's ear, then a message from Ty: 'He wants to talk to them.'

Lock passed it on, and Caffrey's expression shifted from disgruntlement to apoplexy.

By the time Van Straten had reached the barrier, Stokes was no more than five feet away. Silence descended as the taunting and threats fell away, the demonstrators thrown by the proximity of their chief hate figure. A cameraman from CNN tried to elbow his way in front of Lock.

'If you wouldn't mind stepping back please, sir,' said Lock, trying to keep his voice even.

'Screw you, dickwad.'

Lock raised his hands, palms open in placation. 'Sir, I'd really appreciate you moving back,' he added, simultaneously raking the inside of his right boot all the way down the guy's shin.

As the camera operator hobbled a retreat, cursing under his breath, Lock turned to watch Van Straten confront Stokes at the barrier.

'I thought a delegation from your group might like to meet with me this morning,' Van Straten was saying.

Stokes smiled. 'You got my message, huh?'

By now, the media had begun to cluster round. A blonde reporter, Carrie Delaney, was first to be heard above the rapid-fire burst of questions. 'Mr Van Straten, what do you plan on discussing inside?'

Lock caught her eye for a split-second. She made a point of looking away.

A preppy-looking correspondent, with frat boy features and a footballer's physique, broke in before Van Straten had a chance to answer. 'Is this a sign that you're giving in to the extremists?'

Carrie shot the guy a look. *Asshole.* Lock noticed the guy smiling back. *Right back at ya, babe.*

Van Straten held up his hands. 'Ladies and gentlemen, I'll be happy to answer any questions

11

you have *after* my meeting with Mr Stokes.'

More bodies pressed in. A man behind Lock was pushed forward by a surge of the growing crowd. He pushed him back.

Lock glanced around. It looked like every single assassination attempt ever witnessed, five seconds before it went off. A chaotic scrum of bodies, security caught flatfooted, then, from nowhere, someone making their move.

3

As Lock stepped out of the elevator, Van Straten's bodyguard, Croft, was stationed at the door which led into the boardroom.

'Who's inside?'

'Just the old man and Stokes.'

'You check on them?'

Croft shook his head. 'The old man didn't want to be disturbed. Don't worry, I made sure he sat at the top of the table before I left.'

Lock relaxed a notch. There was a panic button fitted directly under that section. Not that he thought even Stokes would be dumb enough to try something here.

'Any idea why the boss wanted a sit-down?'

Croft shrugged. 'Nada.'

'He didn't say anything in the car this morning?'

'Not a word. Just sat in back going through his papers, same as always.'

To be fair to Croft, Lock had found Nicholas Van Straten a tough man to read. Not that he was taciturn or impolite. Far from it, in fact. In contrast to his son, Nicholas Van Straten always seemed to make a point of being overly polite to those who worked for him, sometimes in almost inverse proportion to their seniority in the company.

'So no one knows what this is about?'

Croft shook his head.

13

Lock turned to walk back to the elevator as the door to the boardroom opened and Van Straten stepped out.

'Ah, Ryan, just the man,' Van Straten said, turning his attention to Lock.

'Sir?'

'First of all, I owe you and the rest of your men an apology. I should have given you some warning of my plans.'

Lock bit back his irritation. 'That's quite alright, sir.'

'It was something of a last-minute decision to open direct discussions with Mr Stokes and his group.'

'Yes, sir.'

'Now, in ten minutes or so Mr Stokes and I will be going back outside to make a joint announcement.'

'Sir, if I might make a suggestion.'

'Of course. Please do.'

'Perhaps if we found somewhere inside the building where you could — '

Van Straten cut him off. 'Already thought of that, but Missy thought it would be more visual to be out on the steps. Oh, and could you arrange for some coffee to be sent in? No milk. Mr Stokes doesn't take milk. Something to do with cows finding the process emotionally unsettling.'

'Right away, sir.'

Van Straten stepped back inside and closed the door, leaving Lock alone with Croft.

'Who the hell's Missy?' Lock asked.

'Some gal in the public relations office. The

14

old man put a call in to her about two minutes before you got here.'

'Terrific,' Lock said, trying hard to keep the exasperation from his voice. Now security strategy was being dictated by someone who probably thought an IED was a form of contraception.

'Dude, relax,' Croft said. 'Looks like the war's over.'

Lock stepped in close to Croft. '*Dude*, don't ever use language like that in my presence again.'

Croft was puzzled. 'What? I didn't cuss.'

'In my book, 'relax' beats out any cuss word.'

★   ★   ★

Back outside, word of the sit-down between Gray Stokes and Nicholas Van Straten had got out, drawing even more news crews to the scene. Bystanders and protestors filled the gaps, pilot fish waiting to snatch at whatever morsels of information might float their way.

Lock finished briefing his team stationed on the steps just as Gray Stokes emerged from the entrance, his clenched fist raised in imitation of the black power salute. Next to him, Nicholas Van Straten stared at his feet. A chastened Croft stayed within touching distance of his principal.

'We did it!' yelled Stokes, his voice sounding hoarse in the chill air. 'We've won!'

Two protestors whooped as the pack of reporters surged forward. Lock noticed that Croft and Ty, who were flanking Van Straten, were looking nervous as the reporters pushed up against them, jockeying with one another for position.

Lock stepped between Janice in the wheelchair and a reporter squeezing in next to her, worried that she'd be toppled over by the crush of bodies. 'Folks, if you could give everyone here some space,' he shouted.

Knowing what Lock had done to the cameraman, those nearest to him hastily made some room.

Van Straten cleared his throat. 'I'd like to make a short statement if I may. As of midnight tonight, Meditech and all its subsidiaries, alongside those companies we work with in partnership, will no longer engage in testing on animals. There will be a fuller statement released to all media outlets later.'

Before Stokes had the chance to have his say, a volley of questions came at Van Straten. Even in victory, Van Straten was stealing his thunder, and Stokes didn't seem to be enjoying it one bit. He shifted from foot to foot. 'I have a statement as well!' he shouted. But the reporters ignored him, continuing to throw questions at Van Straten.

'What's behind your change in policy, Mr Van Straten?'

'Have the extremists who desecrated your mother's memory won here?'

Another question, this one more pertinent to a broad section of the audience at home: 'What do you think this will do to your company's share price?'

Van Straten stretched out his arms. 'Ladies and gentlemen, please. I think it would be rude if

16

you didn't at least listen to what Mr Stokes has to say on the matter.'

Struggling to keep his cool, Stokes took a single step to the right. Now *he* was standing directly in front of the Meditech CEO. Now it was *his* face filling the screens directly behind him, and the millions more around the country.

He raised a bunched right hand to his mouth, theatrically cleared his throat, and waited for silence to descend.

'Today has been a momentous one for the animal rights movement,' he began.

But before he could finish the sentence, his neck snapped back. A single .50 calibre bullet had vaporized his head.

4

Lock placed himself in front of Croft and drew his weapon, giving Croft time to spin and sling Van Straten so they were back to back. With his left hand, Croft clasped the collar of Van Straten's shirt, which allowed him to return fire with his right, all the while backing up as fast as he could. Lock remained steadfast among the scrum of bodies as between them Ty and Croft moved Van Straten back inside the building.

Lock looked around for Brand and the rest of the CA team but they were nowhere to be seen. Backing up, he shouted over to Ty, 'Get him upstairs!'

In front of him, people were scattering in all directions, the crowd parting in a V directly in front of the building as another round was fired, this one catching a male protestor in the chest. He fell, face first, and didn't move.

A breath of relief for Lock, as out of the corner of his eye he saw the journalist Carrie Delaney hightailing it for a news van parked on the corner.

Turning to his right, Lock saw Janice Stokes sitting in her wheelchair, her mother struggling to get it to move. At the same time, he saw an additional reason for the collective panic.

A red Hummer was careering towards the front of the building at full tilt, its trajectory an unswerving diagonal towards the one person incapable of getting out of its way. Even if the brakes were applied at that instant, the vehicle's momentum would carry it onwards for at least another two hundred feet. Janice was well within that range.

Lock sprinted forward, his left foot slipping under him as he struggled for traction on the icy steps. Another round flew in, taking out what was left of the glass frontage. Desperately, he tackled Janice from the chair, his momentum carrying them both skidding across the polished stone.

Behind them, the Hummer had started to brake, the wheels locking, its sheer weight carrying it inexorably towards the front of the building and up the steps. Janice's mother stood motionless as it rolled across Stoke's body and slammed into her. She flipped into the air, a spinning tangle of limbs, and landed with a thud between the Hummer's front wheels.

Janice opened her mouth to scream as the Hummer ploughed into the reception area. 'Mom!' she yelled, as Lock pulled her under him, his body covering hers.

He twisted his head round to see one of the Hummer's doors open and Brand emerge. Brand hefted the M-16 in his right hand. He looked around at the devastation wrought by the vehicle and strolled calmly towards Lock, glass crunching under his boots, rifle raised.

Lock rolled away from Janice as a paramedic ran over to them and knelt down next to her. The CA team clambered one by one from the

Hummer and took up position in the lobby, guns drawn.

Brand reached Lock. 'I'll take it from here, buddy.'

Lock felt a surge of anger manifest as bile at the back of his throat. A young woman had just seen her father's head blown clean off and her mother run over by Brand.

Brand smirked. 'Relax, Lock, she was a freakin' tree hugger.'

Lock drew back his right arm and stepped forward. Before Brand had a chance to duck Lock's right elbow connected squarely with the side of his mouth. There was a satisfying crunch as Brand's head jolted back and blood spurted from the side of his mouth.

'She was a human being,' said Lock, hurrying past.

5

Suddenly aware of his laboured breath, Lock took cover behind a Crown Vic parked fifty feet from the front of the building, making sure to stay a good five feet behind the bodywork so that any fragments of shrapnel zipping off were less likely to find him. Getting too close was called hugging cover. Hugging cover got you killed.

Only ninety seconds had passed between Stokes being hit and him making it here. In a one-sided contact like this, it felt like an eternity.

What was it his father had told him as a ten-year-old when explaining the job of a bodyguard? *Hours of boredom, moments of terror.*

He glanced over to see Sergeant Caffrey squatting next to him, tight to the cruiser. Lock grabbed him by the shoulder and pulled him back a few feet.

'What the hell are you doing?'

'You're too close.'

'What do you mean?'

'You want a lecture on appropriate use of cover right now? Just do what I tell you, and stay the hell there.'

Caffrey grimaced, his pasty complexion hued red by a freezing wind and sudden exertion. 'Man, I'd be working the Bronx if I'd wanted to sign up for this kind of shit.'

'I think they're up there,' Lock said, nodding

towards a three-storey redbrick with a ground-floor Korean deli which squatted among its more refined office block neighbours.

'They? How'd you know there's more than one of them?' Caffrey asked, peeking out.

Lock hauled him back in. 'A lone sniper is either a college kid gone wild who can't shoot for shit, or someone in the movies. A professional works with a spotter. And these guys are professionals.'

'You saw them?' Caffrey asked.

Lock shook his head. 'Take my word for it. It's about the only place they can be. The angle of the first shot would have given him the right elevation to take out Stokes above the crowd.'

Lock keyed his radio. 'Ty?'

'Go ahead.'

'Where's Van Straten?'

'Tucked up with milk and cookies. What's the count?'

'Three down.'

A middle-aged man in a suit broke cover to Lock's left. Clutching his briefcase, he ducked out from behind a parked car, only making it a few feet before being blown off his feet by the sniper.

'Correction. Four.'

Automatic rounds chattered from inside the lobby as Brand and his CA team returned fire.

'OK, so, Ty. You leave Croft with Van Straten and get downstairs. Make sure Brand and the rest of his complete asshole team don't light up any more of the citizenry.'

'Will do.'

22

Lock turned back to Caffrey. 'What's the SWAT team's ETA?'

'They'll be here in five. Let's just sit tight until then.'

'When they get here, make sure you tell them that I'm on your side.'

'Where the hell are you going?'

'To give these douchebags the good news,' said Lock, making for the nearest doorway.

He tucked in tight to the entrance of the building directly opposite Meditech headquarters. Now he was on the same side of the street as the shooters he could inch his way up, building by building, all the while narrowing any possible angle. His only real fear was being taken out by friendly fire from Brand's trigger-happy cohort.

The sign on the door of the deli had been switched to 'Closed For Business'. This store didn't even close for Thanksgiving. Lock now knew for definite that he was in the right place. He tried the handle. It was locked. With the butt of the Sig, he punched out the glass-panelled door and stepped through.

Inside, there was no sign of life. The relative calm was unsettling as sirens whooped and screamed in the street beyond. He walked slowly towards the counter, the fingers of his right hand wrapped around the Sig's grip, his left hand cupping the bottom.

Behind the counter there was a young woman crouched beneath the register, her hands cuffed with plastic ties, her mouth sealed with gaffer tape. The space was narrow: these places tried to

23

use every available inch for product. As he knelt down, his hand brushed her shoulder, making her jump.

'It's fine, you're gonna be fine,' he whispered.

He found the edge of the tape with the nail of his thumb.

'This is going to hurt a little but, please, try not to scream, OK?'

She nodded, her pupils still dilated in terror.

'I'm gonna pull it off real fast, just like a Band-Aid. One, two, three . . . '

He tore the tape up and right, a yelp half catching in the woman's throat.

'My dad's through there,' she said, her words coming in short gasps. She nodded towards the corridor, which snaked off from the front of the store to the back. 'He has a heart condition.'

'Who else is here?'

'Two men. Upstairs.'

'You sure?'

'Yes. They haven't come down yet.'

'Where are the stairs?'

She jerked her head back down the corridor towards a brown wood-panelled door.

Lock reached for his Gerber, flipping out the knife into a locked position with a single motion. The woman winced.

'I'm going to free your hands.'

She seemed to understand, but her body remained tense and stiff as he reached behind her to cut through the plasti-cuffs. At first he thought whoever bound her up must have improvised using some plastic ties they'd found lying around, but now he saw these were the real deal. Military issue of the kind used in places like Iraq where you might have to detain large numbers for a short period. Still, the thin edge of the Gerber's blade made fast work of cutting through the thick white plastic band.

'You take care of your father. If you hear shots, get out, but stay on this side of the street.'

Lock stood up and made his way to the door leading to the stairs. He opened it, stepped through, and glanced up. Dust caught at the back of his throat as he moved up the stairs, careful to keep his weight even on each tread. He focused on slowing his breathing as his field of vision, which had unconsciously tunnelled, started to clear again. By the time he reached the second floor his heart rate had dropped by twenty beats a minute.

Footsteps thumped above him. Whoever it was, they were in a hurry. He crouched down, his back to the wall, his 226 aimed at a gap between the iron spindles of the railing on the third floor.

There was a sudden movement as someone broke cover above him, the person a blur. Before Lock could get him in his sights, he was gone.

Slowly, he began to edge his way up the final flight of stairs, the Sig out in front of him, index finger resting lightly on the trigger. At the top of the stairs there was a single door, offset six feet to the left. To the right, another door, this one ajar.

He went right first, down the corridor, pushing the door open with the toe of his boot. The room smelt musty and damp. Inside was a desk. Next to that was a solitary filing cabinet. The window was open. It faced on to the back alley. A metal pin was hammered into the frame; a length of blue climbing rope looped through it snaked out into thin air. Lock crossed to it and leaned out, glimpsing what he suspected were the backs of the sniper team as they ran.

He keyed his radio. 'Ty?' he whispered.

'I'm here.'

'Korean deli half a block down. Second floor.'

'OK, man, I'll pass it on.'

With any luck the SWAT team could throw up a four-block perimeter and find them before they had the chance to slip away. New York might provide the ultimate urban camouflage environment for crazies, but even here a heavily perspiring assassin carrying the tools of his trade just might stand out.

Lock walked back down the corridor, stopping at the closed door he'd seen. He took a single step back and lifted his right leg. The door flew open under the impact of his boot.

There was a deafening boom as a shotgun, rigged to the door handle with a length of fishing line, went off. The force of the impact blew Lock back over the railing. He landed heavily on his back, his head smacking off the wall, leaving a dent in the plasterboard. Then everything went black.

6

A cluster of town cars skulked outside the up-scale apartment block. Engines running, they chugged out a mini smog bank that rolled across the FDR Driveway to the very edge of the East River.

Next to the green-canopied entrance, Natalya Verovsky sheltered under a golf umbrella embossed with a Four Seasons logo. Standing apart from the other au pairs and nannies waiting to collect their charges from the Christmas Eve party, she glanced at her watch. They should be coming out any minute now.

After what seemed an eternity, a gaggle of excited children began to emerge clutching bags of party favours. Last, as usual, was Josh, a loose-limbed seven-year-old with a mop of brown hair. He appeared to be engaged in a comically earnest conversation about the exist-ence of Santa Claus with one of his friends.

Spotting Natalya, Josh broke off mid-conversation with a fleeting 'Gotta go' and made a dash towards her.

Normally this was the signal for Natalya to sweep Josh up in a big hug, lifting him off his feet and matching the embrace with a sloppy kiss, which Josh pretended to think was gross, but which she knew he secretly relished. Today, however, she took his hand without a word, even though she knew he disliked having his hand taken more than being kissed.

'Hey, I'm not a baby,' he protested.

Natalya said nothing, prompting Josh to look up at her, this faintest of blips on his radar registering immediately. 'What's up, Naty?'

Natalya's voice sharpened. 'Nothing. Now come on.' She hurried him towards a town car parked across the street.

As the back door swung open, Josh held back. 'Why aren't we walking?'

'It's too cold to walk.'

A lie. It was cold. Freezing in fact. But they'd walked home in colder.

'But I like the cold.'

Natalya's grip tightened around Josh's hand. 'Quick, quick.'

'Can we have hot chocolate when we get home?'

'Of course.' *Another lie.*

Josh smiled, a victory seemingly won. Natalya knew that his dad hated him having anything sweet before dinner and generally she sided with him, only allowing Josh to sneak some candy as a special treat on Friday afternoons when he'd finished all his homework.

He climbed into the back of the town car. 'With marshmallows?'

'Sure,' said Natalya.

Inside the car, the driver, his face obscured by the partition, pressed down on the horn with the palm of his hand before easing the Mercedes out into traffic. At the end of the block, he made an immediate right down 84th towards 1st Avenue.

Natalya stared straight ahead.

Josh looked at her, his face a pastiche of adult concern. 'There's something wrong, isn't there?'

A dull clunk as the doors either side of them locked. Natalya could see the beginnings of panic in Josh's eyes now. 'It's just so you don't fall out.' *A third lie.*

'But I'm not going to fall out.'

The lights ahead flipped to green. Natalya reached over to secure Josh's seatbelt as the car lurched forward to beat the next set of signals. The park was on their right now, the trees barren and stripped of their leaves. They passed a lone jogger, his face set as he leaned into the biting wind.

At 97th, they turned into Central Park, cutting across towards the Upper West Side. By now any pretence that they were heading home was gone.

Josh unclipped his seatbelt and scrambled up on to the seat to stare out of the back window. 'This isn't the way,' he protested, his voice pitching high with concern. 'Where are we going?'

Natalya did her best to shush him. 'It's only for a little while.' *This part, she'd been promised, was true.*

'What's only for a little while? Where are we going?' He paused and took a shaky breath. 'If we don't go home right now, I'm telling Dad, and he'll fire your ass.'

The partition window slid down and the driver swivelled round. His hair was cut military-short and flaked with grey at the temples. The black suit he'd been crammed into, to lend the appearance of a chauffeur, looked in danger of tearing under his arms.

'Take us home!' Josh screamed at him. 'Now!'

The driver ignored him. 'Either you get the little brat to sit down or I will,' he said to Natalya, pulling aside his jacket to reveal a shoulder holster with a Glock 9mm pistol tucked into it, the handle showing black against his white shirt.

Josh stared at him, the sight of the gun quietening him, boiling down panic to a silent rage.

Beyond the driver, through the clear glass of the windshield, he could see a trademark blue and white NYPD cruiser driving towards them. In a few seconds it would be parallel with them. A second after that it would be gone.

Sensing that this was his one chance, Josh made a sudden lunge towards the front seat. The driver's right elbow flew up, catching the top of his forehead with a crack and sending him spinning back into the footwell. 'Sit the hell down,' he said, pushing a button on the console, the partition gliding back into place.

Natalya pulled Josh back up on to the seat. A welt was already starting to rise where the driver had caught him. An inch or two lower and he would have crushed the bridge of his nose. Fighting the tears was futile.

His eyes burned into Natalya's. 'Why are you doing this?'

As Josh's sobs came, raw and breathless, Natalya closed her eyes, the knot of quiet dread that had been growing in her stomach for the past few weeks solidifying. Knowing now what

30

she'd denied to herself all this time. That she'd made a terrible mistake.

Feet away from them, the police cruiser sped past. Neither cop gave the town car a second glance.

7

Ten minutes after the driver had struck Josh, the partition lowered again and he tossed a backpack in Natalya's general direction. She opened it with trepidation, even though she'd been told what would be inside.

First item out was a plastic bag emblazoned with a trademark Duane Read blue and red logo. Digging a bit deeper, she retrieved a set of children's clothes, brand new and in Josh's size: blue jeans, a white T-shirt and a navy sweatshirt. No cartoon characters, no brand names, no slogans, no distinguishing characteristics of any kind. Plain. Generic. Anonymous. Chosen precisely for those qualities.

'Look, new clothes,' Natalya said, doing her best to coax Josh from the far corner of the back seat.

Josh turned his face to Natalya, half-dried tears like glycerine on his cheeks. 'They suck.'

'Let's get you changed, yes?'

'Why? What for?'

'Please, Josh.'

Josh glanced towards the partition. 'Forget it.'

Natalya leaned in closer to him. 'We don't want to make him angry again, do we?'

'Who is he anyway?' Josh asked. 'Your boyfriend?'

Natalya bit down on her lip.

'He is, isn't he?'

'It doesn't matter who he is.'

'Why are you doing this to me?'

Natalya lowered her voice. 'Look, I made a mistake. I'm going to try and get you out of this. But right now, I need you to cooperate.'

'Why should I believe you?'

'Because you don't have any choice.'

Finally, after more stalling, Josh got changed. Natalya jammed his party clothes into the backpack, the easy part out of the way. Next, she picked up the bag from the drug store, steeling herself, then put it back down. Unless she was going to pin Josh to the ground to do what she had to do, and risk injuring him in the process, this was going to take careful handling.

'You look nice in those,' Natalya said.

'No I don't.'

'They look good.'

None of this was cutting any ice and Natalya could see that Josh was getting jittery again.

He shifted position on the back seat. 'Can we go home? Please? If you want money my dad can give it to you, but I want to go home.'

'It's not that simple.'

'Why not?'

Natalya pulled a pair of hairdresser's scissors from the drug store bag.

Josh's hand shot to his scalp. 'No. Not my hair.'

The car slowed and pulled to the side of the road, as a car behind blared its horn. The partition fell. This time the driver had the gun in his hand. He pointed it directly at Josh. 'If I have to pull over one more time, you'll regret it.'

Shaking, Josh turned his back to Natalya. Legs crossed, she sat behind him, and set to work.

Barely five minutes later the back seat was festooned with long strands of dark brown hair. Josh reached his hand back, ran it through the uneven spikes.

Natalya took Josh's hand and squeezed it. 'You can always grow it back. Now, let me tidy it.'

She made some more tiny adjustments, momentarily getting caught up in the task.

'There. Now you know what would really suit this style?'

'What?'

'A different colour.'

'I guess so,' Josh said, sounding utterly defeated.

Natalya rummaged in the bag again, sighing as she came up with a plastic bottle of hair dye. Quickly scanning the directions on the back of the bottle, she tutted loudly, then leaned forward and rapped on the partition. 'I can't use this now.'

The driver stared at her in the rear-view mirror. 'Why not?'

'It needs water. It'll have to wait.'

'You sure?'

'You think I'm stupid?'

She thrust the bottle through the partition, two fingers covering the part of the label which read 'unique dry application'. The driver grunted, tucked the bottle into his jacket and restarted the car.

'Don't worry, I won't let anything bad happen

to you,' Natalya whispered, putting her arm around Josh.

'This isn't bad?' he demanded.

Natalya pulled him closer and he finally relented, snuggling in to her.

Fifteen minutes later he was beginning to doze off, his head resting against Natalya's shoulder, as the car came to a stop and the driver opened the door, pulling them both out into the cold.

As they stood shivering in a freezing mist of rain, the driver produced a brand-new cordless car vac and used it to suck Josh's hair off the back seat. Someone else would be along later to collect the car.

The area was desolate and semi-industrial, with a road off to the left. They trudged through a sugar coating of powdery snow towards an oversized metal gate which lay smack bang in the middle of a seemingly endless chain-link fence. Cars flitted past in the distance. Other than that they were alone. A man with a gun, Natalya, and the child she'd been charged with looking after and had just so cruelly betrayed.

Natalya looked around, trying to find a point to fix on — a street sign, maybe, or a store — but all she could see was waterfront. Close by she could hear the slurp of waves against a dock.

Everything had changed for her the moment Josh had been hit. Regardless of what was at stake for herself she was determined to make good her mistake. And that meant getting Josh safely home to his father.

She'd have to pick her moment with care,

though. There would be no second chance at escape.

They hadn't driven through any tunnels or over any bridges so she was sure they were still in Manhattan, but it didn't take a genius to work out that this neighbourhood was a long way from the Upper East Side.

The driver pushed Natalya towards the metal gate with the heel of his hand. 'Move,' he grunted.

At the door, a solitary security camera panned round, accompanied by a faint hydraulic whirl. The gate clicked and the driver pushed it open, ushering Natalya and Josh through.

Perched at the end of a pier, a single-engine speedboat was tied up, no one aboard. Painted a dark grey, it sat low in the water. They walked towards it, the driver clambering down into it first, almost losing his footing as a sudden swell rose under the hull. For a split second Natalya considered running, but with the dock stretching thirty feet out into the water she knew they'd never make it in time.

Natalya helped Josh into the boat.

'Get the rope for me,' the driver said, pushing Josh down so he'd be out of view of any passing traffic on the river.

Natalya unhooked the stern line from the mooring and threw it back to him. Now was her chance.

The driver waved her forward with his hand as the boat began to inch away from the dock. 'Quick.'

She hesitated, then caught Josh's terrified eyes.

There was just no way she could leave him. Taking one quick step, she jumped down, the driver catching her hand and half hauling her down into the boat.

The driver gunned the engine and they set off in a wave of spume and diesel oil. Soon the dock was out of sight, a black skyline etched against grey.

Natalya counted off those buildings she recognized. The tower of the Chrysler building. The Empire State. The gaping maw of a breach where the Twin Towers once stood, now replaced by the first nub of the Freedom Tower.

The driver dug into his jacket and pulled out the bottle of hair dye. He squinted at the instructions on the back like they were written in Sanskrit. Finally, he looked up at Natalya. 'Dry application. Bullshit.' He threw the bottle at Josh. 'Make sure you rub it in good.'

8

Lock woke in a bed in a small room, hooked up to a monitor and some kind of IV. He prayed for morphine, but suspected saline. If he was still in this much pain, it had to be some weak-ass morphine.

He wiggled his toes and fingers, relieved to find that they seemed to be responding. To make sure that it wasn't some kind of phantom sensation he flipped back the sheet, surprised that he could move so easily, and amused to find that he had an erection. Maybe it was some kind of evolutionary response to a near-death experience. Either that or a full bladder.

He waited for his excitement to subside, conjuring up the most unerotic of images to hasten its demise. No dice. Not even a yoga-emaciated Madonna could shift it. The blinds weren't closed all the way, and he could glimpse the lights of the city that didn't sleep beyond the window, getting on just fine without him.

Tentatively, he swung his legs over the side of the bed and, with one hand on the bed rail, stood up. For a second or two the room shifted suddenly, but the sensation quickly abated, and he managed to walk gingerly over to the tiny bathroom.

The man staring back at him from the mirror with a deadpan expression was sporting three-day-old stubble and a close-shaven head. Running his fingers across the top of his skull, he found a set of stitches. Whether it was a wound or the result of an incision wasn't entirely clear. He touched his fingertips to it. No real pain, but definitely stitches.

His face was puffy, especially around the eyes. His eyes were set blue amid the deathly pallor of the rest of his skin, his pupils like dots.

He took a moment to work back to how he got here. Relief. It was all there. The protestors, Van Straten's unexpected walkabout, then Lock standing on the steps outside Meditech and the bullet. Correction: bullets. His glimpse of Carrie running for cover. More relief at recalling that. Then him taking on the threat, the young Korean storekeeper tied up, then walking up that staircase, a bang, and a sudden cut to black.

Total recall. He allowed himself a smile at that.

He filled the sink and began to splash his face with cold water, freezing mid-splash as the door opened into the main room. Pressing his back against the wall, he peered out.

In the room, a man in a blue windbreaker looked around, like the empty bed was evidence of some kind of magic trick. For a second, Lock half expected the guy to start shining his Mag light under the covers.

He stepped out of the bathroom, and the guy's face relaxed into a smile. 'There you are.'

'Here I am,' was all Lock could think to say in reply.

Overcome by a sudden wave of exhaustion, he

took a step back towards the bed, and stumbled. The man put out a hand, steadying him. 'Easy there.'

Lock waved him off, keen to get some sheets between him and his visitor. 'Lemme guess, JTTF?'

The Joint Terrorism Task Force's field office in Manhattan was based downtown in the Federal Plaza. Composed of members of the FBI, ATF, as well as NYPD, it was charged with dealing with all incidents of domestic terrorism in the five boroughs and beyond. The campaign against Meditech had fallen under its jurisdiction as the animal rights activists had escalated their actions. Lock had liaised with a number of suits from their office, although the man standing in front of him wasn't one of them, as far as he could recall.

'John Frisk. Just got transferred over.'

'Ryan Lock.'

'Least you can remember your name, that's a start.'

'So where'd they transfer you from?'

'FBI.'

Lock sat back on the bed. Frisk pulled up a chair and sat next to him.

'You're a lucky guy. If you'd been hit a couple of inches either side of your plates you'd be toast.'

Lock had been sporting four plates. Two front, and two back, they slid into pouches either side of his ballistic vest to provide additional protection.

Lock smiled. 'Maybe I should hit Vegas, while

I'm still on this hot streak.'

'Take me with you. I could use the vacation.'

Lock eased his head back on to the pillows and stared at a fixed point on the ceiling. 'What'd they hit me with?'

'Twelve-gauge rigged to the door,' said Frisk.

'Better that than the alternative, I'm guessing. You pick anyone up yet?'

'We were hoping you could help us with that one.'

Lock chewed the side of his mouth. 'Professionals. Both male. Both over six feet. I didn't get much of a look beyond the back of their heels. What did the crime scene team turn up?'

'I can't really say.'

'That many leads, huh?'

It was Frisk's turn to suppress a smile. 'I thought I was the investigator and you were the witness.'

'Old habits die hard.'

Frisk hesitated for a moment. 'OK, from what we can gather, as you said, it was a pro job. High-calibre sniper rifle — we're still working on the exact type, but a fifty cal.'

'Fifty?'

'Yup. If they'd rigged *that* to the door we wouldn't be having this conversation,' Frisk said, super-casual.

'Got that straight,' said Lock. Having seen what the .50 cal had done to Stokes' head, Lock knew that no amount of body armour would have saved him.

'They had the escape route scoped out ahead

of time, not much left behind for forensics. No shell casings anywhere to be seen, not like that would have given us much anyway. Plus the room was bleached down before they exited via the window.'

'What about the shotgun?' Lock asked, leaning over to reach for a glass of water perched on the locker next to his bed.

Frisk beat him to it and passed it over. 'Looking to buy themselves a few extra seconds would be my guess.'

Lock grunted in agreement.

'We traced it to the owner of a house out in Long Island. Place has been vacant since the summer, guy didn't even know he'd been broken into.'

'Did the girl make it?'

'The girl in the wheelchair?'

Lock nodded, took a sip of water.

'She's down on four.'

'She OK?'

'Pretty shocked. Knows about as much as you do.'

'You've got some great witnesses lined up by the sounds of it. What was the final count?'

'Five dead in total.'

'Five?'

'Three shot, one run over, and one heart attack.'

A knock at the door. A young African American doctor in her late twenties who looked like she'd been awake about as long as Lock had been unconscious poked her head round. 'I thought I was pretty clear that I didn't want my patient disturbed until he was ready.'

'It was my fault, doc,' Lock said. 'I was quizzing Agent Frisk, not the other way round.'

'Well, if you have any questions, you can always talk to me.'

Lock glanced back to Frisk. 'Never got to ask Agent Frisk what my federal prognosis was.'

'Well, your weapon was legally held, although how the hell you got a concealed carry in the city these days beats me.'

Lock looked skywards to the ceiling. 'Friends in high places.'

'And your luck doesn't end there,' Frisk continued. 'Seeing as you never fired a shot, there won't be any charges. But next time, leave the cavalry charge to the cavalry, OK?'

Lock bristled. He'd been the only one taking on the threat and here was Frisk treating him like some rookie cop. 'I'd be happy to, if they manage to show up before the final reel. Speaking of which, what's happening to Brand?'

'Police department are keen to go to bat on vehicular manslaughter. But the DA's getting a lot of pressure to go for a lesser charge, or let it slide entirely.'

'If you speak to anyone in their office you can tell them I'd be happy to step to the plate for the prosecution on that one.'

Frisk raised an eyebrow. 'You and he not too close, huh?'

'Different approaches, that's all.'

'Oh yeah, and what's the difference?'

'Mine's correct,' Lock said curtly.

'Mr Lock really does need his rest,' the doctor

broke in. 'I'm sure there'll be plenty of time for you to talk to him tomorrow.'

'What day is it anyway?'

'Thursday,' said Frisk.

'Wait. I missed Christmas?'

The doctor arched an eyebrow. 'You got the gift of life.'

Frisk smirked. 'Sure Santa'll catch up with you next year.'

'OK, he really does need his rest now,' insisted the doctor.

Frisk took the hint and eased out of the room. 'Don't go anywhere,' he said from the door.

When he'd gone, Lock's hand reached up to his head wound. He ran the tips of his fingers over it, like a kid worrying a scab on his knee.

'Pretty good-looking scar you'll have there,' the doctor said, perching next to him on the bed.

'You think it'll make me more attractive to women?'

'Didn't realize that was a problem for you.'

'I'll take any help I can get.'

'Mind if I take another look?'

'Be my guest.'

He bowed his head so she could get a better view.

'You had a pretty lucky escape.'

'So everyone keeps saying.'

'You suffered a slight haemorrhage. We had to drill into your skull in order to take out some fluid. There's a risk that you might suffer some additional blackouts. Oh, and there have been cases where trauma to this particular area of the brain can result in a raised level of — '

'You can stop right there, doc. I think I know where you're heading. So when can I get out of here?'

She stood up. 'Head trauma's a serious business. It'd be best if you stayed here for at least the next few days.'

'Sure thing,' he said, already planning his escape.

9

'Don't you have a home to go to?'

The doctor was back at the foot of Lock's bed, busy looking over his chart as he lay back watching the tube. Even this early on in his convalescence he'd made a number of interesting discoveries, the most surprising being that with a sufficiently high dose of morphine daytime soap operas were damn engrossing.

'Wouldn't have had you pegged as a big daytime soap fan,' she mused as Lock flicked the TV to mute, leaving a cleft-chinned Clooney wannabe to slap around an actress whose Botox-blank face ran the gamut of human emotions from A to B and back again.

'I was waiting for the news to come on.'

'Sure you were.' That killer smile again.

'Are you flirting with me, doc?'

She ignored the question, jotting down an additional note on his chart instead.

'What are you writing?' he asked, doing his best to peek.

She angled the chart so he couldn't see. 'Do not resuscitate.'

Lock laughed. It hurt.

She edged a smile herself. 'Sorry, but I get hit on a lot, and I haven't been home in two days.'

'Who said I was hitting on you?'

'You weren't? OK, now I feel insulted.

Anyway, isn't this all a pointless discussion? You have a girlfriend.'

'Do I?'

'Well there's certainly been a woman putting in a lot of calls since you were admitted. Carrie Delaney ring any bells?'

'Lots, but unfortunately we're just good friends.'

'Unfortunate for you or her?'

'Probably both.'

'I see.'

Lock pushed himself up into a sitting position. 'Y'know, I'd never really thought about it until now, but our jobs have quite a few things in common.'

'Saving people's lives?'

'I was thinking more along the lines of unsociable hours and only getting any real attention when you screw up.'

'What did you screw up?' she asked him. 'Janice Stokes wouldn't be here if you hadn't done what you did.'

'And neither would I.'

She was staring at him now. 'So why did you?'

'This is going to sound like a line from a bad movie.'

'I get lots of those too.'

'I did it because it's what I'm trained to do.'

'So you make a habit of rescuing damsels in distress?'

Lock shook his head. 'No, just a habit of walking through doors I shouldn't. Listen, I didn't even catch your name.'

'Dr Robbins.'

'I meant your first name.'

'I know you did.'

Over her shoulder, Lock caught a glimpse of Carrie fronting the headline report on the TV. Seeing her hurt worse than getting shot. She was standing outside a green-canopied apartment building, a white-gloved doorman flitting in and out of frame behind her, apparently undecided between discretion and getting his mug on the tube.

'That your lady friend?' Dr Robbins asked, following Lock's gaze to the TV and reading the bottom of the screen.

'She was. For a time anyway.'

'Looks too classy for you.'

'I get that a lot. Would you mind if I . . . ?'

'Go right ahead,' said Dr Robbins, stepping out of his way.

Lock turned up the volume, catching Carrie mid-sentence.

' . . . the FBI remaining tight-lipped about this latest twist in the Meditech massacre story which has gripped America. But so far only one fact remains clear: three days after his disappearance, seven-year-old Josh Hulme remains missing.'

The screen cut to a picture of a young white boy with thick brown hair and blue eyes, smiling self-consciously for a family portrait.

Lock moved away from Dr Robbins as she attempted to get a fresh look at the back of his head. 'What's this got to do with Meditech?'

'His father works for them or something.'

Lock felt a jolt of adrenalin. He started to get

48

out of bed, earning a reproachful look from Dr Robbins.

'I need to make a call.'

'Fine, but do everyone a favour.'

'What's that, doc?'

'Put on a robe first. Your butt's hanging out.'

10

Dressed, and with a baseball cap covering what he'd come to think of as his lobotomy patient look, Lock stepped out into the hall. He still felt a little uncertain on his feet and he remained deliberately unshaven. Looking in the mirror as he'd washed his face, he'd figured that slightly altering his appearance might be no bad thing under the circumstances. Clearly the 'Massacre in Midtown', as the press had dubbed it, gleefully unearthing a neat piece of alliteration among the dead, was a first shot rather than a last stand.

Finding a way to call Ty proved tricky. Lock's cell phone was inconveniently back in the bottom drawer of his desk at Meditech and pay phones seemed to be in short supply. Dr Robbins had told him she could arrange for a phone to be brought to his room for a small charge, but he didn't want to wait. Finally, he tracked one down on the ground floor, next to the gift shop.

Ty answered on the first buzz.

'Where's my fruit basket?'

'If it ain't Rip Van Winkle. I was wondering when you were going to surface.'

'Sleep of the just, man.'

'I hear you. Good to have you back.'

Lock was grateful for the relief in Ty's voice. It was comforting to know that someone at the company gave a shit about his mortality.

'Want to give me an update?'

'We're locked down tight. No further incidents. Everything seems to be cool.'

Cool?

'And I thought I was supposed to be the one who took a blow to the head. How are things cool when one of our employee's kids is missing?'

'You heard about that?'

Lock held the phone away from his mouth and counted to three. Slowly.

Ty appeared to read his silence. 'Listen, Ryan,' he said, 'things are a little bit more complicated than you might think. The FBI are involved, it's being left to them to handle.'

'So why the hell have we been paying kidnap and ransom insurance for all this time if we're just going to hand everything over to the Feds?'

'Richard Hulme, the father of the missing boy, resigned his position at the company two weeks ago, which means neither he nor his son are our problem any more. Sorry Ryan, I had the exact same conversation when I heard, but the word's come down from on high. We stay out of it.'

'But the FBI won't pay any ransom.'

'They've got their policy and we have ours.'

'And nine times out of ten our way gets the victim home safe and sound with the only damage being a dent in some insurance company's balance sheet and a bit of actuarial adjustment for next year's premium.'

'I know, man, I know.'

Right on cue, a little girl was wheeled past

him, a Magic Marker-adorned plaster cast covering her leg. She smiled at Lock.

'Listen, Ty, I'm going to get out of here, but first I have to check on something.'

'OK, man. Hey . . . '

'What?'

'Be safe.'

Lock hung up and made a beeline for the gift shop. He grabbed a bunch of flowers that offered a seven-day 'no wilt' guarantee (Lock could relate) and a box of candy. As he paid the lady behind the counter, he glanced at the newspapers on the rack. Josh's face stared out from every front page apart from the *New York Times*, which led on weightier matters in the Middle East: there had been a suspected biological attack on coalition troops on the border between Afghanistan and Pakistan.

He picked up a copy of the *Post* and flicked through it as he walked back through the lobby. On a double-page spread inside there was a picture of him pulling Janice out of the Hummer's way. He didn't like it: a good close protection operative stayed out of the limelight. A double-page spread in a tabloid wasn't exactly staying out of the limelight.

In the elevator, Lock was squeezed to the back by a couple of hospital orderlies wheeling an elderly man on a gurney. One of them eyed him warily. Suddenly he regretted not dragging a razor across his face when he'd had the chance.

Lock handed the orderly the *Post* folded open at his picture. 'Relax, I'm one of the good guys.'

The elderly man on the gurney reached out

his hand for the paper. 'Here, let me see that.' His eyes shuttled between Lock and the picture. 'That's him all right.'

With everyone's curiosity satisfied, Lock got out on the fourth floor, thankful that he hadn't been asked to sign any autographs or pose for a picture. Janice's room was easy enough to spot. It was the one with a cop standing outside, sipping from a Styrofoam cup.

Once Lock had run through the rigmarole with the newspaper again, and the uniform had spoken to someone at her precinct, who'd then had to speak to someone at Federal Plaza, he was allowed through the door.

The blinds were closed but Janice was awake, her face turned away from the door. The room was full of flowers and cards. A few bereavement cards were scattered among those wishing her a speedy recovery. Hallmark's market research clearly hadn't yet unearthed the 'Glad You Survived and Good Luck with the Terminal Illness' niche of the greetings card market.

Lock laid the flowers at the bottom of the bed and pulled up a chair. They sat in silence for a moment.

'How are you feeling?' Lock asked at last.

'Terrible. How about you?' The question was delivered with the hint of a smile.

'I feel . . . ' Lock trailed off, uneasily. 'I'm good.'

She reached her hand across to his. 'Thank you.'

The simple humanity of the gesture threw him

a little. Because he worked for Nicholas Van Straten, Janice and her father had been the enemy for months.

'I'm glad you made it,' he said softly.

She glanced down. 'For now.'

'You don't know that. There could be a breakthrough, some new drug or treatment for your condition.'

As soon as the words were out of his mouth, he regretted them. Even if there was, there was more chance of a Jehovah's Witness agreeing to a blood transfusion than of Janice taking something that would, in all likelihood, have been tested on animals first.

To her credit, she let it slide. Instead she studied Lock's face long enough to make him shift uncomfortably in his seat, before asking, 'Have you ever been to a slaughterhouse?'

For a second, he thought of telling her about the six months he'd spent in Sierra Leone, where Charles Taylor and the Revolutionary United Front had embarked on a systematic campaign of amputating the limbs of the civilian population, including babies. At least killing animals to eat them served some purpose, he thought now. Much of what Lock had witnessed over the years was borne out of a darker human impulse.

He sighed, rubbed the back of his head, finding stitches. 'I've seen a lot of death.'

'Death's inevitable, though, isn't it?' Janice said, her voice rising. 'I'm talking about murder. The animals know they're about to be killed. When they're in the trucks, they know.

You can see it in their eyes, hear it in the noise they make.'

Lock leaned forward and touched her arm. 'Janice, I need to ask you a few questions. You don't have to answer them but I need to ask them all the same.'

'Gandhi said that you can judge the morality of a nation by how it treats its animals,' Janice continued, undeterred.

She was rambling now, her mind on a loop, or so it seemed to Lock. She grasped the bars of the bed frame and pulled herself up into a sitting position. He tried to help her but she waved him away.

'Janice, this is important. I don't think whoever killed your father did it by accident. What I mean is, the more I've thought about it, the more I can't help feeling that this wasn't someone trying to assassinate Nicholas Van Straten and getting it wrong. This was someone trying to kill your father and getting it right.'

'You think I don't know that?' Janice asked, suddenly focused. 'We'd already had threats from your side.'

'What do you mean?'

'Phone calls, letters, saying that if we didn't stop the protesting we'd be killed.'

'You tell anyone about this?'

'And who were we going to tell? The FBI? They were probably the ones doing it.'

'Come on.'

'My mom and dad were saving animals twenty years before a bunch of anorexic bimbos took their clothes off for a photo shoot because it was fashionable. I grew up with our phone being tapped and our mail opened. There wasn't one Christmas went by that I didn't know what my grandma had gotten me because those assholes opened everything. What's changed? Apart from the fact that nowadays there's a hell of a lot more money at stake. For all I know, *you* could have been the one making those phone calls.'

'OK, you got me. Must have been the suppressed guilt that got me to risk my ass pulling you out of there,' Lock fired back, angry now.

Grandma's presents, gimme a break. Talk about brainwashing. Ma and Pa Stokes had done such a nice job that their only daughter was prepared to die a martyr for the cause, rather than compromise her principles and live, while they'd been only too happy to stand by and watch. And for what? To prove their moral superiority over the rest of us.

'Thanks for the flowers, but maybe you should go now,' Janice said, turning away from him.

Lock stood. He took a couple of breaths. 'OK, I'll go. But I've got one last thing I need to ask you.'

'Fine, but make it quick, I'm getting tired.'

'Your father said something to Van Straten when they were outside. Something about him getting his message.'

Janice looked blank. 'I already told you, *we* didn't make threats.'

'I'm not suggesting it was a threat. But if there'd been some kind of back channel discussions going on — '

56

'With Meditech? No way.'

'So what was the message?'

Janice's voice shook with emotion. 'I don't know. And now I never will. My parents are dead, remember?'

Lock got to his feet, his irritation replaced by remorse. 'I'm sorry, I shouldn't have . . . '

But her eyes had already closed, and by the time he reached the door she had fallen fast asleep. The uniformed officer checked on her before allowing Lock to leave. She looked up at Lock as she performed a cursory pat-down, although what he would have wanted to remove from Janice's hospital room was a mystery.

'Must feel pretty good,' she said.

'What must?'

The rookie smiled up at him. 'Saving someone's life like that.'

Lock shrugged his shoulders. He hadn't saved Janice's life, merely postponed her death. He turned his back on the cop and walked back to the elevator.

11

Brennans Tavern was about as authentically Irish as a bowl of Lucky Charms, but it was dark, which suited Lock fine. Even with the painkillers he'd picked up from the hospital pharmacy taking the edge off his headache, bright light was still making him wince.

Getting out of hospital had proved almost more time consuming than leaving the military, with about as many hours of form filling involved. Dr Robbins had warned him that in his present condition he was a danger not only to himself but also others. He'd declined to tell her that his commanding officer had said the same thing.

Eyes adjusting slowly to the gloom, he took a sip of beer. The label on the painkillers no doubt contained a warning about not taking them with alcohol but his vision was still a little blurred, and who could read that kind of small print in this light anyway?

The door swung open, and in strode Carrie. Seeing her, Lock felt suddenly buoyant. And even more light-headed. Without stopping to look around she made a beeline for him, throwing down her jacket and bag on the table, all business, like they'd never broken up.

'Tough day?' Lock asked her.

'About average.'

'How'd you pick me out so quick?'

'Corner table with your back to the wall, a view of the door, and easy access to the back exit. It doesn't take a genius.'

'See, you did get something out of dating me after all.' He stood and pulled out a chair for her.

She pantomimed a curtsy and sat down. 'You always did have good manners.'

They looked at each other across the table, Lock suddenly wishing that the lighting was better.

'Glad you made it out in one piece.'

'Yeah. It was scary for a while there.'

'It was,' Lock agreed. The only people who claimed not to be scared in a violent situation were liars and psychopaths. Fear was hard-wired.

'So how's my hero?'

'I'm your hero?'

'Ryan, let's not — '

He put up his hand in apology. 'You're right. So, let's see, how am I?' He took a sip, reflected. 'I'm sore. If I'd seen it coming . . . '

'It wouldn't have been sore?'

Lock wasn't sure he had the energy to explain. Long ago he'd formed the theory that if you knew you were going to be hurt, if you expected it, the brain could send a signal of anticipation to the body which meant that when pain came it arrived with less of a jolt. Since then, every time he'd gone into a situation the first thing he told himself was, *this is going to hurt. Bad.* And somehow when he did that and the pain came he was able to manoeuvre beyond it and come out on top.

The shotgun rig had been a sucker punch. But

then the world these days was all sucker punches.

'Ryan? Are you OK?'

'Sorry.' He ran his hand across his scalp. 'I was miles away.'

'Evidently. Nice hairdo, by the way.'

He smiled. One of the many things he loved about Carrie was her ability to pull him out of what she chose to call his 'tortured soul' moments. 'You like it?' he asked.

' 'Like' might be too strong a word. It's certainly . . . different. Let me get you a drink.'

'Drinks are on me.'

He flagged down the bartender and ordered Carrie a Stoli rocks with a twist of lime.

'Nice to see you remembered.'

The way she met his gaze as she said it held more than a hint of promise for later. In his current state, Lock couldn't decide whether that was a good thing or a bad thing. On the one hand he couldn't think of anything he'd like better than spending the night with Carrie, but on the other he doubted Carrie would be that impressed if he blacked out on top of her.

That, and it was complicated. They'd first gotten involved vowing that their relationship was only a bit of fun, then quickly realized after he'd stayed over at her place every night for two weeks that maybe it was shaping up to be more. Finally, they reached a mutual conclusion: right person, wrong time. No big argument. No recriminations. Just a slow realization that it wasn't going to work out. Lock ached, then threw himself even deeper into his job.

The bartender brought Lock another beer and Carrie her Stoli rocks with a twist. Carrie's finger circled the rim of her glass. She was thinking about something, Lock could tell.

'Got some pretty good footage of you saving that girl in the wheelchair.'

'No.'

'I haven't asked you a question yet.'

'I know what it is, and my answer's still no.'

Carrie sat back, smiling. 'Will you give me an interview?'

'You know what I think about media bullshit. Present company excepted. And you know what I think about guys doing the job who big-time it.'

'But you saved her life.'

'It's what I'm trained to do. It wasn't bravery, it was reflex. Listen, my job is to be the — '

'Grey man. I know.'

Carrie had made the mistake of curling up on the couch with Lock one evening to watch the Academy Awards. She'd been treated to a stream of invective about the shortcomings of the various 'bodyguards' accompanying the cream of Hollywood up the red carpet. It was also the first time Carrie had heard the expression, presumably picked up from his former British colleagues, 'thick-necked twats'.

'Then you knew what I'd say.'

'Can't fault a girl for trying, can you?' She drained her Stoli. 'Why don't we go somewhere else?'

Lock closed his eyes, tasting the moment.

'You OK?'

'Better than OK. You got some place in mind?'

61

'Maybe.'

Over Carrie's right shoulder, Lock watched a man in his early forties come into the bar. He wore a long raincoat buttoned all the way up but the hair matted to his head indicated that he hadn't had the additional foresight to carry an umbrella. He scanned the bar quickly, clearly seeking someone out, but his manner was off, too much uncertainty around the edges.

The man stopped at the bar, leaning over to speak briefly to the barman, who nodded in Lock's direction. As the man headed towards them, Lock edged his chair back a few inches, giving himself the room to be quickly up and on his feet should the need arise.

'What's wrong?' Carrie asked, looking behind her.

The man got within a few feet of them and stopped.

Lock's focus remained on the man's hands, waiting for them to move inside his coat. But they didn't, and when he finally spoke it was with a slightly affected WASPy accent, the words clipped and decisive. 'Mr Lock?'

Another reporter, no doubt. Lock glared up at the man from his beer. 'Sorry, but NBC already have me tied up.'

'You should be so lucky,' Carrie muttered.

Lock opened his mouth to tell the guy that they were leaving, then stopped as he saw his face up close. He had scaly black bags under his eyes and looked like he was about to burst into tears.

The man's gaze flitted briefly to Carrie, then back to Lock. 'Mr Lock,' he said, his voice breaking, 'I'm not a reporter. My name's Richard Hulme. I'm Josh Hulme's father.'

12

'How did you find me?' Lock asked Richard Hulme.

'One of your friends at Meditech. Tyrone. He gave me a list of places you might be. I think he feels bad about Meditech not being prepared to help out.'

They were alone in a corner booth, Carrie having agreed to catch up with Lock later.

'You want to tell me what happened?' Lock asked.

Richard launched into his story, his voice contained and even. What many would have taken as a lack of emotion, Lock recognized as a father doing his best not to unravel; not through any overweening macho pride, but because stoicism on his part might help get his son back in one piece. Lock had been here before, and like anyone who'd dealt with a child abduction the memory had never abated.

However, as Richard began to lay out the sequence of events, as methodically as one might expect from a scientist, Lock became more unsettled. This wasn't like any other kidnap case he had either been involved in or even heard of.

'I didn't even know he was gone until the next morning. I should explain. I was at a conference out of town. I'd called from my hotel but I just assumed that because Josh was in bed . . . '

'Your wife had turned the phone off?'

Richard swallowed hard. 'Josh's mother passed away three years ago. Cancer.'

Lock said nothing. This was a time for analysis, not platitudes. Josh's mother being dead eliminated scenario one. Something like ninety-five per cent of child abductions were the result of some misguided power play by so-called adults.

'Your au pair, Natalya, she Eastern European?'

'Russian to be precise. St Petersburg, I think.'

'How long's she been with you?'

'About four months or so. You don't think . . . ?'

'It's possible. Take it from me, the part of the world Natalya's from, kidnapping is right up there with alcoholism and wife beating when it comes to ways to pass the long winter nights, so I wouldn't rule it out. The good news is the Russian Mafia doesn't believe in killing their victims. It tends to damage repeat business.'

'There's no way Natalya would be involved.'

'There never is. Until it happens.'

'Josh adored her, and it was mutual.'

'You're not going to like me for asking you this, but . . . '

The way Richard almost flinched, Lock could tell he knew what was coming.

'I wasn't fooling around with Natalya. That's what you were going to ask me, right?'

'Listen, no one's going to judge you if you were. Specially not with your wife having passed away.'

'The FBI asked me the same thing.'

That caused Lock to raise his hand, palm

65

facing Richard. 'If the FBI are involved, why are you so keen to talk to me? Why not leave it to them?' It was the question that had been niggling away at him ever since he'd met Richard.

'They're getting nowhere fast. I'm prepared to deal with whoever I can.' He paused.

'If there's something you need to say to me, spit it out.'

'With Meg gone, Josh is all I have. I need someone who'll do whatever it takes.'

'And you thought that would be me?'

'Yes.'

Lock got up.

'Where are you going?' Richard said, getting up too.

'The FBI are the experts here,' Lock said, hating himself for offering such a transparent platitude. 'Let them do their job.'

Richard grabbed at the lapel of his jacket. Lock stared at his hand until he withdrew it.

'I'm sorry for your loss. I truly am.'

'You're speaking like he's dead already.'

Lock stayed silent.

'So that's it? The company won't help me and neither will you?'

'What did they say when you spoke to them?'

'That I wasn't their problem any more. Neither was Josh. Not quite in those words, but I could tell that's what they meant.'

'You want me to talk to them for you?'

Lock noticed Richard's nails digging into his palms.

'What I want is to find my son. I don't care how it gets done.'

'I can make a few phone calls for you. But beyond that I can't go. I'm sorry.'

Richard's face sank. 'A few phone calls? That's it? I come and ask for your help and you'll *make a few calls*?'

'Listen, Dr Hulme, I work for Meditech — y'know, the people who don't want to help you. What makes you think this is my job?'

Richard rubbed at his face. 'I don't know. Maybe because risking your life to save that protestor in the wheelchair wasn't your job either, I thought . . . '

'Like I said, I'm sorry.'

Richard's hand trembled as he jabbed an index finger in Lock's face. 'You know how this'll end, and so do I,' he shouted, drawing looks from the smattering of patrons dotted around the place. Lock pulled him to the door. 'My son's going to be sacrificed to those lunatics and all you and Meditech can do is feed me some corporate bullshit.'

Lock dropped his voice to a whisper, hoping that what he was about to say might calm Richard sufficiently that his comments about Meditech were restricted to people in a four-block radius rather than the entire five boroughs. 'If I thought I was the best person to help you, Dr Hulme, believe me I would. But the fact remains I'm not.'

Richard took a deep breath. 'You found Greer Price.'

Lock puffed out his cheeks and exhaled slowly, his breath misting in the cold. Richard Hulme had obviously done some digging of his own.

'Haven't heard that name in a long time,' he said.

Greer Price was a four-year-old who had gone missing in a supermarket adjacent to a British military base in Osnabruck, Germany. Despite the fact that there had been at least two dozen shoppers and store employees there at the time, and that Greer's mother had turned her back for a matter of seconds, there had been no witnesses to the little girl's disappearance. Lock was a rookie with the Royal Military Police and the trail had been stone cold a full year before he was given it. Richard was right, Lock had solved the case, but he'd never counted it as a career highlight.

'Greer was dead by the time I found her.'

'You still found her, though.'

'For all the good it did.'

'You brought someone to justice.'

'I brought someone before the courts, where they were convicted and sentenced. Justice didn't enter into it.'

For a second, Lock found himself back in the attic of a small insignificant house, owned by an apparently even more insignificant old man. A former accountant, given to ordering everything, even the unimaginable. Lock had spent two days in that attic, searching through box after box filled with clear plastic Ziploc bags. Each bag contained mementoes of an abused child, the bags marked in black ink with the date of their abuse. Greer had been discovered a few days later, buried in the back garden.

He suppressed a shudder at the thought of a

place he never wished to revisit, not even in his mind's eye, as Richard Hulme stood there waiting for an answer.

'OK,' Lock said finally. 'Finish your story. Maybe I'll catch something that the FBI missed. But if I don't, will you leave me alone?'

Richard nodded.

They left the bar and walked to Richard's car, a late-model Volvo station wagon. The windows fogged as the heater worked overtime to keep them from freezing.

'So you get home, and no one's there.'

'Yeah. I tried to reach Natalya on her cell but it must have been switched off.'

Lock made a mental note. The only way for a cell phone not to be traced was for it to be completely off, otherwise the authorities could triangulate its position from the masts in the area.

'Go on.'

'I thought maybe Natalya had forgotten her phone. I didn't like intruding on her privacy, but under the circumstances . . . So I searched her room, gave it an extra hour, then called the police. They called in the FBI.'

Lock knew this was standard procedure in these cases, when someone of what the Feds euphemistically called 'tender years', meaning a minor aged twelve or under, went missing. Over twelve and there had to be some suggestion of the person crossing state lines before they'd step in.

'Last time they were seen?'

'A few of the other au pairs at the party said

they saw Natalya pick him up. They got into a car, and that was it.'

'What kind of car?'

'A grey Lincoln town car.'

'That usually how Natalya and Josh got around?'

'Natalya has the number of a town car service I have an account with in case the weather's really bad during the school run.' Richard sighed and rubbed at his eyes. 'But they had no record of Natalya requesting a car in the past week.'

'Did the FBI talk to their drivers?'

'At length. They were all accounted for when Josh went missing.'

'But he was definitely seen getting into the car with Natalya?'

'That's right.'

'Was there any sign of a struggle? Of him being forced into the car?'

Richard shook his head.

'And you're still sure Natalya's not involved?'

'I know how it looks. Maybe she thought she'd ordered a car and forgot.'

Lock sensed that Richard was clutching at straws, refusing to accept the inevitable: that a woman he'd hired was responsible for the kidnap of his only child.

'Did she come into the country on a visa or was she already here?'

Richard bristled slightly. 'I used an agency. I wouldn't employ someone illegally.'

'So they would have done a background check.'

'They assured me they'd checked her out thoroughly.'

70

'Have you had any previous threats?'

'Of course. Everyone at Meditech gets those.'

'No, I mean stuff that came directly to your home. Letters? Phone calls?'

'One or two crank calls, just before I resigned. And some emails.'

'Was that why you decided to leave Meditech?'

'One factor, yes.'

'The other factors?'

'All laid out in my letter of resignation.'

Lock was starting to get irritated. 'Help's a two-way street, Richard.'

Richard shifted awkwardly in his seat. 'I disagreed with the animal testing, but more on scientific grounds than ethical.'

'But you were involved with it?'

'For most of my career, yes.'

'Was the pressure starting to get to you?'

'It was a decision that I arrived at after a lot of consideration. I wouldn't have resigned if I didn't think it was bad science.'

Lock had heard enough about the debate around animal testing over the past few months, and certainly didn't want another lecture like the one he'd endured from Janice. He moved on. 'And were there any threats after that?'

'Not that I made my resignation public, but no.'

'And since Josh disappeared, what contact has there been?'

Richard's gaze fell to the floor. 'That's just it. There hasn't been any.'

Lock was disbelieving. 'No ransom demand? No demands of any kind?'

'Nothing.'

Scenario two could be crossed off the list. Beyond a parent or step parent snatching a child, three per cent of abductions fell into the category of kidnap for ransom. Due to the prohibitive sentences handed down by the judiciary since the Lindbergh kidnapping, only dumb or hardcore felons in the US viewed kidnap for ransom as any kind of business opportunity. Elsewhere, however, it was one of the big growth areas of criminal enterprise, up there with counterfeiting, internet fraud and trafficking. In these cases, where profit was the motive, the ransom demand swiftly followed the abduction, usually accompanied by dire warnings that the victim's family should not, under any circumstances, contact the authorities.

Lock chewed his bottom lip. What lurked behind the door of scenario number three didn't bear thinking about. The animal rights activists were people who didn't mind digging up an old lady and dumping her remains in the middle of Times Square to make a point.

Richard looked at Lock, his pupils wide with fear. 'It's bad, isn't it?'

Lock took a moment before answering. 'Yes, it's bad.'

13

Half of the 19th Precinct must be on guard duty, thought Lock, as he and Richard stepped from the elevator and walked towards Richard's front door.

The patrol officer reacted with a mixture of alarm and relief as he saw them. 'You're not supposed to leave without letting us know,' he said to Richard.

Richard blanched, like a kid caught breaking curfew. 'I'm sorry, I hope I didn't get you into trouble.'

As Richard ushered Lock into the apartment, the cop was already on his radio, letting his superiors know that he was back — with a guest.

Like most of the rest of the building, the apartment lay in near darkness. It was close to midnight, and in this part of town the streets were quiet. Lock figured that the kind of money that had to be generated in order to afford a place in this neighbourhood required most of its residents to favour early nights over bar hopping.

Richard flipped on a light switch to reveal a narrow hallway, off which were three bedrooms and a bathroom. Beyond that it opened out into a large open-plan living area.

'How long you lived here?' asked Lock.

'Since before I got married. It was Meg's place

from when she was a graduate student.'

'Pretty swanky part of town for a grad student.'

'Rent controlled. An aunt of hers died,' said Richard as he went to turn on the main light.

'You may want to close the drapes first.'

'I forget sometimes. Plus, with Josh gone, I'm not sure I care any more.'

Like every other Meditech employee above a certain level, Richard would have gone through a security awareness programme and review. Lock knew that he would have been advised to alter his daily routine as much as possible, and to watch out for the absence of the normal, like a doorman missing from the front of the building. Ditto the presence of the abnormal, like a doorman suddenly appearing in a building which didn't have one. All of the advice boiled down to remaining vigilant and employing simple common sense.

Lock wandered over to a tiny kitchen area at the far end of the room. Two couches. No TV. Built-in shelving ran along one wall, crammed with books and papers. A family portrait. Richard, Josh and a strikingly attractive blonde woman that he wouldn't have put with Richard in a million years.

'Meg,' Richard said, saving Lock an awkward question about his dead wife. 'There's been no one since we lost her. I didn't feel it would have been fair on Josh. Actually, that's not strictly true.'

Lock said nothing. Let him continue.

'There's been my work. Maybe I've used that

as my way of not confronting things,' Richard added, before rubbing again at his eyes.

Lock was starting to feel Richard coming off a little too noble. 'You mind if I look around the rest of the place?'

Richard shrugged his agreement.

Lock headed back down the corridor, the walls blank either side of him. He couldn't help feeling that the place resembled more of a college dorm than a family home.

The first bedroom was similarly utilitarian, although the lack of personal touches was more easily forgiven here. Natalya clearly hadn't brought much with her when she'd moved. A portable CD player lay on the bed, an already ancient relic. On the bedside table there was a picture of an older man and woman, presumably her parents. What Lock assumed to be her brother stood in front of and to one side of his father, edging him by a good foot in height, even though he couldn't have been more than fifteen. Natalya stood next to her mother, long dark hair pulled back into a ponytail, her eyes and smile bright and confident. No pictures of a boyfriend, nor anyone else for that matter.

An attractive young Russian girl, and, by her standards, a wealthy widower not past his prime. Lock wondered how truthful Richard had been when he'd claimed that there was nothing going on between him and Natalya. From the look of Josh's mother, Richard could attract good-looking women. Perhaps he'd not wanted to complicate things for the sake of his son. Either that or he was lying.

Although the FBI would have been all over the place with a fine-toothed comb, Lock made a quick search of his own, coming up with nothing that seemed significant. He stepped back into the corridor and pushed open the door of Josh's bedroom.

In contrast to the neat, almost antiseptic feel of the rest of the place, Josh's room was a mess of toys, sporting equipment and comic books. A single sleigh bed was backed against one wall. Atop the duvet sat an FAO Schwartz teddy bear, the only concession to his tender years. A catcher's mitt had been placed on its head at a rakish angle.

Lock's mind flashed back to Osnabruck. He'd never been able to let go of the sense of failure he'd felt after the Greer Price case. Even though he'd known when he was handed the investigation that Greer was almost certainly long dead, it still gnawed away at him.

It was the loneliness of her death that had got to him more than anything. The feeling of abandonment she must have experienced in her last moments had left him hollowed out. Even at the end of the rope there was no act of vengeance that came close to balancing the murder of a child; if there had been, he would have put a bullet through the skull of Greer's killer himself.

He squared his shoulders, took a deep breath and walked out of Josh's room.

In a corner of Richard's room, a twirling strand of DNA bounced around a twenty-inch flatscreen computer display, which sat atop a desk. Lock moved the mouse and it disappeared, defaulting to a log-in screen.

'The FBI have already been through everything on there,' said Richard, framed in the doorway. 'But if you think they might have missed anything . . . '

'You mean, in case you're involved?'

The notion seemed ludicrous but Lock knew he couldn't dismiss it out of hand. It wouldn't have been the first time a perpetrator had brought about his own discovery by trying to employ a private investigator as a smokescreen to bolster his appearance of innocence.

Richard looked shocked. 'No, don't be ridiculous. I mean, maybe there's an email, something that might be a clue.'

It couldn't hurt to look.

Richard pulled up Firefox. 'I burned all my work emails to disk before I left.'

'You have a copy?'

'Here,' Richard said, pulling a DVD from a carousel next to the computer.

'Any other email account?'

'Hotmail, but I hardly use it.'

'Did the FBI look at your Hotmail account?'

'Why would they? I didn't get any threats through it.'

'You mind if I do?'

'Go right ahead.'

Richard opened Firefox, which defaulted to Hotmail. He typed in his username and password, handed Lock the disk with his work emails, and left him to it.

Lock doubted that the email threats would yield anything. Or the letters, for that matter. Anyone who went to the trouble of mailing a death threat wasn't likely to sign their name, either directly or by licking the envelope and leaving their DNA all over it. And the emails would have been sent from an internet cafe or via multiple proxy servers. One of the things he'd learned about the animal rights people who'd targeted Meditech was that they were savvy as well as motivated. Many of them were college-educated and as up on the science involved as anyone Meditech had to offer.

A half-hour later, Lock was no further forward. There were no specific threats to anyone by name, apart from Richard. Family was mentioned in a catch-all manner; there was no reference to a son, or even a wife, deceased or otherwise. As poison-pen correspondence went, it was all fairly insipid.

He switched back to the web browser. Idly, he clicked on the deleted emails folder and scrolled through the spam offering to enhance the recipient's sexual performance or asking to use their bank account to rest millions of dollars.

Then he spotted it. Unopened, like most of the rest of the spam. No subject line. A Gmail address. It had arrived the day of the shooting, maybe an hour before Josh was last seen with Natalya. He clicked it open.

Now you will feel the pain you have inflicted on others.
Lone Wolf

78

When he walked back into the living room, Richard was standing by the window with the lights off. Lock considered asking him about the email. Richard had been pretty adamant that the threats had ceased once he'd stopped working for the company so he decided to let it go. It had made no reference to Josh or the kidnapping, and crucially it registered as unopened.

A car drew up directly opposite the apartment block and Lock watched as a man got out. As he darted across the street and passed under a streetlight, Lock's gut instinct was confirmed. It was Frisk.

Lock met the FBI agent at the door.

'Get the hell out of here, Lock,' Frisk grunted, 'we can handle this.'

Lock was still riled from their encounter back at the hospital. When Frisk had given him that bullshit speech about no charges being pressed as if he was doing Lock some kind of personal favour.

'You seem to be doing a bang-up job so far, Agent Frisk,' observed Lock.

'It's early on.'

Lock pulled the door closed, so Richard wouldn't hear the rest of the exchange. A pissing contest meant some hard facts might come to light, and Lock wasn't sure Richard was ready for them.

'Early's when you put it to bed. You know that and I know that. But seeing as you're here, Hulme came looking for me, not the other way round.'

'Fifteen minutes of fame not enough for you,

79

huh?' said Frisk aggressively.

'OK, we can stand out here and compare dicks, or we can try and help each other out,' Lock said, lowering his voice.

'And what possible help are you going to be?'

'Well, for a start, you might want to take another look at his computer.'

'One of our tech guys already did a data dump from the hard drive.'

'Which wouldn't help you with a web-based email account. Check the spam folder. You're looking for an email from someone calling themselves Lone Wolf. Arrived the day it all went down at Meditech.'

Frisk's stony face reddened. Some tech was going to get his ass chewed when he got back to Federal Plaza, Lock could tell.

'Anything else?'

Lock shrugged. 'That's it . . . for now.'

'So what's your take on all this? Come on, if you've got some dazzling insights, I'd love to hear them.'

'Find the au pair and you find the boy.'

'Get with the programme, Lock. We already did. The harbour unit pulled her out of the East River a half-hour ago.'

14

A visit to the morgue was a grim affair at the best of times, and this was a long way from the best of times. The fact that there was still no sign of Josh, dead or alive, counted as good under the circumstances, although the river could have been waiting to offer up its misery in instalments. The bad news was that the task of identifying Natalya's body had fallen to Richard Hulme. As if the poor bastard didn't have enough to deal with, thought Lock, as he listened to Frisk make the request.

Richard had been stoical about it, agreeing without argument. Even if he hadn't already offered to help, Lock figured it was the least he could do to tag along as a shoulder to cry on. That, and there might be something to glean from Natalya's recovery. Something that might just help them to find Josh. If he was still alive.

It was hot in the corridor outside where the identification took place. Lock's head was still pounding. He found a solitary chair, sat down and made the mistake of closing his eyes.

He came to as Richard was led in, eyes rimmed red, hands trembling, the heavy weight of realizing that very bad things could happen to good people bearing down on him. Things that a person might never wholly recover from. Lock had seen that look before, when he'd stood across from the family of Greer Price as her coffin was lowered into the ground. He'd hoped never to see it again, but now here he was, offering a silent prayer that history wasn't about to repeat itself.

From what little Frisk had told him about the FBI's investigation, Lock had gathered that they'd garnered the same amount of significant information Lock had managed to glean in his few hours talking to Richard. Almost nothing. So, Lock did something which went against every fibre of his professional being: he made a phone call to a member of the media. A phone call which he knew in all likelihood would get him fired, and might even ensure that he never worked private security again.

That said, he didn't flinch from it. His approach when backed into a corner was always the same: fast, aggressive action with determination. Which didn't have to mean using your fists.

'I need a favour.'

On the other end of the line, Carrie sounded bleary. 'Ryan?'

'You know how I said I'd think about giving you an interview . . . '

He could see her sitting up, reaching over for the pad and pen that lived on the left bedside table.

'You'll do it?'

'No.'

'You woke me up to tell me that?'

'No, I called to make you an even better offer.'

★　★　★

82

Frisk's voice echoed so loud against the tiled walls of the mortuary that one of the orderlies actually asked him to keep it down.

Lock wasn't entirely sure what decibel level had to be reached to wake the dead, but between Frisk's outburst and the retina-busting strip lights, the headache he'd been feeling since discharge was about to go nuclear.

'Are you out of your mind? Whackjobs like this love this kind of attention,' Frisk shouted, poking a finger into Lock's face.

Lock didn't react. 'It's already out there in the public domain.'

'So you want to put him on national TV?'

'International. I'm sure other countries will pick it up.'

'And what if this pushes the kidnappers over the edge?'

'If they were going to kill him, if that was the plan, they'd have done it by now.'

'And what if they haven't?'

'Someone has to have seen something. Someone must know where he is. At the very least we'll get their attention.'

'You say that like it's a good thing.'

'So what's the alternative? Sit back and wait for a break?'

'You're interfering in a federal investigation.'

'So arrest me.'

'Don't be too sure I won't,' said Frisk, heading back through to check on Richard Hulme.

★ ★ ★

As the freezer cabinet clanged shut on the body, Richard shivered involuntarily. 'I can't tell.'

Even with the work that had been done to piece together what remained of Natalya's face, the hollow-point bullet and the river had done their work. It might be Natalya. Likely it was. But he couldn't be certain.

Frisk put an arm on his shoulder. He was used to this type of uncertainty with witnesses, less so at the morgue. 'Don't worry, Dr Hulme, we can do a match with the DNA we picked up back at your place. It'll take a little longer, but that's OK.'

* * *

Outside, Lock paced the corridor. If he'd been a smoker he'd have been breaking open his third pack of the day by this point. He thought about the body laid out a few feet away and tried to reconcile it with the photograph in Natalya's room. He thought too about her parents and the phone call they'd be getting. Your daughter, the child whose nose you wiped and tears you dried, the one who grew up into a beautiful young woman, the one who had her chance of a new life in America . . . she's been murdered.

Lock took in a lungful of air. He knew he had to pack away such thoughts. He couldn't afford them right now. There'd be plenty of time for all that later. Too much time. Now he had to focus on the living.

He was still sure that Natalya, even in death, was the key. Perhaps even more so in death. If

84

she had no significance, why take the trouble of killing her? Natalya was the last person seen with Josh. Natalya had led him into the car. Active accomplice, or unwitting rube, Natalya's story was the story of this abduction. He was sure of it.

The door down the corridor clicked open, and Richard emerged alone. He saw Lock and shook his head. 'I couldn't tell. She'd been . . . ' His knees folded under him, and he sank to the floor.

Lock wished some of the animal rights people were here to witness this, given how ready they'd been in the past to caricature men like Hulme as heartless vivisectionists who got a kick from inflicting suffering on helpless animals.

Richard looked up at Lock, his skin dishwater grey. 'They shot her in the face.'

Lock helped him back to his feet. 'Listen to me, you have to believe that Josh is still alive. If someone had wanted him dead, they wouldn't have gone to all this trouble.'

'But say something went wrong? Like they tried to escape and that's how it happened? Josh can be pretty wilful at times.'

'In a situation like this, wilful's not necessarily a bad thing. Wilful might just keep him alive.'

'Really?'

'Absolutely,' Lock lied.

15

The room was white and smelled of fresh paint. The door was grey and so heavy that the driver had struggled to open it when they'd arrived. Josh had heard him grunting with the effort, although he couldn't see him. He'd put a hat over Josh's head and pulled it down over his eyes for the last part of the journey.

The floor was grey as well. It always felt cold when he stepped on it. There was a bed. It was longer than the one he had at home but not much wider. There was no window, but there was a light. It was a clear plastic dome and was mounted on the ceiling at the farthest end of the room from the door. It never went off. Next to it was a camera, like the kind he had seen in stores sometimes. There was a television, which was hooked up to a DVD player and a selection of DVDs. All stuff for little kids. Stuff he would have watched when he was maybe six.

There was a toilet and a sink. Both of these were silver and shiny. The toilet was directly under the camera so he didn't think anyone could watch him pee. That was something at least.

And that was it. The entire contents of his room. Apart from him of course. And his clothes. And the photo album. But he didn't like to think about the album. He didn't even like to touch it.

It had been there when he arrived. Next to the DVDs. It didn't look like anything, just an album with a grey cover and a red spine. No title on the front or anything saying who wrote it. He'd made the mistake of opening it. Every time he'd gone to sleep since then he'd had nightmares about the pictures in it. Horrible pictures of horrible things. Now he was afraid to go to sleep.

There was a metal flap at the bottom of the door. It would open and food would be pushed through. Mostly cereal, sandwiches, or potato chips, with juice. If he got down on his knees he could see a man's hand push it through. He thought it might be the driver's hand but he couldn't be sure because the person never said anything.

The worst part of it was being alone. He wondered if people were looking for him. His dad must be. He tried to imagine the door opening and him walking in. He'd close his eyes and think of him scooping him up in his arms and cuddling him. Like Natalya used to do.

Then his mind would flash on to what happened to Natalya in the boat. Or worse, a picture from the album. Then he'd have to open his eyes again. And when he opened his eyes his dad would be gone, but the album would still be there. Then he'd start to cry again.

16

It was close to four in the morning by the time Lock got back to his own apartment, a studio in Morningside Heights, within spitting distance of Columbia University. There was nothing more that could be done now anyway. The lab was busy running the match to the body they thought was Natalya. From what Frisk had said, it was almost certain to come back positive. NBC were already trailing Carrie's exclusive with Richard Hulme, which was due to air later in the day. And everyone else with a job to do in the morning was asleep. Lock decided to join them, crashing out on top of his bed, fully clothed.

Less than four hours later he was awoken by a sliver of low winter sun creeping across the room. It took almost as much resolve not to throw a pillow over his head and go back to sleep as it had to storm the sniper position opposite the Meditech building. In the bathroom, he realized that limited time meant the choice was shave or shower. He wouldn't have time for both. Prioritizing body odour over smooth skin, he undressed quickly and climbed under the blast of hot water.

Standing with a towel around his waist, he rifled through his wardrobe. He wasn't short on dark colours, but suspected that blackout gear and a ski mask wouldn't be considered appropriate attire for a funeral. In the end, he compromised with black trousers, white shirt left open at the collar and a black parka jacket bulky enough to cover a multitude of sins, and his gun — returned to him last night after another heated exchange with Frisk.

As he dressed, he opened his fridge, only to be met by a mouldy and festering collection of food items worthy of a Gordon Ramsay smack-down. Grabbing a black garbage bag, he dumped most of the contents. Breakfast would have to wait.

The buzzer went. Lock pressed the intercom button. 'State your business.'

'It's Ty.'

Lock cracked the door open and went into the bedroom. When he came back out, Ty was standing in the kitchen, rifling the cabinets. Ty was almost always hungry but no matter how much Lock watched him eat it didn't appear to make a difference to his lanky six foot four basketball player's frame.

'You don't even keep cereal in this dump?' Ty asked him.

'I'm never here.'

Ty turned, stopped and stared at Lock. 'Wow, man. Just . . . wow.'

'I look like shit?'

'No, more like . . . ' Ty paused, ferreting out the word. 'Roadkill.'

Lock scratched at his stubble. 'Late night.'

'Dude, I've seen guys who've spent ten years on the pipe that look better than you. Anyway, shouldn't you be resting up?'

'I should be.'

'So why ain't you?'

'They found Josh Hulme's au pair.'

'Good. What she have to say for herself?'

'Not too much. She'd been shot in the face and dumped in the East River.'

'Harsh,' said Ty, his expression unchanging. He studied Lock's apparel. 'That why you're all duded up like Walker, Texas Ranger?'

'You saying I look like Chuck Norris?'

'Chuck on a bad day. Look, Ryan, you do remember me telling you that we're not getting involved.'

'We're not. I am.'

'Ryan, you're an employee of Meditech, same as me.'

'And while I'm convalescing, I thought I'd do some pro bono work.'

Lock grabbed a towel, walked into the bathroom and closed the door.

Ty shifted some stale underwear from a chair and sat down as Lock disappeared into the bathroom. He smiled to himself. It had to be said, this was classic Lock. The guy had never found a lost cause he didn't like.

It was how Lock had been ever since they'd first hooked up in Iraq, Ty in the Marines and Lock, bizarrely, in the Close Protection Unit of the British Royal Military Police. Lock had become a source of instant fascination to Ty. Although he walked, talked, even chewed gum like an American, here he was working with the limeys, having flown to England to enlist straight out of college. The decision, Lock later explained, came courtesy of a Scottish émigré father who'd served in the same unit but had fallen in love and married a girl from California — in the days before the Beach Boys let the rest of the world in on the secret.

Post-Iraq, and both finally out of uniform, Ty had hooked Lock up with the Meditech gig. He wasn't even fazed when he found out that he'd be working as Lock's second-in-command. Putting aside his own ego, he knew that when it came to close protection work the RMP Close Protection Unit was as good as it got. No bravado. No special forces heroics. They simply got the job done with the minimum of fuss.

Lock emerged from the bathroom. Ty resolved to give it one more shot.

'This isn't a good idea, brother. Brand's after your job.'

'Tell me something I don't know.'

Both Lock and Ty knew Brand had been looking to step into Lock's shoes ever since his appointment.

'And he's been whispering in Stafford Van Straten's ear. Saying how you were grandstanding when it all went down at headquarters,' Ty said.

'Pot. Kettle.'

'Maybe so, but Stafford's been at his old man to dump you entirely. Listen, you're on their payroll and they don't want to get involved with this kidnapping.'

'Richard Hulme worked for them long enough. They owe him this much.'

'Not how they see it. Tell me to butt out if you want, but leave this alone.'

'They send you?'

'Hell, no. They don't know anything about this.'

'So what they don't know can't hurt 'em.'

Ty's face split into a grin. If that was how Lock saw things, then hell, he might as well go along for the ride.

17

Carrie looked straight down the barrel of camera two. 'It's every parent's nightmare. A crime which grips the public like no other. Your son or daughter snatched, by a person or persons unknown. Who can possibly imagine the torment felt by a loving father' — they cut from Carrie to a close-up of an uncomfortable-looking Richard Hulme as he straightened his tie for the umpteenth time — 'for whom that nightmare is reality? In a few moments we talk to Dr Richard Hulme. His seven-year-old son Josh disappeared after leaving a Christmas Eve party on the city's Upper East Side. A body believed to be that of Josh's au pair, Russian-born Natalya Verovsky, was found yesterday. But, as of this hour, there is no sign of little Josh. Tonight his father speaks about his son's disappearance, and the role his work as chief research scientist for controversial company Meditech may have played in his abduction. That's coming up, right after these messages.'

The teaser finished, and they cut to commercial. Carrie turned to Richard who was sitting beside her, ashen-faced.

'I never agreed to speak about Meditech.'

'Then just don't answer those questions,' she replied, a hint of steel in her voice.

'But then I'll look like someone who has something to hide.'

'Well, do you?' she challenged.

Richard looked away.

Carrie leaned in closer to him. 'I'm here to help you find your son. But I also plan on getting to the bottom of this story. With or without you.'

Back from the commercial break, Carrie set about laying out the timeline of Josh's disappearance, aware that as she did so Richard was doing his best not to break down, his face caught in a slowly creeping zoom. 'Every morning I wake up and it's like being underwater,' he said, his voice cracking. Carrie nodded sympathetically. After the next break she planned on making her move, changing up a gear and moving on to Meditech and the animal rights people. Lock had given her a couple of questions that he wanted out there, like why had Meditech cut Richard loose? They both knew that Richard wouldn't have the answers but by putting them out in the public domain they could rely on the rest of the media to broaden the focus.

As Carrie segued to the next break, she could hear her producer, Gail Reindl, in her ear: 'I need to talk to you before we come back live. I'm on my way down.'

Carrie made sure that a production assistant refilled Richard's glass of water as she headed to the back of the studio to meet Gail.

Gail pulled Carrie into a corner. 'Lose the Meditech questions.'

'Why?'

'Don't ask.'

'This is total BS,' Carrie said, breaking away. 'I

know, don't tell me: one of their publicity people has been on the phone hollering about pulling their ads from the network. Damn flacks.'

Gail ignored the comment. 'Listen, the emotional stuff is dynamite. We won't be losing anything by not asking him about it.'

'Apart from the truth, you mean?'

Gail snorted derisively. 'You're coming off like some first-year journalism grad student at Columbia.'

Carrie bristled. 'No, I'm going after the story. How can we not mention that he worked for a company outside whose headquarters several people were just killed? It'll make us look like idiots.'

'OK, ref it when you come back, but move straight on.'

'To what?'

'You'll think of something.'

And with that Gail was gone, in a swish of black cashmere and a trail of Chanel No. 5. Carrie had to speed-walk across the floor to make it back to her position in time.

The eyes of the nation back on her, Carrie didn't miss a beat. 'Richard, until a few weeks ago you used to work for the Meditech Corporation.'

'Yes, yes I did.'

'And how long did you work for them?'

'In total, approximately six years.'

'And what did your work involve?'

'I was involved in a number of areas.'

'Which involved testing on animals?'

Richard didn't hesitate. 'That's correct. I

believed that the benefits to mankind out-weighed any suffering caused to the animals.'

'But recently you left Meditech's employ?'

'A few weeks before Josh went missing, yes.'

She could hear Gail, out of breath from having run all the way back to the booth, in her earpiece: 'OK, now back to the kid.'

'What was the nature of the work you did for Meditech?'

'That I can't discuss in any detail. There are confidentiality issues.'

Gail again: 'Back the hell off, Carrie.'

Carrie smiled evenly across at Richard, her next comments directed right back at Gail, and whatever asshole in a suit had decided to try to do her job for her. 'I understand, and your loyalty is commendable, particularly in light of the fact that your previous employer won't assist you in finding your son — isn't that correct?'

Richard hesitated this time. 'Yes . . . that's correct.'

As they went to the next break, Gail was back by Carrie's side. Carrie braced herself for the onslaught. Gail Reindl in attack mode was a sight to behold.

Instead she studied the studio floor and said, 'Wrap it up with Hulme.'

'But we still have ten minutes.'

'I do realize that, but we have a call. I want you to take it live on air.'

Carrie's heart quickened. 'We have a lead already?'

'We have every crank from Long Island to Long Beach jamming the switchboards, but this one's a bit different. The CEO of Meditech wants to clarify a few points.'

Carrie did her best to suppress a smile. Not at the thought of more ratings dynamite, more at the last thing Lock had said to her when he called to set up the interview with Richard Hulme.

Let's see if we can't rattle a few cages.

From the very corner of her vision, Carrie could see Richard being led out by a production assistant. As the floor manager counted her back in with a silent folding of three fingers, she stared straight down the lens.

'On the line now we have Nicholas Van Straten, majority shareholder and chief executive officer of Richard Hulme's former employer Meditech. Mr Van Straten, thank you for getting in touch. Our viewers will certainly appreciate your perspective.'

18

There was no need for masks. There were no cameras inside the apartment, and the only witness was the person they'd come to kill. The taller man knocked first, while the smaller of the two men stood off to one side of the door.

No one answered at first. The men traded worried glances, but said nothing. The taller man knocked again. Maybe the TV was up too loud. Or she'd gone out. They were just about to leave when the door cracked open and the side of the woman's face pressed between door and frame. It was that kind of neighbourhood.

The taller man smiled. 'Mrs Parker?' he asked.

'I told you people already, I don't know where they're hiding.'

'It's not about that, Mrs Parker.'

'Did someone complain about my cats?'

'I'm sorry to disturb you, ma'am, but may I come in?'

He could see her thinking about this, taking in that he was polite, well dressed and, most important of all, white. She closed the door so she could slide back the chain, then opened it again and let him in. He stepped inside.

'Let me get that for you,' he said, closing the door, but not all the way.

The smell was overwhelming. He didn't know how anyone could live like this. A cat vibratoed a miaow and rubbed itself against his legs. He stepped over it and followed the woman into the living room. Sure enough, the TV was on, Cesar Milan lecturing an anorexic woman about how to talk to her Rhodesian Ridgeback. So much for people looking like their animals.

'Now, let me tell you something about these people next door to me. They don't like my cats, y'see.'

'And they're such lovely creatures,' he said, moving so that if she was to stay facing him her back would be to the door.

'You think so?'

'Absolutely. My favourite domestic animal. By some way.'

'Do you have one?'

She was side on to the door now. Almost in position.

'No, afraid I live in a co-op with a no-pets rule.'

'That's a shame.'

The smaller man appeared in the doorway now, the woman oblivious to his presence. But the half-dozen cats dotted around the room weren't. With some kind of feline sixth sense they began to yowl. First one, then another.

The smaller man moved fast, taking the last few steps in under a second, flicking off the plastic cap of the syringe as he did. As she turned, he plunged the tip of the syringe into her left buttock and pushed down on the barrel.

As she started to scream, the taller man wrapped his arms around her. The smaller man clamped his free hand over her mouth. A cat hissed and jumped on to the TV set where it stared, unblinking, as its owner slumped to the floor. Her mouth was open. So were her eyes. The expression on her face was one of complete bewilderment.

'OK, let's get her into the chair.'

Together, they hauled her into the solitary armchair, hands resting in her lap. The smaller man folded down her eyelids with thumb and index finger, then stepped back to admire his handiwork.

'She looks too posed,' said the taller man.

'You're right.' The smaller man bent down and pulled at her right foot so that one leg was splayed at an angle. A final check. 'Perfect,' he said, bending down to retrieve the plastic cap of the syringe.

'What about the cats?'

'What about them?'

'Well, won't they starve?'

The smaller man took one final look at the dead old lady in the armchair.

'They got a good three weeks' supply right there.'

19

Stafford Van Straten appeared to be on the edge of an aneurysm. He combed his mane of blond hair with one hand while his mouth opened and closed with all the articulacy of a goldfish. 'You're putting Lock in charge of this?'

His father pulled him to one side, out of earshot of his entourage. 'I know you and he don't get on, for whatever reason, but we can use him right now,' he said, ignoring the fact that they both knew the reason Stafford and Lock didn't see eye to eye. As reasons went it wasn't one Nicholas Van Straten was likely to forget either. It was a reason that had cost him no end of sleepless nights, and a quarter of a million dollars.

'But Richard Hulme's not our problem.'

'Listen to me. Whatever our problems with Richard Hulme, or whatever our lawyers are saying — ' Nicholas Van Straten stopped, lowering his voice to an urgent hiss. 'A child is missing. What if it were you?'

Stafford smirked. 'I'm hardly a child.'

'Precisely, so stop behaving like one.'

Dismissing his son with a turn of his shoulder, Nicholas Van Straten waved Ty over. 'Tyrone?'

'Yes, sir.'

'Any luck getting hold of Ryan?'

'He's still off comms.'

'In English please, Tyrone.'

101

'His cell's switched off.'

'OK, as soon as you get hold of him, I want him in here for a briefing. In the meantime, can you start actioning our other procedures?'

'Yes, sir.'

★ ★ ★

Stafford strode into his office, picked up the putter leaning in the corner and swung it like a baseball bat, narrowly avoiding his desk. He was the heir apparent, the man who'd be running the company one day, and he wasn't even asked for his opinion. The building's super had more say in the running of the company than he did.

The door into the executive bathroom was ajar and he caught sight of his own reflection. He paused, pleased by his own image, by the bright blue eyes and thick blond hair, both inherited from his mother. Only his father's weak chin let him down. With a solid chin it would have been a face for the front cover of *Fortune* magazine. The face of a man born to greatness.

'You look real pretty.'

Stafford spun round to see Brand framed in the doorway. He let the club fall into a more conventional position and mimed sinking a twelve-footer. 'Don't you know to knock first?' he asked, feeling like he'd been caught with his pants down.

Brand put a hand on his shoulder. 'Don't let the old man get to you.'

'This was our chance to get past all this animal rights crap. Why couldn't he have given this to one of your guys? I mean, anyone but Lock. I hate that guy.' Stafford kicked out at the wall with the point of his English-made leather Oxford brogues.

'You're not the only one.'

'So what do we do about him?'

'Can't you have a word with your old man? Maybe suggest to him that it's time Lock pursues other opportunities outside the company.'

Stafford smiled. 'And make you head of security?'

'Hey, that's not a bad idea.'

'He won't go for it. Not after what's happened. He thinks the sun rises out of Lock's asshole.'

'There's an image. You know what I think? Lock's probably the one who set up this interview. The broad who's doing it, Lock was seeing her for a while.'

'Maybe I can use that.'

Brand clapped Stafford again on the shoulder. 'Your chance'll come, Stafford. You and me, we're the ones to watch. Your old man and Lock, they'll be history soon.'

20

A 'For Lease' sign hung like a white flag outside the Korean deli. Further down, the Meditech building looked the same as it had before the shooting, albeit with one or two muscular additions in the form of half a dozen Metalith™ anti-ram barriers. The glass frontage had been made over too, the tint of the windows, even in this light, hinting at blast-proof capabilities.

They threw back Lock's reflection at him as he stood outside, studying the face of an ever-changing stranger. What had once been a shadow was now the approach of a full beard. His eyes had large dark half-moons underneath them. His pupils were wide but the whites bloodshot. He was reminded of someone else. It took him a moment to think of who. That was it. He looked like Richard Hulme. He took off his ball cap, reached up and rubbed at the stitches in his scalp. Maybe they'd all end up looking like Richard Hulme before Josh was found.

He took three steps into the foyer.

'Excuse me, sir, who are you here to see?'

It was one of Brand's team. A baby-faced former Marine who went by the name of Hizzard.

Lock glanced at the bulge under the guard's overcoat. 'Hizzard, it might be freezing out there, but it's eighty degrees in here. You look like a moron.'

Hizzard reluctantly took off his coat to reveal a

Mini Uzi with what Lock guessed from first glance was a fifty-round mag.

'Jesus, second thoughts, put your coat back on before someone sees that thing. What the hell is this? *Get Rich or Die Tryin'*?'

Hizzard looked sheepish.

'Listen up, Fiddy,' Lock said, 'you pick a weapon based on its suitability for the job. No other reason.'

Footsteps echoed on the marble floors behind them. Lock looked over, pleased to see Ty loping towards him across the lobby.

'They want you up on twenty-five. We can talk on the way up.'

'Damn straight,' said Lock, glancing from Hizzard to Ty.

Ty directed a 'kids these days' shrug at Lock as they headed for the first bank of elevators that would take them as far as the twentieth floor. They got in and Ty pressed the button. The doors slid shut. A camera concealed in the front right corner of the elevator was on them. Lock turned so his back was to it and counted to ten.

'What's with all the hardware, Tyrone?'

'I told you, man, with you out we got the mother of all pissing contests here. Brand's marking his territory.'

The doors opened on twenty. Waiting for them were two more members of Brand's CA team. This time they were minus overcoats but both with the same model of machine pistol the boys downstairs were sporting.

Lock and Ty shared a look. The lunatics had clearly taken over the asylum.

21

Walking into the boardroom on the twenty-fifth floor, Lock felt about as much at ease as a crack-head crashing the Rainbow Room. Not that anyone said anything — far from it. No one commented on his appearance. Or asked how he was. Or enquired as to how he was getting on as 'official' Meditech point man in the search for Josh Hulme. Instead, they all studied whatever pieces of paper they had in front of them and waited for their boss, Nicholas Van Straten, to start.

Nicholas Van Straten sat at the head of the table. Stafford was directly to his father's right, Brand to his left. Not a good sign. Ty took a seat next to Lock, a few seats down. Scattered around the other chairs were five or six other employees. Some of them Lock could put a name to, some he couldn't. It was a big company.

Stafford looked Lock up and down. 'I didn't realize it was dress-down Friday.'

The woman from the media relations department tittered like a schoolgirl.

Lock stared at Stafford. 'My tux was at the cleaners.'

Nicholas Van Straten closed a thin manila folder with an expensively manicured hand and looked down the table, meeting Lock's gaze for a second. 'Thanks for being here, Ryan. I certainly appreciate it. How are you feeling?'

Lock directed his answer to Brand. 'Ready for duty.'

Brand smirked.

Lock took a breath, and did his best to centre himself. 'I apologize for my appearance. It's been a hectic day or two.'

Lock could see Ty studying the table, trying hard not to laugh.

'Quite,' said Nicholas. 'Now, shall we discuss where we go from here?'

The woman from public relations, who it transpired was the Missy of 'outside press conference' legend, launched into an enthusiastic pitch as to how best to handle the Josh Hulme kidnapping situation from a public relations perspective. Like the true professional she was, she started out with a little light ass-kissing. 'Well, Mr Van Straten, with your brilliant intervention we've made a great start at wresting back control of this very delicate situation. Clearly our initial lack of involvement did some damage, but that shouldn't last too long now that we're being seen to help.'

The 'being seen to' jarred with Lock but he remained silent. The terrain had clearly changed a lot in a very short space of time and he needed to get an overview of it before he said anything.

As Missy continued, using words of three syllables or more when two would have been sufficient, Lock studied Brand. A square head on an equally square torso, he was sitting ramrod straight, staring directly at the woman speaking. His hands were folded on the conference table, his fingers interlocked. He gave the appearance

107

of someone listening intently when, in fact, Lock knew from his experiences with him that he had pretty much no idea what was being said. Still, he looked impressive. Calm and in control.

'So, in summary,' Missy was saying, 'I think this is, in fact, an excellent opportunity to not only build brand awareness but reposition our company as one which truly cares about the wider community.'

Holy shit. Only in corporate America could a child abduction which had already yielded one dead body be seen as a way to make a business appear warm and cuddly.

'I've an idea,' Lock said.

All eyes swivelled round to him.

'Maybe if we get the kid back in one piece we could do a tie-in with one of our drugs. You know, like Ritalin, or something.'

No one laughed. Or looked pissed. Missy jotted something down. 'Or perhaps set up some kind of foundation?'

'I think you'll find Mr Lock was being facetious,' Nicholas Van Straten said, drily.

'Oh,' she said, looking at Lock like he'd just taken a leak in the corner of the room.

'If I may?' Stafford interjected.

'If you must,' said his father.

Stafford pressed the palms of his hands together in apparent supplication and paused for a moment. 'I don't think we have a problem here. This is a public relations snafu, nothing that'll affect us. And certainly nothing that'll worry our shareholders. The animal rights protestors, now *that* was a problem for us. But

108

seeing as they're out of the equation we can get back to concentrating on our bottom line.' Stafford stood up. 'Now, this is what I propose . . .'

Lock shifted uncomfortably, his recurring headache beginning to gnaw away again at the front of his skull. As he watched Stafford drone on, his mind drifted back three months, to the first time he'd run into the man.

Lock had been supervising a sweep of the upper floors of the building, taking the newly recruited Hizzard through proper civilian search procedure of a location while the place was quiet. Even those employees desperate to avoid returning to an empty apartment, or clocking up unpaid extra hours to impress their line manager, had long gone.

Lock had left Hizzard to check one half of the floor while he did the other. Lock had one office to try. Stafford's office. A floor down from his father's, Stafford's was close enough that he could feel important, but not close enough that his father had to see him all that much. The door was slightly ajar, and as Lock pushed it open he saw a woman bent double over the desk. In Stafford's right hand was a hank of her hair; his left hand was working its way up between her thighs. The woman was doing her best to fight him off, clawing at Stafford's face with a free hand.

'Shut the hell up, bitch,' Stafford growled, sharply yanking her head back.

'You're hurting me,' she pleaded.

Stafford's face moved closer to hers. 'Bet you

like it rough, don't you?' he whispered.

Lock had seen enough. He stepped through the door.

'This office doesn't need cleaning, go somewhere else,' barked Stafford, not bothering to look behind him.

When no answer came, Stafford let go of the woman's hair and reached down to unzip his trousers.

Covering the distance between them with six large strides, Lock stopped as Stafford glanced round. The look on Stafford's face wasn't shame, or guilt, or anything approximating either of those. He just looked irritated that someone would have the audacity to disobey him. Never before had Lock felt such a strong urge to wipe a look from someone's face.

He did it with a single strike to Stafford's face, the ridge of his elbow meeting his nose with a soft crunch. If there was one thing guaranteed to make a rapist lose wood it was a severe jolt of pain. It usually worked a hell of a lot faster than a cold shower.

The woman disentangled herself and turned round. She was breathing heavily from the struggle. She put both hands up to her face and rubbed at it, as if wishing away a nightmare. She looked to Lock to be in her early twenties, either an intern or fresh out of college.

'Are you OK?' Lock asked.

She nodded, struggling to pull back up her torn pantyhose. Hizzard, the new recruit, blustered into the room and froze as he took in the scene.

110

'There's a bathroom just down the hall,' Lock said to the woman. 'Hizzard here will take you.'

She hesitated.

'Don't worry, you're safe now,' Lock said.

'OK.' Her voice wavered slightly. Pulling down her skirt, she walked out, head down, avoiding eye contact with Stafford. Hizzard padded after her, careful to keep his distance.

Lock reached past Stafford for the phone. He was pleased to see a flicker of panic in Stafford's eyes.

'Hey, wait a minute.'

Lock pressed nine to get an outside line. He could see that Stafford was desperate to make a lunge for the handset, but too much of a coward to go for it. He cradled the phone between his shoulder and chin. 'What you gonna tell me? Rough was how she liked it? She'd been coming on to you for weeks now? Why else would she have stayed late on a Friday night with just you and her left in the building?' He pressed down on another nine.

'Lock? That's your name, right?' Stafford said, his voice suddenly falsetto with panic.

Lock hit a one. Only one digit to go.

'Look, man, I'm not going to make any bullshit excuses. I don't know what I was thinking. I've got a problem.'

'You do now,' Lock said, pressing down on the final one. 'Police department, please.'

A second passed as he was put through, Lock perched casually on the edge of the desk, enjoying Stafford's obvious discomfort. In his gut he knew one thing for sure: this might have

111

been the first time Stafford had been inter-rupted, but it sure as hell wasn't the first time it had happened.

'The hell with you, man,' Stafford blurted. 'What you saw adds up to nothing in court. It won't even go to trial. It's her word against mine.'

Lock replaced the handset. What Stafford had read as a scare tactic on Lock's part was far from it. Lock had put down the phone not because he'd scared Stafford enough but because Stafford was right. A call to the police would change nothing.

He removed his Sig and levelled it at Stafford's bloodied face. The movement was relaxed to the point of casual. 'You like guns?'

Stafford's face was white with shock now. 'I was in the ROTC at college,' he stammered.

'Remember the first thing your firearms instructor told you? The cardinal rule?'

Stafford swallowed. 'Never point a gun at someone unless you intend to shoot them.'

'Very good. Ten out of ten. Now, outside.' Lock waved Stafford over to the door.

There are lots of ways a man might think he'll react when a gun is pointed at him. In combat, Lock had known blowhards lose control of their bladders, and cowards find a relative calm in which they could fight back. But the first surge of emotion is the same for everyone. Fear.

Stafford walked meekly to the door. In the corridor, Lock holstered his gun but made sure that Stafford was ahead of him and didn't look back. Behind them, Hizzard stood sentry outside the ladies' washroom.

Lock guided Stafford to the elevator. Confirmation that they were being watched came in the form of a voice from the control room in Lock's ear.

'We're fine. Just taking a little night air,' Lock replied.

They got out on the top floor. From here they could access the roof. Lock punched in a key code and pushed Stafford through the door with a shove.

Outside it was dark. High forties at best. A sensor light snapped on, throwing both men's shadows to the very edge of the roof.

The walk appeared to have given Stafford the opportunity to compose himself a little. 'So what now? You gonna shoot me?' he asked.

'No,' replied Lock, 'you're going to jump.'

'What? Are you crazy? You walking me up here is all on disk.'

'You mean the hard drives that are gonna be accidentally wiped on my command about the same time as you're hitting the sidewalk?'

'What about the girl?'

'You think she's going to say anything after what you did?'

'There's no way you could explain this away.'

'I was ten years in the Royal Military Police. You seriously think I couldn't cover my bases?'

Keeping his gun trained on Stafford, Lock paced across to the edge of the roof. 'I catch you trying to rape a junior member of your staff. I pull you off her. All that'll be corroborated, right?'

Stafford didn't answer.

'There's no cameras up here, no one to know you've admitted to anything,' Lock continued, moving his gun up a fraction so it was pointing directly at Stafford's face.

Stafford put his hands up. 'OK, so I accept that she'd support that version of events. What difference does that make?'

'Well, I have a duty to report you. You beg me to reconsider. You have an offer for me. We take it up on the roof, where no one can overhear us. All that's on tape is two guys taking a walk up here. We get up here, under the stars, nice and cosy, you make your offer. But I won't accept it. In fact I'm going to mention it when the case comes to court. My saying you offered to bribe me makes her story a whole lot more convincing, wouldn't you say?'

Lock had circled round, so he was facing Stafford and Stafford had his back to the edge. As Lock had been talking he'd advanced on him. Just enough to crowd his personal space. Stafford had instinctively inched back, unaware that he was even doing it. He was maybe six feet from the void now.

'You're distraught. Sobbing. Not making any sense. Because you know what happens to rapists in prison. Especially handsome young ones like yourself. You'll be catching instead of pitching. Plus the shame to your family. So' — Lock wrapped his finger round the trigger of his Sig — 'you jump.'

'No one'll believe that,' Stafford said, taking a step back.

'Oh, some people won't. It's a hell of a story, isn't it? But in a court of law it'll boil down to my word against yours. And you won't be doing any talking.'

Stafford glanced over his shoulder. Startled by how close he was to the edge, he took a step forward, but Lock waggled the gun. 'Wrong direction.'

'I won't do it. I'm not going to jump.'

'Then I'll throw you. It won't be the first time I've done it.'

Lock holstered the Sig and punched Stafford hard in the solar plexus. As he went down, winded, Lock kicked him in the groin, then in the face. 'No one's going to notice a little extra trauma on the body of a jumper,' he remarked, grabbing the back of Stafford's jacket and shirt and hauling him to the edge.

'Help me! Someone!' Stafford screamed.

'We're on our own, Stafford. Not even Daddy can rescue you now.'

There was a concrete lip at the very edge of the roof. Lock pulled Stafford up on to it.

'Please. Please, don't do this!' Stafford begged.

'Why shouldn't I? Give me one good reason.'

'I don't have one.'

'You don't want to die, do you?'

Stafford shook his head, tears streaming down his face. 'No, I don't.'

Lock stood back, the gun still on him. 'OK, so here's what you're gonna do.'

Lock briefly outlined Stafford's obligations and what would happen to him if they weren't fulfilled. Then he retreated back inside the stairwell, leaving Stafford alone on the roof for the night to think about what he'd done.

A few days later the intern had contacted Lock to thank him. A day after the attack a certified cheque in the amount of two hundred and fifty thousand dollars had arrived in the mail at her apartment. Along with a legal agreement that she would take no further action.

Lock knew that it was a cheap way out for Stafford and he felt bad about that. But he also knew what the conviction rate was in sexual assault cases.

Once again, justice hadn't come into it.

22

'I want Ty to work the recovery with me.' Lock phrased it as a statement rather than a question. It was quicker that way, and they'd already wasted thirty minutes on bullshit that had zero to do with the safe recovery of Josh Hulme and everything to do with Meditech's share price and Stafford's ego.

'Agreed,' said Nicholas. 'What else do you need?'

'We'll need someone to liaise with the JTTF.'

'Wouldn't you be the best person to do that?' Nicholas asked.

'I'm gonna have my hands full. Plus, my being involved hasn't been a popular move with them.'

'OK, what else?'

'We'll need a team of people to sort through all our previous threat assessments. Particularly those relating to Richard Hulme.'

'Already done,' Stafford piped up. 'And I've had a briefing go out to all employees warning them to be vigilant and report anything suspicious to local authorities and our security personnel.'

Maybe Stafford's midnight sojourn on the roof with him had finally knocked some sense into him, Lock thought.

'So who's to hold the fort here while you're out playing detective?' asked Brand.

'By the looks of it, I thought you'd already

stepped into the breach,' Lock fired back.

'Well, someone had to.'

Nicholas Van Straten rifled his papers, signalling the end of the meeting. 'That's everything settled, then.'

★ ★ ★

Ty and Lock rode back down together in the elevator.

'You sure about leaving this place to Brand?' Ty asked.

'Nope.'

'Me either. You know, I don't have the kind of investigation experience you do.'

'So?'

'So maybe I'm not the best man to be helping you out.'

'You fit all three of my main criteria,' Lock said.

'Oh yeah, and what are those?'

'I need someone I can trust. And investigating comes down to one thing those chumps back up there don't possess. Common sense.'

'That's only two. What's the third?'

'If there are any more closed doors, I need someone in front of me.'

'Now, that I can buy. I'm still getting a feeling there's something else.'

Lock sighed. 'OK, the political activists we're going to be dealing with aren't your right-wing Bill O'Reilly crowd, right?'

'Meaning it'll be a hell of a lot more difficult for them to tell a black man to go take a jump.'

'Got it in one. We need to locate the enemy's weak spots. If that so happens to be a liberal conscience, that's what we use.'

'So you'd use the colour of my skin to game someone?'

'Absolutely.'

Ty thought about that for a second. 'OK, I can be down with that.'

The elevator's floor counter ticked down to single digits.

'So, what do you think our chances are?' Ty asked.

Lock thought about it. The doors opened into the lobby.

'Well, we got no ransom demand, no sightings since the kidnap, and the one person who does know what happened was just confirmed dead. Apart from that, I'd say we're in excellent shape.'

23

'We'll take my car.'

Ty gave Lock a look.

'What?'

'Nothing.'

'You got something to say about my car, you'd better say it.'

'OK, but if we take your car,' Ty said, pulling out a black i-Pod, 'we gotta dock my tracks.'

It was Lock's turn to eye-roll Ty. 'Maybe I should have picked Brand as my ride-along after all.'

Ty faked outrage. 'That cracker listens to country. I got stuck in the CAT vehicle with him once. Made me listen to a tune called 'How Can I Tell You I Love You With a Shotgun in My Mouth?' And they say rap lyrics are messed up? Damn.'

'Point taken. My ride, your music.'

'Calling your vehicle a 'ride' is stretching it.'

'So's calling the shit you listen to music.'

Forty minutes later they pulled up at the gates of the cemetery, still debating the pros and cons of Lock's car and Ty's taste in music.

Ty scanned the other arrivals. 'Don't these folks look in the mirror before they leave home?'

At the top of the hill a *Who's Who* of the animal rights crowd were gathering to watch

Gray and Mary Stokes being laid to rest, alongside their long-deceased pets, dogs, cats, rabbits, and even a donkey.

'Not an animal lover?'

'Had a pit bull once. Loved that dog, man.'

'What happened to it?'

'Tried to eat my little cousin Chantelle. Had to shoot the asshole. I mean, she was pulling its ears and shit, so it wasn't entirely unwarranted biting her, but family's family.'

'Ty, I get a lump in my throat listening to stories about your upbringing. It's like the Waltons on crack.'

Ty smiled. 'Screw you, white boy.'

'Listen, you stay here with the car.'

'Aw, man. Do I have to?'

'What's the problem now?'

Ty regarded the interior of Lock's Toyota with a look of repulsion. 'Someone might think this piece of shit's mine.'

★　★　★

A familiar face greeted Lock as he started up the hill. The sergeant voted 'most likely to be high on cholesterol but low on patience' lifted a fillet o' fish with extra cheese in greeting. Who the hell puts cheese on a fillet o' fish? Lock wondered.

'If it ain't Jack Bauer,' said Caffrey, swiping at a smear of mayonnaise, which slicked under one of his chins.

Lock was as pleased to see some variation in Caffrey's diet as he was to hear that the cardiac

121

time bomb's sarcastic repartee extended to both sides.

'How's that sandwich?'

'Food from the gods,' Caffrey mumbled, mid mouthful.

'You really get around, don't you?'

'JTTF seconded me,' spat Caffrey.

'That a new tactic? Al-Qaeda attack, we Spurlock them till their livers burst.'

'Spurlock?' Caffrey asked, missing the reference.

'Guy who made the movie about eating nothing but burgers for a month.'

'A month?'

'Yup.'

'Lucky bastard.'

'Well, it's been nice chatting.'

Lock started past, but Caffrey blocked him. 'Don't go upsetting any of these folks, Lock. I'll be lucky to finish the last set of paperwork you generated by the time I retire.'

'I'm just here to pay my respects.'

Caffrey stepped out of his way, and took a sloppy bite of mystery fish. To a man who'd missed breakfast, it looked pretty damn good.

Lock carried on up the slope towards a spot where he could see a couple of blacked-out SUVs. As subtle as a brick, the decals on the numberplate might as well have read 'FBI Surveillance'. Then again, maybe that was the point: the FBI letting the stragglers of the animal rights campaign know they were being watched.

122

As he passed the FBI vehicle, Lock narrowly resisted a juvenile temptation to tap on the windows. He stopped fifty yards back from the funeral party as it gathered around the plot. Two graves. Side by side.

As Lock got closer he realized that he shouldn't have worried about his attire. He was about the best-dressed person there. The mourners were a rag-tag mixture of decaying hippies and twenty-something New Agers. One kid in his early twenties had turned up in blue jeans and a brown faux-leather jacket, presumably hand-crafted from tofu. Lock would have forgiven him black, but *brown*?

A few of the mourners turned their heads at Lock's approach but no one said anything. At the centre of the group he glimpsed Janice sitting in her wheelchair, staring into the void as the two coffins were simultaneously lowered into the earth.

A man in his sixties with an ashen pallor and long greasy hair stood, hands clasped and head bowed, and said a few words. As Lock stepped closer, he caught the last of it.

'Gray Stokes goes to his grave a hero. A martyr for the cause of animal rights. He was a man who saw genocide where others chose to look away. A man who chose to confront those who ran the death camps. A man who chose to speak up for those who have no voice. But his death will not be in vain. The movement to liberate animals from suffering and torture will go on. And his spirit will travel with us on our journey.'

Martyrdom, sacrifice, struggle. Lock wondered where he'd heard all those words before. Maybe John Lewis, the FBI's deputy assistant director for counterterrorism, had it right when he'd warned a Senate committee a few years back that animal rights extremists were becoming a real threat. But then al-Qaeda had leapt straight to the top of the terror charts with a boxcutter rather than a bullet, and most everyone had forgotten that terrorism wasn't restricted to guys with a penchant for virgins in the hereafter.

People on the fringes of the group began to drift away back down the slope once the man had finished his eulogy. Lock approached Janice, a couple of the remaining mourners shooting him a dirty look as they passed him. The younger man in the brown jacket was speaking now, head tilted in defiance. 'They're gonna pay for this. You'll see. They'll be filling whole graveyards by the time we're through.' His dire predictions were aimed at everyone and no one. Janice shushed him as Lock came closer.

Lock reached out and touched her shoulder. 'I'm sorry for your loss.' The words seemed inadequate. He braced himself for another outburst from the uber-casual hothead, maybe even a punch, but the young man drifted off as well.

Janice kept her eyes on the two coffins. 'Why did you come here?'

'To pay my respects.' Lock flicked his head in the direction of the hothead. 'Who's he?'

Janice's eyes flicked from Lock to the two

hulking JTTF SUVs. 'Why don't you ask your friends?'

'Don't you think things have gotten too serious for us to be playing any more games?'

'Why are you really here?'

'Answer my question and I'll tell you.'

'That's Don,' Janice said. 'He wasn't really part of our group. He didn't agree with our way of protesting.'

'More of a direct action kind of a guy?'

'He's been involved in some liberations.'

'Liberations' was the term used by the activists to describe their forcible entry into labs that used animals, in order to free those animals. Occasionally they'd hit farms as well, usually ones with vast sheds of battery chickens.

'So what's he doing here?'

'Same as you.'

'This guy bothering you?' said someone, tapping Lock's shoulder for emphasis.

Lock half turned to see the guy in the brown tofu jacket. He was tall, but he struggled to be imposing. Lock ignored him.

He tapped again. Harder this time. 'Why don't you leave her alone?'

'Don, it's OK. This is Ryan Lock — you know, the guy who saved me.'

Don looked awkward and studied the ground. 'Guess I owe you a thank you.'

As apologies went it settled somewhere on the wrong side of grudging.

'Sure you would have done the same,' Lock said.

'Yeah, I would have.'

'So, what do you know about Josh Hulme?'

Don blinked at Lock's sudden shift of direction. 'I know what his father does. You live by the sword, you — '

Lock moved in quickly on Don, making sure he had eye contact and didn't break it. 'We're talking about a young boy here. I'd appreciate it if you gave my question some proper consideration.'

Janice edged her chair up between the two men. 'There's no need for this. Especially not here. And not today.'

'Under normal circumstances, I'd agree. But as long as Josh Hulme's missing, I'd argue that normal rules no longer apply. Especially as I think you, and your buddies, might know where he is.' Lock grabbed Don's wrist and twisted, just enough to make it interesting. 'Now, Don, maybe we could start with your full name.'

No one moved from either of the two blacked-out SUVs, although Lock would have bet the farm that they had shotgun mikes catching every word of the exchange. Their decision not to intervene didn't surprise him, even though he'd just committed assault. Government agencies were big on outsourcing these days and Lock would do as well as any Syrian jailer with a cattle prod and some time on his hands. Plus he wasn't quite as restricted by the niceties.

'Why the hell should I tell you anything? You're not a cop.'

'That's right, Don, I'm not. Which means I'm not bound by proper procedure.'

Don glared at Lock, his eyes full of hatred.

'Stop it!' shouted Janice. 'We've just buried our parents!'

Lock dropped Don's wrist. 'What do you mean 'we'?'

'Don's my kid brother.'

24

Lock wondered how much of an extremist you had to be to fill the role of the Stokes family black sheep. It did kind of explain some of the young man's over-righteous anger, though. He almost regretted adding injury to insult by hurting Don's wrist. Then he thought of Josh Hulme, and his momentary feeling of sympathy ebbed away, as quickly as it had appeared.

Don worried at his wrist. 'Man, I could use a drink.'

The way he said it, Lock assumed he wasn't talking about a lactose-free protein shake. Lock had always assumed the animal rights crowd weren't much for liquor. Lentil casseroles, for definite. Cheap whisky, not so much.

'There's a place about five blocks from here. I can give you a ride,' he offered.

Don seemed unsure.

'He's OK,' said Janice.

Don still said nothing. Lock didn't want to push it, but this was a great opportunity. Get a few drinks in him and who knew what Don Stokes would cough up?

'Listen, I shouldn't have laid my hands on you back there, man. I'm sorry.'

Don almost managed a smile. 'Forget it, you saved my sister's life.'

'We good?' asked Lock, offering a hand.

Don shook with his left. 'I'm usually right-handed, but some asshole almost broke it.'

In the language of men, that was a yes. The tension between them lifted.

Lock helped Janice back down the slope. It had never occurred to him before, but if getting a wheelchair up a slope was an effort, getting it back down was an adventure. At the bottom, he could see Ty fully engaged in the seemingly impossible task of trying to make it look like he had nothing to do with Lock's Toyota while standing right next to it.

Lock made the introductions. Once those were out of the way, Lock, Ty and Don helped Janice into the car and then spent the next ten minutes collapsing the wheelchair and trying to load it into the trunk.

'Shoulda brought one of the Yukons,' Ty observed helpfully as they set off, the FBI surveillance vehicle slotting in behind them.

Lock drove, Janice next to him in the passenger seat, giving Ty and Don a chance to buddy up in the back.

'You must really like animals, huh?' said Ty.

'Guess I do.'

'I had a dog once,' Ty continued, earning a *please don't go there* glance from Lock in the rear-view. 'Man, I loved that dog.'

'That the one who died at a ripe old age?' Lock asked, pressing down on the gas, eager to get to the bar.

'Nah, I'm thinking of a different one. Y'know, the pit bull. I'm sure I told you this story, right?'

'Which is why I don't need to hear it again.'

129

Lock glanced in the mirror. The JTTF SUV was still behind them, keeping the regulation half-block distance.

Ty smiled at Don. 'Lock gets real emotional when I tell it. It was kind of an Old Shep type of situation.'

'Well, here we are,' interrupted Lock, turning so hard into the bar's parking lot that Ty and Don were thrown around on the back seat.

Having helped Don wrestle the wheelchair from the truck, Lock left him to reassemble it. Then he pulled Ty out of earshot. 'What are you doing, Tyrone? These people love animals more than they do people and you're gonna tell him about shooting your dog?'

Ty glanced over at Don. 'Hey, if they think I'm cold enough to shoot my own dog, maybe it'll get them thinking about what might happen to them if they don't cough up that kid.'

25

Josh woke to the sound of boots in the corridor outside. He tensed as they stopped outside the door. Backing up, he found the wall. The camera whirred, its Cyclops eye tracking his movement. His breathing quickened. He glanced across to the album which lay like an accusation on the dresser.

The door began to open. Josh closed his eyes. When he opened them again, Natalya was standing in the doorway.

But how? Natalya was dead. Josh was sure she was. OK, he'd closed his eyes after the man had raised the gun. But he'd heard the shot. Followed by the splash. There had been blood at the far end of the boat.

Natalya smiled at him. 'It's OK, Josh. You can go home now.'

Josh stayed where he was. 'How can I believe you after what you did?'

'Don't you want to go home, Josh?'

'Yes.'

'Then come with me.'

Natalya held out her hand. Josh took a step towards her, stretched out his. Almost there. A matter of inches between fingertips.

Then a loud bang as the door closed on both of them, and Natalya evaporated from view.

Josh sat bolt upright. His back was sore. The flap in the door was open. A tray was pushed through it. Breakfast.

He sank back down on to the bed, listening to the sound of the boots, this time retreating. He got to his feet and rushed the door, pounding against it with his fists. 'Let me go! Let me out of here!' The boots faded to silence.

He looked down at the tray. Dry cereal. Toast. OJ. He was ravenous. He ate the cereal with his hands, stuffing it into his mouth, oblivious to the camera. His mouth began to dry and he gulped down the juice. It tasted like the stuff that you made up yourself at home. Gritty. Horrible.

Then he spotted the piece of paper, folded under the plastic cereal bowl. He pulled it out and unfolded it, bracing himself for something horrible like the images in the album. But it was only a note. He sipped at the orange juice as he read it.

Josh —
Keep doing as you're told and you can go back to your family soon.
Lone Wolf

Josh read it slowly, making sure he understood every word.

Lone Wolf. He was sure he'd heard that name before. Maybe it was something to do with the phone calls they'd had at home. He would pick up the phone and no one would speak. He was sure it was something to do with his father's work for the company. Josh'd been so happy when his father had told him that he was leaving. And then this happened.

He looked again at the note, took another sip of juice. It said nothing about what would happen if the demands were not met. If it was aimed at reassuring him, it was having the opposite effect. First chance he had, he planned on getting out of this place.

He sat back down on the bed. His body felt heavy, especially his legs. The horror of Natalya's visit was receding. He felt safe again somehow.

Sinking back down on to the bed, he closed his eyes. Within a few seconds he was asleep again.

26

Lock, Janice and Don grabbed a table near the rear of the bar next to an old Wurlitzer jukebox. Ty stayed outside, chasing up a Yukon to take Janice and Don home. It would take twenty minutes to get there, which gave Lock just about enough time.

The bar smelled of stale beer and old men's farts — an unfortunate side-effect of the state's smoking ban. Lunchtime trade was sparse, but the barflies seemed to compensate for their lack of numbers by drinking industrial quantities of beer and whisky chasers.

Predictably, Lock took the chair facing the door and studied Don as he got their drinks at the bar. If he was directly involved in Josh's disappearance he was doing a very good job of covering it. Even the more disengaged criminals Lock had encountered in his previous professional incarnation had given away something, some tiny 'tell', as poker players liked to call it. Nor had he gone out of his way to convince Lock of his innocence — something else the guilty were fond of doing when faced with an authority figure bearing down on them with awkward questions.

When everyone was properly settled, Lock raised his glass — Coke in his case. 'What should we drink to?'

In the present company, a thornier topic was hard to imagine.

'How about survival?' offered Janice.

'And those who didn't make it,' Don added.

Lock didn't have a problem with reflecting on either of those. They clinked glasses, earning a few watery-eyed glances from the men at the bar. Lock found himself studying Janice's face as she sank her bourbon in one and stared into the bottom of the glass as if some secret might be engraved there. He wondered how much her current composure was a result of having had to face her own death.

'What about those we can still save?' Lock asked, directing the question to Don.

'What I said back there, about the kid.'

'Emotions are running high on both sides right now.'

'There's no way anyone involved with us would do something like this.'

'So who would?'

'How would we know?'

'So who's Lone Wolf?'

Janice and Don shared a blank look. But not before both of them had glanced down at the table for a split second. It was the first false note Lock had detected.

'Gimme a break.' Lock had dropped his voice so it was barely discernible. 'Who's Lone Wolf?'

He uncrumpled the copy of the email he'd printed from Richard Hulme's computer and spread it out flat on the table.

Another glance between the siblings.

'We don't know who you're talking about,' Don said.

Lock slammed his glass down on to the table with enough force to get the whole bar's attention. 'Stop lying to me or, so help me God, I really will do you some damage this time.'

Don drained his glass of beer. 'It's not any one person. I mean, it's like Spartacus or something. People in the movement adopt the name.'

'When they want to make a death threat?' Lock asked.

'When they want to make a stand,' Don said.

'Oh for God's sake, Don, stop this,' Janice said. She turned her face so she was looking directly at Lock. 'Lone Wolf is a man called Cody Parker. He was the one who had the idea of digging up that old lady and dumping her in Times Square.'

'And he took Josh Hulme?'

Don was on his feet. 'There's no way, man, no way Cody would do something like this.'

Lock stared at him. 'And how would you know?'

Don looked away, answering Lock's question for him.

Lock flipped back to Janice. 'What do you think?'

'Don's right. He wouldn't have done something like this.'

'OK, then let's go ask him.'

Don threw his head back and laughed. 'And how are you going to do that? The government's been looking for him for years and they've never even got close.'

136

Lock thought it over for a moment before speaking again. 'Have you got a quarter?' he asked.

'What?'

'For the jukebox.'

Don looked at Lock like he was nuts, but dug out a handful of quarters and handed them over. 'Ladies' choice. Any preferences?' he asked Janice.

She shrugged, as confused as her brother.

Lock took the coins and pumped them into the Wurlitzer. He selected something by a band with the word 'death' in its name. Then he crossed back to the bar and slapped a hundred dollars down on the counter. 'Drinks are on me, but I need you to max the volume.'

Lock sat back down next to Don and Janice as the first few bars of distorted guitar and pounding drums drowned out everything else. He leaned in closer so that his face was inches from theirs. 'All that concerns me right now is the safe return of Josh Hulme to his family. Just so you're both clear on my personal position, I don't really give a shit about furry little bunnies having shampoo poured into their eyes, and presently I don't give much of a shit about Meditech either. So I'm going to give you both a choice. It's entirely non-negotiable, and you have until this song ends to make your decision. With what you've already told me I can hand this to the FBI and you'll both face conspiracy charges. Janice, you'll die in a correctional facility, probably before you reach trial. Don, with the way child abduction's viewed by the courts, not to mention guards and inmates, so might you. In fact, I'll take the stand to maximize the chances of that happening. That's option one.'

The song was building, the lead guitarist working his way down the fretboard to find notes discernible only to dolphins. At the bar, a shoving match had broken out between two guys over who was to be served next. A glass smashed on the floor.

'What's our other option?' Janice asked.

'You take me to Cody Parker.'

Don rocked back in his chair. 'What happened to the dog?'

The question threw Lock. 'What dog?'

'Your friend in the car. His dog.'

'The dog attacked Tyrone's cousin, and, see, Ty's real sentimental when it comes to children,' Lock said, reaching over and grabbing Don's sore wrist. 'More sentimental than he is about animals. So you want to know what happened to that dog he loved so much? He shot it dead. And if you dick us around, I'd say there's a good chance he'll do the same to you.'

27

'I bet you follow round comedians shouting out the punchlines before they can get to them,' Ty said, tossing Lock his keys.

'Hey, it worked. They're gonna help us out.'

Ty stared at Don, who was busy getting his sister back into Lock's Toyota. 'They'd better,' he said, clambering up into the cab of the Yukon.

'You know what to do, right?' Lock asked him.

'Roger that.'

As Ty pulled out of the bar's parking lot, Lock walked back to see if Don needed any help.

He had to admit, they made for one hell of a strange-looking search party: a girl in a wheelchair with a left leg prone to random spasms, a young man pushing her with one hand while massaging his wrist with the other, a guy with a patchy buzz cut intersected by a nearly new six-inch scar, and a six foot four African American with no hair and a lot of tattoos.

As Lock pulled his car out of the lot, the black SUV holding the JTTF surveillance team was waiting for them. To ensure that Janice and Don Stokes' choice of option two didn't bleed into option one, his first task was to lose the tail. Seeing as the Royal Military Police had been the branch that taught the rest of the British military defensive and, when the need arose, offensive driving techniques, the prospect didn't overly worry him.

His phone chirped. He flipped it open, driving with one hand.

'Hey, cowboy.'

'Carrie?'

'How many other hot blondes who just scored a thirty-five share of the audience do you have calling you?'

'Thirty-five's good?'

'Ten years ago it was good. These days it's spectacular.'

'Should Katie Couric be worried?'

'Peeing in her pants.'

'Listen, can you do some digging for me? But I need an embargo on it.'

The request for an embargo was met by silence.

'Carrie?'

'Yeah, OK. What is it?'

'The lowdown on a gentleman by the name of Cody Parker.'

'You got it.'

'Thanks,' Lock said, ending the call.

Turning to Don, he asked a question he already knew the answer to: 'So, where first?'

Don gave him an address. It wasn't the one he had given him a few moments earlier.

Don glanced over his shoulder at the JTTF SUV. 'Won't they be able to hear us?'

'Nah, they're too far back,' Lock lied, punching on the radio and turning up the volume as an apparent afterthought.

★ ★ ★

140

In the back of the black SUV, the comms member of the three-man surveillance team smiled broadly. 'We got an address.'

The driver glanced back at him. 'For what?' he asked.

'Find out when we get there, I guess. You might as well ease back. This is gonna be easy.'

★　★　★

Don glanced nervously over his shoulder as they stopped at a light.

'Don't worry about them,' Lock said. 'While we may be in a twelve-thousand-dollar Toyota compact and they're in fifty thousand dollars' worth of specially modified government-issue steel, we have a few things in our favour.'

'Oh yeah?'

'Well, for starters, I'm driving a stick,' Lock explained, banging it into gear and accelerating away as the lights turned green.

Don glanced over his shoulder again to see the SUV also lurching forward. 'I don't think that's going to be enough somehow.'

'You didn't let me finish,' Lock said, continuing to accelerate as they reached the next intersection. 'More importantly, the problem with what they're driving is that not only is it an SUV, it's also up-armoured. Which means . . . ' He concentrated hard on his next manoeuvre, changing down as he came into the corner, braking at the apex and accelerating out again. 'That it corners like a rubber brick.'

Behind them, the black SUV had dropped

back. Too far back. As Lock had predicted, the driver sped up when he should have slowed in an attempt to reel in his target. He took the corner too fast and the wheels of the heavy high-sided vehicle lost traction. As the SUV lurched from one side to the other the driver eased down on the brakes to bring the vehicle back under control.

Behind them, Ty, driving the Yukon, took his opportunity, braking a second too late and rear-ending the FBI vehicle. It lurched forward suddenly, both front airbags deploying. Both vehicles came to a halt.

Ty made his way over to the FBI vehicle, pulling open the driver-side door as the driver pushed the airbag out of the way.

'Sorry, man,' Ty said, 'you kinda slowed down too fast for me. Braking distance on these things is a bitch, ain't it? Listen, you want to take down my insurance details?'

Ty peered yokel-mouthed into the back where the comms guy was pulling off a set of headphones while simultaneously trying to extract the front seat from his mouth.

'Ah, shoot, you fellas ain't cops, are you?'

28

Lock took a deep breath and charged through the apartment door. A blast of a very different kind almost knocked him off his feet. The air reeked of death and decay. His stomach lurched as he stepped down the narrow hallway, matted with old newspapers and other, less salubrious organic matter.

Outside, at the bottom of the stairs, he could hear the homeless man he'd passed on the way in, engaged in a one-sided philosophical discourse. 'Damn bitches. Draining a nigga dry. Where's the justice, brother?'

Don and Janice were in the car, Janice exhausted by the day's events and Don unwilling to face Cody.

If Cody was here.

Lock toed open an already semi-open door leading into a living room area. An elderly woman, sat in an armchair, the TV still on, the volume turned down. She wasn't breathing. Her eyes were closed.

A big ginger tom cat sat on her lap, gnawing away at her hand. From the scratches on her face, it was obvious her hand hadn't been the only part of her body to get attention.

Lock stepped towards it. 'Get.'

The cat waited long enough to show who was boss, then jumped back down on to the floor.

Lock left the body and checked the other

143

rooms. Even with a Vicks inhaler up each nostril, a trick employed by cops and emergency medical technicians, no one could have borne the stench for more than a few minutes.

Back out on the walkway, his body got the better of him, and he threw up. Black shapes swam in front of his eyes. Here it comes, he thought. The first blackout. But it didn't. His stomach stopped rolling in on itself and his head cleared enough to enable him to dial 911.

* * *

In this part of the Bronx, Lock guessed that a dead body alone in an apartment didn't merit a dash to the scene, and the cops took their own sweet time. If the authorities didn't care too much how this woman had lived, why would it change now that she was dead?

He walked back down to the car. Janice blanched when she saw him. 'Are you OK?'

Concern from a dying woman made him feel worse. Don got out of the car and Lock told him what he'd found inside.

'That'll be Cody's mom.'

Lock got Don to give him a quick description. It checked out. He didn't want to ask Don to go inside and take a look. Not today.

'Listen, Cody might be a little crazy, but there's no way he would've — '

'I know.'

There had been no sign of any major trauma, stabbing or bullet wounds.

'Were Cody and his mom close?'

144

'Yeah, I think so.'

'She involved in the movement?'

'That's what got Cody started.'

Perfect. Lock reached into his jacket for his cell and handed it to Don. 'Start putting the word out. But don't say anything to anyone about her being dead, just say that something's happened. That she's in a bad way. Oh, and get back in the car, we need to keep moving.'

If they were to find Cody Parker, he wasn't going to do it in convoy.

Lock drove as Don made the calls in the back, Lock insisting it stay on speaker so he could hear both ends. Six calls in, they were getting warmer. A woman at an unofficial 'animal shelter' out on Long Island confirmed that Cody was out getting supplies, but that he'd be back.

As primed by Lock, Don told her to warn off Cody from going to his mom's place. 'The cops are all over the place.'

'You found her?' the woman asked Don.

'Pretty much.'

'Then Cody'll want to speak to you.'

29

On the way, they dropped off Janice at a neat suburban house in Dix Hills, owned by a woman whose daughter had also suffered from MS and who had met Janice in a support group for families affected by the condition. The woman took one look at Lock and hustled Janice into her home, slamming the door without a backward glance.

Lock called back in to Meditech and got Brand, who informed him with delight that Ty was being held by the Feds, and that both Van Stratens were far from happy bunnies. Lock thanked him for the update. None of it mattered: they were getting closer to Josh. Lock could feel it.

On the way to the shelter, Don filled Lock in on Cody's background. Run by volunteers, and used to house animals 'liberated' by the movement, there were shelters dotted around the country. A kind of Underground Railroad for quadrupeds, Lock thought. When animals were taken, they were still technically the property of the company that had been using them for experiments, so the shelters where they were kept tended to stay off the radar. Only the most trusted of activists knew their location, which made Lock wonder just where Don Stokes fell on the spectrum of extremism.

The shelter they were about to visit was run by

a woman with whom Cody had an on-off relationship.

A chorus of barking from the back of the house greeted their arrival. Lock checked his Sig. When he saw the gun, Don's attitude shifted.

'No guns,' he said.

'What?'

'It's one of the rules.'

'One of the rules for you whackjobs maybe. I've got my own rules. And right around number six is, when confronting a wanted felon, carry a gun.'

'You're not gonna turn him in, are you?'

'That all depends.'

'On what?'

'If he has Josh Hulme,' Lock said, failing to add that if Cody did have him, he'd be turning him in as a corpse.

'He doesn't. You have to believe me.'

'Let's go see, then.'

In truth, Lock had no intention of handing Cody Parker to the authorities. Not yet, anyway. If Cody was arrested, Lock knew the first thing he'd do would be to lawyer up and take the Fifth.

The house had been painted white but had faded to yellow, and the front yard was overgrown. Don led the way round the side. Lock followed a few steps behind. They were greeted by a pack of dogs who bounded up to them, a blur of wagging tails and lolling tongues. A boisterous yellow Labrador Retriever, shaped like a bowling ball and carrying about the same momentum, shoved its nose into Lock's crotch.

147

The top of the dog's head showed a rectangular scar pattern where its skin had been peeled away. Lock wondered if it was the poster dog for the Meditech protests. He scratched behind its ears and it nuzzled in even closer to him.

'That's Angel. She was pulled out of a lab in Austin.'

They turned the corner to find Cody Parker, lugging an industrial-size bag of puppy chow. He stared at Lock for a second before turning to Don, but made no move. Nor did he seem to register any grief. Maybe the woman Don had spoken to hadn't yet broken the bad news.

'They got her, huh?' he said to Don.

Uh-oh, thought Lock, here we go. All aboard the paranoid express.

Cody threw down the sack of chow. 'Who's this?'

'Ryan Lock.'

Cody was a big guy with a hooker-blonde ponytail that snaked halfway down his back. Six four and two hundred and ten pounds, none of it fat.

'I remember now. Meditech. Come to kill me too?' Cody asked, shifting another bag.

'You don't really believe that?' Lock said, caught flat-footed by the question.

'That my mother was murdered or that you're here to kill me?' Cody stood, feet apart, arms by his side, way too relaxed to believe the second part. 'If it's the latter, I don't see why you'd have brought a witness.'

'OK, so why would someone have wanted to murder your mom?'

'Because they think I've got something.'

'What's that?'

'I said they think I have, not that I do.'

'One of the places Cody was staying got robbed a few weeks back,' Don said, filling in.

Lock thought back to the apartment in the Bronx. How low did a burglar's ambitions have to be to target a shithole like that, never mind kill an old lady?

'What'd they take?'

'Papers mostly.'

'What was in them?'

'Details of places they torture animals.'

'You mean laboratories?'

'Among other places.'

'But Meditech are discontinuing their animal testing.'

'That's what they all say.'

'Listen, I'm here to find Josh Hulme.'

'He thinks you took him,' added Don.

Cody didn't blink. 'And why would I want to do that?'

'Because you're capable of it,' Lock interjected.

'Everyone's capable of some serious shit if they're pushed hard enough.'

'So would you mind if I had a look around?'

'Go right ahead.'

Lock crossed to the screen door at the back of the house. Cody, Don and the Labrador followed him inside. He tried to shoo the dog away but it plodded on after him.

'Must be more messed up in the head than we thought,' Cody mused, with a nod to the dog.

149

Lock scratched at her scar as she rubbed against his legs. If Cody had Josh here, he was remarkably calm.

'You know a girl called Natalya Verovsky?'

'Know the name, sure. Same as I know the name of Richard Hulme. And his son. Been all over the news.'

'You know the FBI are looking for you?'

'Not about this they ain't.'

'Only a matter of time. I doubt grave robbery to kidnapping would be much of a stretch for a jury. Unless you're denying digging up Eleanor Van Straten as well.'

Cody looked straight at Don. A dead giveaway. Cody knew it too. 'Have to plead the Fifth on that one, my friend,' he said. 'But lemme ask you a question.'

Lock stopped in the middle of the living room. 'Go ahead.'

'Why'd Gray Stokes get his head blown off? And don't give me that stale bullshit the media have been feeding the folks at home about the sniper aiming for Van Straten and missing. That was some cold shit right there. One shot. One kill.'

'I can't answer that question.'

Cody stared straight at him. 'Well I can.'

Lock sat down on a couch matted with dog hair. Angel dropped her head in his lap and stared up at him with thousand-year-old brown eyes. 'Enlighten me, then,' he said.

'Are you for real, brother? Stokes and everyone else in the movement had been yanking Meditech's chain for months. The way we saw it, if we could get them to stop using animals, a big power-house corporation like that, all the others would fall into line. But they dug their heels in. Just kept hiring more and more guys like you. Then, out of the clear blue sky, they cave. How come?'

Lock was silent.

'Man, I might not have all the answers, but at least I've got some of the right questions,' Cody said.

'Say they got tired of the intimidation,' Lock offered. 'It happens.'

Cody burst out laughing. 'To individuals, sure. But to a company who're going after a big contract from the Pentagon?'

'What?'

'Oh, but nobody's supposed to know about that, are they?'

'So how come you do?'

'You think we don't have people on the inside too? People might join a company like Meditech, buying into all the soft soap about curing cancer, but some of them open their eyes. It's all about the money. Always has been. Always will be.'

'So what's this got to do with Josh Hulme? Or Gray Stokes, for that matter?'

'Like I said, I've only got the questions. But it doesn't take a genius to figure that settling should have been the last thing on Van Straten's mind. Big contract like that means more testing. More animals tortured, like your new best friend there.' Cody nodded towards Angel, who'd now fallen asleep with her head on Lock's lap. 'But call a truce is what they did, and next minute

151

Janice is picking her pa's brains off the sidewalk. He knew something, my friend. Knew something big enough to get them to back down and get him killed at the same time.'

'OK, so what did he know?'

Cody clapped his hands together. 'Bravo, Mr 'Take the Corporate Dollar'. Now you're asking the right questions. Listen, I got some stuff around here somewhere, might help you out. Let me get it for you.'

'Thought all your stuff was stolen.'

Cody's lips parted, forcing a smile. 'Not all of it.'

Cody stepped out of the room. Less than five seconds later there was the sound of a screen door slamming shut and Cody running. Lock was immediately up and on his feet, turfing Angel on to the floor. Angel righted herself and slammed into Lock's legs. He stumbled, but stayed on his feet.

As he hit the doorway, Don made a point of blocking his way. Lock shoulder-charged him to the ground and bolted outside, just in time to see a red pick-up take off down the driveway, snow and mud spinning up from its rear tyres.

Lock pulled his gun, but the truck was already out of effective range to hit the tyres, and he didn't think shooting an unarmed civilian, even a wanted fugitive, without proper authority would go down too well. He re-holstered the Sig as Don came outside.

Don read the look Lock gave him. 'I'm sorry I got in your way, but Cody's my friend.'

'And you'd make a sacrifice for your friends, right?'

'And for the movement.'

'Well, I admire your principled stand,' Lock said, grabbing Don's wrist and finishing what he'd started. It snapped with a dull crack.

Don screamed in agony. 'Son of a bitch! You broke it! You broke my wrist!'

'Do something like that again and I'll break your neck.'

30

Lock pulled away from the house with an ageing yellow Labrador riding shotgun in the front passenger seat, instead of Josh Hulme. Angel had followed him and Don out to the car, jumped in, and then refused to budge. Lock had stared at her, and she'd stared right back. Screw it, Lock had thought, what's one more damaged case in a car full of them?

'Where we going now?' asked Don from the back seat.

Lock flicked down the button to secure the rear doors. 'You, asshole, are going to jail.'

'I found him for you.'

'And then you helped him get away.'

'He doesn't have the kid.'

'So why'd he run?'

'He's wanted, that's why. But not for this.'

Lock swivelled round. 'He is now.'

'You should have listened to him,' Don pleaded.

'Gimme a break. You people think everyone's out to get you.'

'OK, fine, so why did my dad know he was going to die?'

'He told you that?'

'He didn't have to.'

As Angel stuck her head as close to the climate control vent as she could get it, Lock studied Don in the rear-view. 'Keep talking.'

154

'You ever hear that speech Martin Luther King gave in Memphis before he was shot?'

'The 'I Have a Dream' one?' Lock ventured.

'No. This one was about climbing to the top of the mountain, about how the civil rights movement was winning, but about how he might not be there to see the final victory. Something like that anyway. But the thing about it is, when you see the film of it, it's like he knows that he doesn't have long left.'

'People had tried to kill King before.'

'Yeah, but this was different.'

Lock's anger at Don had settled enough to rekindle his interest. 'So what's that got to do with your father? You think he knew someone was going to try and take his life?'

'No, nothing that specific, but, well, it's like he knew something was up. Just the odd thing he'd say. About how things were about to change, that we had to stay strong.'

'Janice told me you'd had threats. You get any in the days leading up to it?'

'No, everything had gone really quiet on that front.'

'Maybe your folks didn't want to say anything,' Lock suggested.

'Believe me, I would have known. What's the point of making a threat otherwise?'

'Maybe you should ask your sister that. Or your buddy Cody.'

Don had a point, though. Lock had to acknowledge that. In a crowd, he never worried about the crazy guy shouting obscenities, working himself up into a lather and making all sorts of threats. You only had to worry when they went quiet. There was an ocean of difference between someone telling you they were about to commit an act of violence and someone resolving to do it. Someone who'd resolved to do it wouldn't feel the need to tell the world about it. In fact, the last thing they would do is broadcast the fact and give the other person the jump.

As Don sulked in the back, Lock dropped back down on to the Long Island Expressway. Angel had somehow managed to push her head under the steering wheel and rest it on Lock's lap again. It made shifting gears tricky. Lock rested one hand on the steering wheel and stroked the dog's head with the other, grateful for the relative calm and the time it gave him to decide what to do next.

He'd leave the FBI to chase down Cody Parker. They could have Don too. That left him back at square one. And neatly etched inside that square was a dead woman.

Lock stopped off at a convenience store next to the West Jericho Turnpike and picked up a bag of dried dog food, bottled water, and two bowls. Angel dined al fresco in the freezing parking lot before sauntering over to a patch of grass at the rear of the store and carefully selecting the right spot to take a leak. Then she followed Lock back to the car and jumped on the front seat.

'This is a temporary arrangement, so don't go getting any ideas,' he told her. 'And if they somehow need you to cure cancer I'm kicking your ass to the curb. Comprende?'

Angel cocked her head.

'And you can knock off cute shit like that.'

Don leaned forward through the gap between the front seats. 'So where are we going now?'

'We aren't going anywhere,' Lock replied. 'I'm going back to work, and *you're* going to jail.'

31

What Federal Plaza really needed was a bigger set of revolving doors, thought Lock as he pushed Don in one direction while Ty was being led out by Frisk in the other.

'Trade you,' said Lock, propelling Don towards Frisk.

'I was letting him go anyway,' said Frisk with a nod of the head towards Ty.

'Really? I thought damaging federal property was a serious offence.'

Ty took in Don's limp hand. 'So's breaking some guy's wrist.'

Frisk reached down to tickle Angel's ear and noticed the scar. 'So what'd the dog do to you?'

'She was like that when I found her,' Lock said. He glanced back at Don. 'For the record, so was he.'

'Uh-huh.'

'I don't think he believes you,' said Ty.

'Being suspicious is what I'm paid to be,' Frisk said. He jerked his head towards Don. 'What's his story?'

'Black sheep of the Stokes family.'

'That must take some application.'

'That's what I thought. But he did find Cody Parker for me.'

This seemed to pique Frisk's attention. 'Where is he?'

'Gone,' said Lock.

'But you saw him?'

'Briefly.'

'You see the boy?'

'I don't think he has him.'

This got a reaction from all three men. Don seemed the most surprised. 'That's what I've been trying to tell you,' he said.

Lock silenced him with a glance. 'When I want your opinion, Donald, I'll be sure to give it to you.'

'So how come you think Parker doesn't have the boy?' Frisk asked.

'He's not the type.'

'That's it?'

'Hey, I spoke to him. More than you guys have managed.'

'And then you let him go.'

'He escaped. There's a difference.'

Frisk put a hand on Don Stokes' shoulder. 'OK, well, let me see what I can get from this chump.'

'You might want to get him some medical attention for that wrist. He caught it in the car door when Parker was making a run for it.'

★   ★   ★

Ty and Lock waited until they were a block clear before they spoke.

'So what's really going on?' Ty asked.

'What I told Frisk. Apart from Don getting his hand stuck in the car door. I broke it.'

'Well, duh.'

'Ever decreasing circles, Tyrone. Whisper it,

159

but I don't think the animal rights people have Josh Hulme.'

'So who does?'

'Maybe it's just a straight K and R.'

'Mighty big coincidence.'

'Or not. Meditech's in the news. Everyone knows they're big enough to have a sizeable policy. Kidnapper's not going to go near someone like Van Straten for fear of getting offed, so they grab the kid of the chief research scientist. Week before, it could have been the CEO of Microsoft. We just got unlucky.'

'Only Richard Hulme isn't covered.'

'Could be they didn't know that.'

'So where does that leave us?'

'I can't get past the au pair.'

'Because she's Russian?'

'What's one of the fastest growing crimes for profit internationally over the past five years?'

'Kidnap for ransom.'

'And who has led the way?'

'Islamists, Colombians and Russians.'

'Except the Colombians stay on their own turf, as do the Islamists — which leaves the Russians. The wave's been moving west though. Remember that banker's family they took in Frankfurt? And the stockbroker in London? He traded half his firm's cash reserve without anyone knowing. It was only going to be a matter of time before they made it to North America. And not knowing the territory, they go after whoever has the highest profile and the lowest security.'

'But there ain't been no ransom demand or

warning of any kind, man. I don't buy it,' Ty said.

Lock chewed his bottom lip. 'No . . . but explain Natalya getting into that car with Josh Hulme for me.'

'I can't.'

'Me either.'

32

It seemed like a long time since Lock had been
in Carrie's apartment but it couldn't have been
more than three or four months. Not one to
follow any set of rules, Carrie had invited him
back there pretty much on the first date,
stressing that she wasn't normally that kind of
girl. He wasn't normally that sort of guy either,
but the attraction between them had been both
immediate and powerful, more connection than
hook-up. Being back here, especially with all the
shit that had been flying, calmed Lock.

He'd called Carrie from his car and she'd
met him at the outdoor rink at the Rockefeller
Center before suggesting that it might be
warmer back at her apartment. Lock hadn't
thought to argue.

As he hung his jacket in the hall closet, it hit
him just how much he'd missed her. The
intensity of work had allowed him to push those
feelings to the side. But the quietly ordered
domesticity of her apartment, the fresh flowers in
a vase on the coffee table, the sharp smell of
furniture polish, the warm air flowing gently
through the floor vents, all of it conspired to
send a wave of regret through him.

Any sense of an opportunity missed was
compounded as soon as he flopped down on the
couch. He glanced over at the framed photographs on the mahogany sideboard. Lock was

162

familiar with most of them, apart from one recent addition.

It must have been taken on a skiing trip. Carrie was standing with her arms wrapped around a man's waist, both of them grinning for the camera like newlyweds. He was about Lock's age with an expensively acquired natural tan and not so naturally acquired bleached teeth. Lock hated him on sight.

Carrie walked in from the bedroom, having changed into a pair of jeans and a sweater. She saw Lock looking at the picture. 'That's Paul,' she said. 'He's one of our producers. Divorced last year. We've been seeing each other for a while now.' She seemed keen to get past the awkwardness of the moment.

'Hey, it's a free country,' Lock came back, a little too quick to be convincing.

'He's a really great guy. You'd like him.'

'I doubt that somehow.'

In a show of support, Angel jumped up on to the couch, lay down next to Lock and began to lick her genitals.

'Well, this is awkward,' he said, averting his gaze from the dog.

'Gal's got to have a hobby, right?'

'We still talking about Paul?'

Carrie laughed.

'So, is it serious?'

'Oh, Ryan. So if I said to you right now that I'll ditch Paul and we can give it another try, what would you say?'

He knew where this was going. Like a trial lawyer, Carrie's profession ensured that she rarely asked a question she didn't know the answer to.

'I'd say I have a little boy to find.'

'And I love you for that, but it doesn't get us anywhere, now does it?'

They lapsed into silence. Angel finished licking herself and made a move to snuffle Lock's face. 'It's not that I don't appreciate the thought, but you're really not my type,' Lock said to the dog, gently deflecting her head with one hand.

Carrie busied herself preparing some pasta and salad while Lock opened a bottle of red wine. She could, he thought, make even something as mundane as boiling water seem elegant. Everything she did was so precise, done with such attention to detail.

'Oh, I almost forgot.' She crossed to a stool, picked up her bag, pulled out a folder, handed it to Lock. 'Everything you always wanted to know about Cody Parker but were afraid to ask.'

Carrie had accumulated not just the regular press clippings, she'd also gotten hold of arrest reports, court transcripts from Cody's early transgressions of the law, and some classified profile and wire tap information from the JTTF.

'How'd you get all this stuff?'

'I could tell you, but then I'd have to kill you.'

'Long as I eat first,' Lock said, settling down to speed-read through the mass of information.

Don must have been right about the influence of Cody's mom on his beliefs because his criminal record started early. Fourteen in fact. But almost every offence was against property. He was prime suspect in the exhumation and

164

dumping of Eleanor Van Straten, but even that, it could be argued, involved an inanimate object. The only thing that came even close was a bomb threat against a construction company building a new animal testing and research facility down by the former Brooklyn Naval Yard. The client was Meditech.

'Who'd you get to do this piece of research?' Lock slid the piece of paper across the marble towards Carrie.

'That would have been me.'

'Well, don't go clearing any space for that Pulitzer on your shelves just yet.'

'Oh, and why's that?'

'Because I know all of Meditech's facilities. And I've never heard of one down at the naval yard.'

Carrie nibbled on a piece of radicchio. 'I'll double-check for you, if y'like.'

'Probably someone else's typo. Lot of these companies have similar names.'

'So what do you say to Cody Parker taking Josh Hulme?'

Lock picked up the file. 'Don't see it from any of this. Y'know, he was dropping some hints that all roads lead back to Meditech.'

'Of course they do. And 9/11 was organized by the CIA. And the Jewish-controlled media are in on the whole thing.'

'He did say one thing that made me think though.'

Carrie crossed to the sink and began to rinse the rest of the radicchio under the cold tap. 'And what was that?'

'Did you hear about this contract that Meditech is going after with the Pentagon?'

Carrie shrugged, shaking the excess water off the lettuce and placing it in a bowl on the counter. 'So what? The government's been pumping billions into biotech companies ever since it realized the Department of Defense couldn't keep up. You should know that. There's been forty-four billion dollars handed out since 2001. Every pharma and biotech company's fighting each other to get on the federal teat.'

'Bio-terror is bullshit. Terrorists that are any good go low tech. Fertilizer. Boxcutters. Stuff that's easy to acquire,' Lock said, passing Carrie a glass of red.

'What about someone slipping something into the water?'

'It's possible, I guess.'

He took a sip of wine.

'Would you do some digging for me?'

'Into this contract?'

'And Richard Hulme. I still never got out of him why he resigned.'

Carrie grimaced. 'Me either.'

Lock knew this was a rare admission. It wasn't something that happened to her very often.

'Can I give you some advice, Ryan?'

'Sure.'

'When I'm trying to break a story I always try to keep it simple. It's easy to see things that aren't there. Make connections that don't exist.'

'Like this contract with the Pentagon?'

'Precisely. Think about it for a second. If anything, wouldn't a contract like that make it

166

less likely for Meditech to give up on animal testing, not more?'

'That's what Cody Parker said. But Meditech *have* given up testing.'

'No, they *said* they had. Those are two different things.'

33

The Kensington Nanny and Au Pair occupied a small corner of the top floor of a five-storey walk-up within spitting distance of Alphabet City. Ty had tracked it down as the company Meditech had used to source childcare for its senior employees. 'Had' being the operative word. Several complaints that the people referred were wholly unsuitable to care for goldfish, never mind children, had led to it being dropped as an outside contractor.

On the fourth floor, Lock and Ty both had to stop to catch their breath.

'Man, we are some unfit motherfuckers,' Ty observed, gulping for air.

'Hey, I just got out of hospital, what's your excuse?'

'Too much good living.'

They continued on to the top floor. The door leading into the office was ajar and they could hear a woman inside fielding calls. Lock pushed it open with the toe of his boot and they walked in.

The woman appeared to be in her late forties. Holding the phone in one hand, she rifled through a stack of papers on the desk in front of her. A cup of coffee sat full and untouched next to the papers, the milk congealing in a white paste on the top. The rest of the office was a mess, papers scattered randomly over every conceivable surface. 'Yes, and I'm very sorry that things haven't worked out, but I simply don't have anyone else available at the moment,' she was saying into the phone. She acknowledged Lock and Ty's presence by holding up her hand and waving them in, directing them to two seats on the opposite side of her desk with another sweeping gesture.

Lock picked up the stack of files that were resting on top of his chair and laid them down on top of a filing cabinet.

'Listen, I have someone in the office right now,' the woman continued. 'If anyone becomes available you're top of my list.'

Lock could still hear the person on the other end of the line as she put the phone down on them.

When she spoke, the English accent seemed to drop away, revealing something more akin to Brooklyn. 'Just so you both know, I've got a three-month wait list before I can find someone to mind your little bundle of joy.'

'Er, we're not together,' Lock objected.

'Yeah,' she said, checking out Ty from head to toe before diverting her gaze back to Lock, 'he is a little out of your league, sweetie.'

Ty snickered as Lock tried to decide whether or not to be offended.

'Hey, you guys aren't nannies by any chance, are you?' she asked with a beleaguered smile.

'Only for grown-ups,' Ty smiled. 'And I'm most definitely, one hundred per cent, straight.'

Only Ty could turn this into a hook-up opportunity, thought Lock.

169

'This how you find your staff? Anyone who manages to hit the door?' Lock asked.

'You with the FBI? Because I've already told one of your guys everything I know. Shit, you're not a reporter, are you? Because if you are I'm making no comment.'

'We're here in a private capacity, Ms . . . '

'Lauren Palowsky.'

'Ms Palowksy. Josh Hulme's father asked us to help find him.' Lock deliberately kept Meditech's name out of it.

'The FBI said I shouldn't discuss any of this.'

'The FBI are fully aware of our involvement,' Lock assured her.

'Then speak to them.'

Lock's face set, any trace of amiability falling away. 'I'm speaking to you. And if you don't mind me saying, you seem remarkably composed for someone who's had an employee brutally murdered and the child who they were looking after kidnapped, and possibly murdered too.'

Lauren studied the film of milk floating on top of her morning coffee. 'I'm trying not to think about it. But let's be clear about one thing: I didn't employ Natalya. I'm a broker, that's all.'

The phone rang again, but Lauren let it go to voicemail.

'Your lawyer tell you to say that?'

'No. And anyway, don't you think I've been worried sick about that child since I heard?'

'I've no idea. You tell me.'

She looked down at her desk, grabbed a random handful of papers, held them up at him. 'All these people are looking for someone to parent their children because they don't have the time. They all want Mary Poppins, but they're only prepared to pay minimum wage. Then when something goes wrong, suddenly it's my fault.'

'I'm just trying to figure out what happened,' Lock said, lowering his voice and leaning forward. 'Tell me about Natalya.'

'There's not much to tell, really. Same story as most of the girls who contact me looking for work. Her English wasn't great, but a lot better than some. She seemed pleasant enough.'

'How long had she been in the country?'

'Not long, from what I could tell.'

'Years? Months? Weeks?'

'Months, probably.'

'Did she say anything else about her circumstances?'

'She'd been doing bar work, travelling into the city every day from Brighton Beach or somewhere. She thought a live-in position would suit her, give her a chance to save some money.'

'Where was she bartending?'

'I deal with dozens of applications every week. I'm lucky if I can remember any of the names.'

'What about her visa? She had one, right?'

There was a pause.

'I'm not the FBI, or the INS, or Homeland Security. I understand that you probably cut some corners,' Lock prompted.

'The clients sign a contract that says they, as employers, have final responsibility for checking that kind of stuff. Look, it's not like I'm smuggling people into the country here.'

'So what's the difference between using you

and putting an ad in the paper or posting on craigslist?'

Ty answered for Lauren. 'About four thousand bucks a pop, right?'

'I'm kind of going off you,' she said to Ty.

'Right back at ya, babe,' said Ty.

Lauren sighed.

'If these girls were legal, most of them could go get a job that paid them more than seven bucks fifteen an hour, know what I mean? Everyone bitches about illegals, until it comes time to put their hand in their pocket.'

Lock sensed this was a favourite gripe Lauren rolled out when challenged about the ethics of her business. But it wasn't helping him with working out what part Natalya had played in Josh Hulme's disappearance.

'Did you get any references from Natalya's previous employer?'

'I gave all that stuff to the FBI already. They took copies.'

'May we take a look?'

The phone rolled to voicemail again. Lauren sighed, and with what seemed to be a huge effort got up from behind her desk and crossed to the filing cabinet. 'I didn't want to give them the originals in case this whole thing comes to court.' She stopped in the middle of the room. 'Now, I know I put it all somewhere safe.'

Lock guessed that 'safe' in the context of Lauren Palowsky's chaotic filing system meant somewhere it would probably never be found again.

The phone rang for a third time.

'Would you mind if I . . . ?' she asked.

'Listen, do you want me to take a look?'

'Could you? If I don't keep on top of my calls I'll be here till midnight.'

Lock opened the top drawer of the nearest filing cabinet and set to work. He motioned for Ty to start checking one of the numerous teetering piles.

A full hour later, Lock was wondering how people spent their whole lives in offices doing exactly what he was doing now. Not that he suffered from claustrophobia per se, but his mind and body were inherently restless; always moving, rarely still. Even in sleep, his dreams were vivid and kinetic.

The search did double duty: it gave them access to all of the agency's records and allowed Lock time to weigh up Lauren. One thing had rapidly become clear: she wasn't involved in any kidnapping. Kidnapping took a level of organization that was way beyond her. She'd probably end up sending the ransom note to the wrong address.

As they picked up and glanced at one piece of paper after another, Ty and Lock had soon discerned that invoices, applications, every piece of paperwork imaginable were simply thrown together with no rhyme or reason. There were applications from prospective nannies going back over ten years and details from parents of children who were probably in college now.

Ty lifted out one green hanging file whose tab read 'telephone account', so naturally it contained company credit card statements. Beneath

173

it, on the bottom of the cabinet drawer, was a piece of paper. He lifted it out. It was a letter of reference. He went to place it with the others when he noticed the name. Natalya Verovsky.

Ty walked over to Lauren's desk, waved it in front of her. She covered the phone with one hand.

'Did the FBI see this?' he asked.

'What is it?' She looked at the letter. 'Shoot. It must have got separated from her application.'

Lock had joined Ty at the desk, and he took the single sheet of paper from Lauren and studied it. No letterhead. Handwritten. The writing was spidery longhand. Natalya's name was written in block capitals about a third of the way down, then the actual reference was scrawled beneath. Just a few lines.

Natalya has worked for me for twelve months now. She has been a very good worker. She is very good with the customers and always on time. I am happy to recommend her services to you.

Then there was a gap of maybe an inch, and it was signed 'Jerry Nash'. There was an address, but no phone number. No reference to what Natalya's work had been either, and no mention of what the relationship between Natalya and Jerry had been. Boss? Co-worker? Friend?

It took Lock and Ty another forty minutes to locate Natalya's original application. When they found it, there was nothing on it that they didn't already know. Crucially, it didn't list her last place of employment. Or any other employers. So the reference remained significant, the only new lead Lock was aware of in an investigation rapidly going cold.

Unbelievably, there was no computer in the office, and no way of checking the address on the reference, or whether it even existed. With no phone number, Natalya could have concocted the whole thing herself.

Lauren was still on the phone. Lock waved the reference at her. She made a face at him. 'What now?'

Lock took three steps, bent down, and yanked the phone jack from the socket. He held the reference directly in front of her face. 'Did you even check the address on this?'

'Of course. There's a letter I wrote here somewhere. Don't think I ever got a reply.'

'You ever heard the phrase 'not worth the paper it's written on'?' Ty asked her.

She looked at him slack-jawed. Lock felt like crumpling the damn thing up and making her eat it.

'I'm doing my best here,' she protested.

Lock folded up the reference, jammed it in his pocket, and walked out of the office. He called Carrie from the street. It took her less than ninety seconds to call him back — quicker than the FBI.

'Well, it's a real address. Real business too,' Carrie said.

'What kind?'

'The world's oldest.'

175

34

'Now this is the kind of investigation I'm down with,' said Ty, surveying the day-glo pink frontage of the the Kittycat Club from across the street.

Before they'd headed there, Lock had gone home to change. Dressed in black cords, a white shirt, sports coat, and wearing a pair of non-prescription clear glasses, he approached the club parallel to the entrance. There were two bouncers on the door, big guys who relied on their height and steroid-induced muscle to carry out their duties. To get in the front you had to go past them.

Over the years Lock had dealt with enough of these guys to know that the key to getting past them was to appear as non-threatening and compliant as possible. They were wired to see a slight where there was none. Direct eye contact was a definite no-no. The glasses, he hoped, would help, as well as give him a geeky look. Amazing how schoolyard stereotypes became hard-wired into us as adults.

He marched along the sidewalk and took a sharp left turn into the entrance, keeping his eyes down and doing his best to appear nervous. Nervous tended not to come naturally to Lock, though, and one of the men stuck a hand across his chest.

'What's your hurry, buddy?' the other guy asked him.

'Let's see some ID,' the bouncer with his arm out added.

The last thing Lock wanted to do was show them something with his name on.

'Don't have my wallet, fellas.'

What had been the firm pressure of the man's hand turned to a light push. 'No ID, no entry.'

Lock allowed himself to stagger back a step before regaining his balance. He reached into his left pants pocket, pulled out a money clip and peeled off two twenties. 'Here you go, fellas.'

They took the money, pocketed it, and the hand dropped away from his chest like a drawbridge being lowered.

'What happened to your head?' the bouncer asked as he put his hand back in his coat pocket.

'The wife. Found someone else's number on the back of a cocktail napkin from the Lizard Lounge in my wallet. Hit me with the side of the iron. I was in hospital for a week,' Lock said. He delivered the story with his eyes on their feet. It explained the absence of the wallet, his nerves and, more importantly, the four-inch scar on the top of his skull.

The two bouncers snickered. They were both thinking exactly the same thing. *What a loser.*

'OK, we just gotta give you a quick pat-down.'

Lock raised both his arms to shoulder level, the loose change in his sports coat pocket heavy enough to stop it riding up and giving them a good view of his Sig. This was Ty's signal.

'Yo!' Ty appeared seemingly from nowhere.

Lock smiled as Ty pimp-rolled his way across the street in long, loping strides. He lowered his arms again as the two bouncers stepped from the curb to confront him.

'How much is the door entry?' Ty asked them as Lock stepped past them, gun undiscovered.

The bar ran the length of one wall. Behind it, the solitary bartender was female. And topless. It certainly complicated ordering a drink. She had a motel tan and limp blonde hair pulled back tight, giving her face a Projects facelift.

'Beer, thanks,' Lock said.

She noticed him avoiding looking at her breasts even though they were right there at eye level. 'It's OK to look at my tits if you like,' she said jauntily.

All Lock could think to say to the offer was, 'Thanks.' Truth be told, he wasn't much of a breast man. Not much of a leg man either. He liked eyes. And lips. Yeah, give him a great pair of eyes, ones that showed some sparkle. And expressive lips. Maybe throw in a nose that was in proportion to the rest of the face. Which must make him a face man, he guessed.

'Kinda why I took this gig,' the woman continued. 'I mean, guys stare at your tits anyway, so why not cut out the whole charade? Make better tips too.'

'Been working here long?' Lock asked, making it sound as much like a lame pick-up as he could.

'This your first time, sweetie?' she shot back, teasing him.

'First time in this place. Just got a new job down the street. Boiler room financial racket.'

She slid his beer over to him. He took out the

money clip and paid, leaving her a generous tip. 'Keep the change.'

'Just so we're clear, with me, a tip's just a tip. If you're looking to get your pipes cleaned, it's the dancers you have to take care of.'

'Of course.'

A few moments later, Ty sat down at the other end of the bar. Lock acknowledged his presence with a raise of the head.

A crank-thin redhead approached Lock. She introduced herself as Tiffany and he bought her a ten-dollar Coke. He was waiting for an invitation to go through to the back for a private dance, but it never came. Tiffany elected to launch into her life story instead. Lock smiled politely and did his best to listen.

For reasons only known to the young women who frequented these kinds of businesses, he seemed to give off some kind of a father confessor aura as soon as he entered. It had become a running joke with his buddies in the army. He must have been the only soldier in the history of the armed forces who ended up giving out a back rub to a hooker as she poured out her deepest, darkest secrets. He knew the narrative off by heart now: a missing or abusive father followed by a quest to rediscover him in a litany of equally vacant men.

At what felt like an appropriate break in the story — Tiffany had just lost her daughter to social services, which sent her into a tail-spin of ketamine abuse — Lock excused himself from her company and eased off his bar stool,

179

ostensibly heading for the men's room.

'You want me to hold it for you?' she said with a smile, remembering the bottom line in places like this.

'No thanks, but I really do appreciate the offer. You're a good kid.'

She slid down the bar to sit next to Ty.

Beyond the door marked 'gangstas' for the men's room and 'ho's', presumably indicating the ladies', there lay a short stretch of dark corridor which dead-ended with three doors. One led to the men's room, the other to the ladies', which classily doubled as the dancers' changing area, judging from the sound of rap emanating from behind it; the third, up a short flight of stairs, was marked 'No Entry'. The sign made it a no-brainer.

On the way, Lock unholstered his Sig, chambered a round and then decocked it using the lever on the left of the pistol grip. Then he holstered it again. It left him ready to go. He did it every time he was about to walk through a door when he didn't know for sure what lay on the other side and there was a chance it was something bad.

At the top of the stairs he stopped, took out his Gerber, and eased a section of painted-over wire away from the door frame. Cutting through it, he jammed the wire into his pocket before pushing open the door.

A solitary desk lamp cut an arc through the gloom. The smell was of stale sweat and cigarette smoke. An overweight elderly woman with her hair up in a bun sat behind a desk.

She fumbled for the panic button.

Lock held up the sliver of wire he'd cut out from around the door frame. 'It's not working.'

There was a phone on the desk, but the woman made no move for it. She seemed remarkably composed, as if an armed man storming her office was an everyday occurrence. Lighting a fresh cigarette from the dying embers of the previous one, she sucked down on it, browning the filter with one drag, seemingly resigned to whatever was coming next.

'What do you want? I'm busy.'

Lock reached inside his jacket and pulled out the picture of Natalya with her parents. He laid it on the desk in front of the woman. She glanced at it, then looked away.

'So?'

'You know her?'

She eyed him suspiciously. 'Who the hell are you?'

'She's dead. But before she died a little boy she was looking after was abducted. I'm trying to find him. And you're going to help me.'

'I don't know what you're talking about.'

He was getting nowhere fast. Sooner or later someone would realize that a customer who'd gone to the men's room hadn't reappeared. Then one of the gorillas would come scouting.

He pulled out the letter of reference, placed that on the desk alongside the photograph and pointed to the signature. 'This is you, isn't it? You're Jerry.' He could see that right now she'd deny being in the same room as him, so

181

he kept going. 'Now, you can either answer my questions or I can turn this over to the FBI.'

'It's my name, but I didn't sign it. My name's spelled with an i not a y.' She picked up the letter and took her time studying it. 'She worked here. Until, maybe . . . ' She paused, making an effort to recall. 'Five months ago. Then she left.'

There was a knock at the door. Then, a man's voice. One of the bouncers. 'Hey, Jerri, we need you downstairs.'

'Answer him,' Lock whispered.

'Give me five.'

They listened as the man clumped back down the stairs. Then they heard him push open the door to the ladies' room and bark something to one of the dancers.

Jerri dragged on her cigarette as Lock rifled through the files on her desk.

'Listen, if I treated Natalya so bad, why did she come looking for her old job back?'

Lock looked up from the filing cabinet. 'What?'

'Didn't know that, did you?' Jerri said, a smirk passing across her face.

'When was this?'

'Let me think. A month, six weeks ago.'

'Did she give a reason?'

Jerri blew a smoke ring and shrugged. 'She didn't say. But it'll have been a man. Always is.'

'She mention anyone in particular?'

'Some guy called Brody, I think.'

'Could it have been Cody?'

'Yeah, might have been.'

'Cody Parker?'

'She just called him Cody.'

Shit. Lock had been wrong. The guy wasn't innocent, merely cool under pressure.

'Did she say anything about animal rights?'

'Animal what?'

Lock took that as a no.

'You ever meet him?'

'He might have picked her up once or twice.'

'Was he older? Younger?'

'Than her? Older. Listen, our five minutes is up. They'll be coming back up here and there'll be trouble.'

Right on cue there was another knock at the door. This one more insistent.

'Jerri?'

Before she had a chance to respond the door opened and one of the bouncers got a face full of gun.

'Relax,' said Lock, 'I was just leaving.'

The bouncer blanched. 'OK, man. I ain't gonna try and stop you.'

Lock pushed past him and headed down the stairs, taking them two at a time. In the bar, Tiffany was perched on Ty's lap.

'I gotta go,' Ty told her.

She threw her arms around Ty's neck. 'Will you call me?'

'Sure.'

Ty fell into step with Lock. Behind them they could hear the bouncer screaming into his cell phone as he careered down the stairs. 'Yeah, he's got a gun. I need someone here now!'

In the office, Jerri lit a fresh cigarette and

cradled the phone against her shoulder. 'I don't know,' she said, blowing a perfect smoke ring and watching it slowly dissolve in front of her face. 'But if I were you, I'd start closing this thing down fast.'

35

'So we had him and we let him go,' said Ty, pacing to the window of Lock's living room and faking a punch at his own reflection. 'If they've harmed that kid . . . '

Lock sat on the couch, his head in his hands, the tips of his right fingers worrying at his scar. 'It might not be Cody, y'know.'

'Ah, come on, Ryan. He knew Natalya, then magically she pops up as Josh Hulme's nanny.'

'Au pair,' Lock corrected him.

'Whatever.'

'I guess we should call Frisk. Hand this back over to the Feds. People might not have wanted to cough up Parker when he was the Che Guevara of furry animals everywhere, but this might change his image.'

Lock pulled out his cell from the pouch on his belt. It buzzed in his hand. The prefix was for the Federal Plaza. 'Speak of the devil.' He flipped to answer.

'What the hell are you playing at?' The voice was unmistakeably that of Frisk.

'Just the man I wanted to speak to.'

'The hell with you, Lock.'

'We know who has Josh Hulme.'

'That's great. You know who has his father too?'

'What?'

Ty read Lock's face. 'Wassup?'

185

Lock waved him away. 'Richard Hulme is with your guys, isn't he?'

'He was until about an hour ago.'

'What happened?'

'He left his apartment and now we can't find him.'

36

Stafford Van Straten took some papers from an eight-hundred-dollar leather attaché case and laid them out on the back seat of the Hummer. 'I spent most of the day negotiating with our insurance company,' he said.

Richard looked down at the documents, a glazed expression on his face.

'I managed to convince them that because there's only been a short window between your terminating your employment and your decision to rejoin the company, they won't void the policy which covers you in relation to kidnap for ransom. In other words, you'll still be covered.'

Stafford smiled to himself. He would have made a great door-to-door salesman.

'It wasn't an easy negotiation under the circumstances. They're placing a limit on any ransom of two million dollars. Usually they'd go to five. But I think we were lucky to get them to extend their cover at all, don't you?'

Again, Richard said nothing.

'In the event that any ransom that's paid exceeds two million dollars, Meditech have agreed to cover the excess beyond two to the usual ceiling of five. We can write it off against tax, in any case.'

Finally, Richard looked up at him. 'This is my son's life you're putting a figure on.'

Stafford loosened his tie, undid the top button

187

of his shirt. 'I'm sorry, Richard. I don't mean it to sound so clinical. I'm not really the best guy when it comes to dealing with emotions. I tend to suppress things, you know. It's easier for me to try to fix things than worry about why they went wrong in the first place. I understand that you'd give anything to get him back.' He eased a contract across the seat with the fingertips of his right hand.

Richard looked down at the thick sheaf of laser-printed heavy bond paper. 'What's this?'

'Well, in order for this to work you have to be in our employ for at least the next twelve months. Any less and the insurance company would void the policy again. Along with the cover for other employees. Which in turn would make it near impossible for us to be insured with anyone else. And *that* would present major difficulties, especially for our overseas operations. Major difficulties for you too, as you'd be liable for any ransom. And I'm guessing if you had a spare few million lying around we wouldn't be here now. You do see what I'm saying here, Richard, don't you?'

Richard hesitated, then reached out for the contract. He began to flip through it, looking for where his signature was required.

'It's all fairly standard stuff,' Stafford said quickly, handing him a Mont Blanc. 'All the usual caveats, in particular with regard to the commercial sensitivity of your work.'

Richard stopped flipping. 'I won't go back to using animals.'

'And neither will we. Our word is our bond on that issue.'

Richard flicked to the last page and signed his name. Stafford handed him the copy. He signed that as well.

'You're talking about a ransom,' Richard said, 'but there hasn't been any demand yet.'

'That's not entirely true.'

'What do you mean?'

'We had to resolve some other issues first. Before we told you.'

For a moment Stafford thought Richard was going to stab him through the throat with the pen.

'The kidnappers have contacted you?'

'They were obviously confused about your status with the company. Didn't you think it was strange when you didn't receive any demand?'

'Why didn't you tell me?' Richard sounded disbelieving.

'If we had, you'd have told the FBI, and where would that have gotten us? Listen, Richard, you've been a bit of a loose cannon for the company. Even prior to all this. All your objections to the animal testing didn't go down well with senior management.'

'It's bad science. The genetic structure of a primate isn't close enough for something of this nature. Fine if you want to come up with something to treat, say, diabetes, but there's no margin of error with these agents.'

Stafford cut him off. It was tough love time. 'Well, while you were busy baring your soul on national TV, I was hard at work trying to get the company to sort out this damn mess. The people who have your son have made it plain they don't want news of any ransom demand getting to the FBI. Nor do we. How many kids of our employees would be snatched if this were made public? Millions of dollars involved. Every scumbag loser in the country would be looking to repeat the trick. Every child whose parents were employed by a major corporation would be a target. Do you want that?'

'Of course not. I wouldn't wish this on my worst enemy.'

'Good. So no telling anyone else. Especially not the FBI. If they find out, they'll block it, and your son will likely die.'

'How can we be sure he's still alive?'

'Proof of life?'

Richard nodded.

Stafford reached back into his smart leather attaché case and retrieved a clear plastic bag with a bright blue Ziploc sealer at the top. Inside were four locks of brown hair. 'We've had it analysed using our own labs. It's definitely Josh's. And they sent us this.'

Aware that a Polaroid avoided any suspicion that the image had been doctored, Stafford produced a white-edged snap, and passed it to Richard. In it, Josh stood, blinking against the flash, hair shorn and coloured, holding a two-day-old copy of the *New York Post*.

'Oh Jesus. My son. What have they done to him?' said Richard, breaking down at last.

37

Close to midnight, lights still shone from inside the Korean deli. A pool of hard commercial reality illuminating the 'For Lease' sign.

'This'll only take a minute,' Lock said, pushing open the door.

'You could just send a card,' Ty objected.

On the way back to headquarters they'd got word from Carrie that the old Korean man hadn't made it, that his heart had stopped working.

His daughter was behind the counter. She stiffened as Lock walked in. Even more so when Ty followed in his wake. Lock sighed: some things in the city never changed.

He took off his ball cap and held it against his chest. 'I'm sorry about your father.'

She looked away, grief still catching her unawares. Tears welled. Ty studied the ground.

'That's all we came to say, really.'

'Thank you.'

They started back to the door.

'Wait,' she said, moving from behind the counter. 'My father thought you were a hero. You know we'd been robbed once before. And people did nothing. Just stood there and watched it happen.'

'Have the police said anything about the men who broke in?'

'They've asked about the people who were

doing the protests down the street.'

'That figures.'

'Why?' she asked.

'Doesn't matter. When the shooters came in, what did they say?'

'They didn't say anything.'

'Nothing at all? Not even 'get down' or 'don't move'?'

'They gave us each a note.'

'What do you mean?'

'Instructions on a piece of paper. The one they gave my father was in Korean.'

Lock felt suddenly wide awake. Ty, who had picked up a newspaper to kill time, put it back on the rack.

'And what did it say?'

'Just told us what to do.'

'And the notes were definitely written out in Korean?'

'And English. Yes.'

'Did you tell the police this?'

'Of course.'

'And what did they say?'

'Nothing. Why?'

'Did you give them the notes?'

'The men didn't leave them behind.'

Lock looked at Ty, both thinking the same thing. They told her again how sorry they were to hear about her father's passing and left.

A civilian cop wouldn't have made the connection. To him or her it would just have been a neat trick, perhaps a way of making sure that the victim didn't pick out an accent. But to Lock and Ty the written instructions meant something else. Something heavy.

In Iraq, when military patrols conducted raids on houses where they didn't have access to a local interpreter, they used cards written out in all the local dialects. They relied on the fact that the Iraqi population was an educated one, and that although literacy levels were high, it wasn't guaranteed that people could speak English. They also knew that a failure to understand instructions led to misunderstanding, and misunderstandings led to death. So the cards were brought in.

Lock felt a jolt of adrenalin. Whoever had taken over the store had been military, or ex-military.

Speed-walking along the sidewalk, they made it to the entrance of the Meditech building in under a minute. They spoke only once they'd reached the elevator.

'Cody Parker have any service?'

'Don't think so.'

'Don Stokes?'

'Are you shitting me? With that kid's attitude he'd last about two seconds.'

Brand was sitting behind a desk as they filtered into the makeshift ops room. Above Brand's head a huge poster-size blowup of Josh Hulme gazed down on them.

Brand pushed back his chair, put his hands behind his head. 'The wanderers return.'

Lock leaned over the desk so his face was inches from Brand's. 'Where's Hulme?'

'Safe.'

Lock took a step back, lifted his boot and used

it to roll back Brand's chair into the wall. 'I said where, not how.'

'I know what you said, Lock. But while you've been trawling the titty bars of the five boroughs for fresh skank, the situation's moved on. He's up at the Bay, if you must know.'

'Brand, cut the shit. What's going on?'

'Relax, it's all being taken care of.'

'I'm in charge here, and you know it. When things happen, I need to be told.'

'Correction. You *were* in charge.'

Brand stood up and picked up two white business envelopes from the desk. One was addressed to Lock, the other to Ty. He passed them over.

Lock ripped his open. The single line in bold upper case beneath the letterhead left no room for interpretation: NOTICE OF TERMINATION.

38

Stafford stood on the deck of the family's Shinnecock Bay compound, phone in hand. Ten thousand square feet of property porn with nothing between it and Europe, save the Atlantic. New money fronting the old world.

He ended the call and turned to the two men standing behind him. One was his father, the second Richard Hulme. 'It's agreed,' he said.

Richard's shoulders slumped, gravity seeming to return to normal for him. 'Tell me he's OK. Tell me my son's safe.'

'He's fine, Richard.'

'So when can we — '

'If everything goes smoothly, this'll all be over in less than twenty-four hours.'

Richard nodded to himself, desperate to believe this, as Stafford knew he would be.

Nicholas Van Straten walked to the edge of the deck, arms still folded. 'How much?'

'Three million.'

Nicholas's eyes narrowed as he stared beyond the swimming pool beneath them to the ocean. 'A small price to pay.'

'Especially when we have someone else picking up most of the tab,' added Stafford.

'Richard, would you allow me a moment with my son?'

'Of course.'

Nicholas waited until Richard was out of sight.

195

'Well done, Stafford.'

It was the first unqualified piece of praise Stafford could recall his father ever giving him. Even as a child, any compliment had always been tempered by an immediate addendum that while he'd done well it was the least that could be expected given the advantages of his birth.

He wanted to savour it. But all he felt was resentment.

'Thank you, sir.'

'Perhaps I should have involved you earlier.'

'Perhaps you should have.'

And then it came, the ubiquitous qualification: 'Let's just hope the handover goes smoothly, shall we?'

39

The room snapped to darkness. Josh felt his way on his hands and knees over to the TV set and pushed the power button, but nothing happened. The fear he'd pushed away over the past few days was back as a pounding in his chest, and a dryness in his mouth.

The absence of light was total. The room was so dark that he could feel his hand against his face but he couldn't see it. He shouted for help, but no one came.

Then, maybe a minute later, maybe five minutes, he heard the door being opened. Outside the door was dark as well. Then a sharp blinding light burst on, directed at his face. He squinted into it, black shapes edged in yellow swimming in front of him. He sensed someone behind the light. Then a bag was thrown into the room, landing at his feet.

'Merry Christmas,' a man's voice said.

Josh stared down at the bag.

'Go ahead, Josh. Open it.'

He reached down and undid the zip. His hands shook. *Don't be a baby*, he said to himself.

Inside were a pair of sneakers.

'Put them on.'

He sat down on the floor and hurriedly threw them on to his feet, fumbling with the Velcro fasteners.

'OK, now turn round so you're facing the other way.'

He did as he was told.

'Now, I'm going to put a hat on you. A big hat so you won't be able to see anything. But I'm not going to hurt you. Do you understand?'

'Yes,' Josh said. His voice sounded strange to him. Then he remembered he hadn't spoken in days.

He turned round and the man pulled the hat down over his face.

'OK, do you promise not to peek?'

'I promise.'

'Good, because if you do, you can't go home ever again. Do you understand me?'

'Yes.'

'OK, I'm going to hold your hand and show you where to go.'

Josh felt rough skin against his hand as the man led him out of the room. The air was colder, and he could hear the echo of the man's shoes as he walked next to him. There was a click, like a door being opened. The man pushed Josh forward and then there was another click. He guessed that was the door closing again. Then the man took his hand again and they kept walking forward. Josh struggled a little to keep up, rushing every few steps to stay level. The last thing he wanted to do was make the man mad.

There was a buzz and the click of another door opening, and then an icy blast of cold air.

'Watch your step,' the man said, almost hauling Josh off his feet. 'This way.'

There was the sound of a heavy car door being opened, and then he was shoved inside, bundled into the back.

'Here, sit down.'

He felt a pressure against his chest as the man forced him back down. The seat felt soft, cold and smooth against his bare hands. There was the sharp clip of a seatbelt.

'Keep the hat on. I'll be watching you.'

A moment or two later the engine started. Josh placed his hands in his lap. He could feel the wool of the hat tickling his skin but resisted the urge to scratch. He dug his fingernails, which had grown since he'd been taken, into the palms of his hands, to distract himself.

The car smelled the same as the one he and Natalya had got into after the party, what seemed like an eternity ago. It brought back memories of things he'd tried not to think about. The panic he'd felt as they drove away. The smell of the river. The spine-stiffening crack of the gun. He clenched his hands tighter, his nails pressing deeper into his flesh, the pain pushing it all away.

In the front seat, the driver made the first of three phone calls. The first one worried him the most because he had no idea if the person he needed to reach would answer. He was relieved to hear the voice on the other end of the line. He'd spent hours familiarizing himself with it, listening over and over to the threats made by the man who possessed the voice.

'Yeah?'

'I know what happened to Stokes, and why.'

'Who is this? How'd you get this number?'

'If you want to find out, you need to meet me in one hour,' the driver said. Then he gave him the address and ended the call.

Human nature would do the rest.

40

Ty and Lock slid into a booth. Opposite them, Tiffany stirred a hole in the bottom of her coffee cup with a spoon.

Ty slid a picture of Cody Parker across the table. Tiffany glanced at it for less than a New York second and shook her head.

Lock leaned across the table towards her. 'But that's him, that's Cody Parker.'

'He didn't look nothing like that.'

Lock used his hand to crop the top of Cody's head, reasoning that for all he knew Cody's long flowing locks could have been a disguise, grown at a later date. 'Look again.'

She kept stirring her coffee. Lock reached across and plucked the spoon from her hand. She went to snatch it back but he held it out of reach.

'I said, look again.'

'I don't have to. That looks nothing like him.'

Lock handed her back the spoon and she resumed her stirring.

'OK, so what did the Cody Parker that Natalya was seeing look like, then? And if you say 'not like the picture' I'll take that spoon from you and wedge it up your ass.'

Tiffany glanced at Ty. 'Your buddy's really intense.'

'I know,' said Ty, 'and that's one of his better qualities.'

'Let's start with height,' said Lock.

'Like his height,' she said, indicating a squat Hispanic busboy who was clearing the detritus from a nearby table.

'Around five eight?'

'If that's what that guy is, then yes.'

'White? Black? Hispanic?'

'White, but his skin was all messed up. Like he'd had really bad acne when he was younger.'

'What kind of hair?'

'Brown with some white. Cut short.'

'Like mine?'

She put the spoon down on the table, a tiny slick of coffee clinging to its bowl. She looked up at Lock like she'd only just noticed him. 'Yeah. Kind of.'

'How old?'

'Forties. Maybe fifty.'

'But he said his name was Cody?'

She regarded Lock like a particularly impatient teacher might look at a defiantly obtuse pupil. 'Yeah.'

'You stay with her for five minutes,' Lock said to Ty. 'Make sure she doesn't go anywhere.'

'Why? Where are you going?'

'To get some more pictures.'

41

The town car bumped across the rough ground of the abandoned lot. The driver parked, killed the engine, got out and walked away, across the street. He then made two more calls. The first was to Meditech headquarters. The second, a full ten minutes later, was to the FBI.

When he finished the last call he switched off his cell phone. He crossed back to an abandoned building next to the vacant lot. At the back of the building was a previously boarded-up door. He stepped inside and made his way through the garbage which littered the hallway to a set of stairs and began the climb to his observation post. From there he could see the lot with the town car parked in the middle of it.

Fifteen minutes later two hulking GMC Yukons screeched to a halt at the edge of the vacant lot. They sat there, engines ticking over, as if unsure about what to do next.

Brand sat in the front passenger seat of the lead vehicle, the fingertips of his right hand tracing the mini craters on his face. Hizzard sat in the driver's seat. Brand had chosen him specially when they had got the call barely ten minutes ago.

Richard Hulme sat in the rear. As they came to a halt, he sprang forward, his hands clasping the back of Brand's seat. 'What are we waiting for?'

'It's not that simple. We verify he's there first. Then we make the transfer. When that's validated, *then* we can get him out.'

'Why not just grab him?'

'I already told you why. These people aren't fooling around here.'

'Let me go look,' Richard said.

'He might get upset if he sees you. Once it's done you can get him out, I promise you.'

'What if he's not even in that car? What if this is some kind of sick joke?'

Brand twisted round to face him. 'Hizzard, you go.'

Hizzard opened the door, exited the car and jogged over to the town car. When he got within ten feet he slowed and knelt down, taking a long, hard look underneath. Then he crossed to the rear passenger door nearest to him. He touched the handle, took a deep breath and opened the door. There was a little boy inside. He was sitting almost casually, his legs swinging over the edge, a hat pulled down over his face.

'Hello?' he said, his voice hoarse, the question tentative.

'Josh?'

'Yes.' The voice was a whisper.

'I've come to take you to your dad. But I need you to be patient for just a little while longer. Can you do that for me?'

'I think so.'

'Good. You're being really brave. Now, I'm going to reach in and take off this hat so you can see.'

'OK.'

Hizzard reached in and peeled off the hat. Josh stared back at him, recognizable, just, from the pictures he'd seen. They'd cut his hair, and dyed it, but it was definitely him.

'Now, I have to go for a few minutes. But I'll be back real soon. You have to do one thing for me, OK? You have to stay here until I come back for you. Whatever you do, do not leave this car.'

He closed the door, leaving Josh on his own. He jogged the whole way back and climbed back into the lead Yukon.

Richard grabbed at him as he sat back down. 'Is it him? Is he OK? Have they hurt him?' His voice was cracking, the questions stacking on top of each other.

'It's him. He's fine, Dr Hulme.'

Brand hit speed dial on his phone. There was a second's pause before his call was answered by their assigned lead at the insurance company.

'This is Brand. We have a positive ID.'

'I'll action the transfer now, Mr Brand,' the woman on the other end of the line replied.

Brand ended the call.

'What now?' Richard asked.

'The insurance company makes the transfer. Once they verify it's been made, they contact me and we can go get him.'

'And what if they don't hold up their end of the deal?'

'They will,' said Brand. 'If they don't I'll scour the earth for every last one of them. They know that.' He flashed a reassuring smile at Richard. 'It's all over. We're gonna get your boy back real soon.'

From his vantage point three floors above, the driver watched as a beat-up '96 Ford pick-up drew parallel to the lot and parked. The driver switched his cell back on and made another call. He said three words: 'We got it.' Then he hung up.

Down below, he watched as all four doors of each Yukon flew open and men rushed towards the town car. The first man to reach it threw open the rear door with such force that he bent it back on its hinges. Then his head and upper torso disappeared inside. He re-emerged with a small bundled figure and raced back towards the Yukons. A man in a sports jacket and chinos he guessed was Richard Hulme grabbed the little boy from the man's grasp. The other men pulled him, still carrying the boy, back to their vehicles.

Across the street, Cody Parker pulled up just in time to secure a ringside seat for the transfer.

'Son of a bitch.'

He threw the transmission of the truck into drive just as the first FBI vehicle car swept down on him, its nose cutting across the front of his pick-up. He looked in the rear-view mirror, ready to back up, as another car ploughed into him from the rear.

Up above, the driver waited until the doors of both Yukons were closed and then he made his final call.

Inside the town car, the cell phone stashed under the seat barely got the chance to chirp into life. The car exploded, sending a cone of fire into the sky. The windows shattered, glass fragments spinning out in every direction. The blast wave

206

pushed the main body panels off the car, and they spun up and out, one of them slamming into the nearest of the Yukons. A second later a secondary explosion shot another burst of flame from the rear of the town car as the gas tank ignited.

In the back seat of the lead Yukon, Richard watched the windowless shell of the town car burn as Josh buried his head in his father's chest. Sobbing with relief, he leaned down and kissed the top of his son's head, his fingers running quickly through his hair. Across the street, he could see a well-built man with a greasy pony-tail being dragged out of a pick-up truck by four men wearing blue windcheaters emblazoned with the letters JTTF. The man mouthed a stream of obscenities as his arms were wrenched behind his back and he was lifted up to his feet.

'Let's get the hell out of here,' Brand said.

Hizzard needed no prompting to press down on the gas and accelerate away from the town car's smoking carcass.

In the back seat, Richard held on tight to his son. 'It's OK, Josh, you're safe now. You're safe with me.'

42

'In a new twist to the Josh Hulme abduction case, self-styled animal liberator Cody Parker, also known to police as Lone Wolf, will be arraigned Monday on federal kidnapping charges for the alleged abduction of seven-year-old Josh Hulme.'

Carrie stopped, flicked back some hair which had worked its way loose and fallen over her left eye. 'Sorry, Bob, let me try that again,' she said to her cameraman, straightening up and setting her face to concerned.

'In a dramatic twist to the Josh Hulme abduction case, thirty-seven-year-old animal rights activist Cody Parker, also known to the authorities as Lone Wolf, is due to be arraigned Monday on federal kidnapping charges. Parker is also being investigated over the exhumation of the body of seventy-two-year-old Eleanor Van Straten. He is, however, denying any involvement in the Hulme kidnapping.'

She held her expression for a count of three. 'How was that?'

'Great, if that's what actually happened,' Lock said, skirting round the fountain outside Federal Plaza.

They hadn't spoken since dinner at her apartment. For Lock, it had been a night spent with Paul, Carrie's new squeeze, gloating at him from the sideboard. Even Angel the rescue dog had deserted him for the plusher confines of Carrie's bedroom, where she'd nestled herself into the pillows and steadfastly refused to budge. Between then and now, Carrie had been busy trying to keep up as the Josh Hulme story unravelled at breakneck speed, while Lock too had been doing more digging. They'd played phone tag a few times but Lock wasn't willing to trust anything he'd discovered to voicemail.

As her cameraman broke down his equipment, Carrie joined Lock at the fountain. 'So what did happen?'

'I don't have all the pieces yet, but I can tell you one thing: Cody Parker didn't have anything to do with the kidnap of Josh Hulme.'

'The FBI don't agree. They seem to think they have a pretty strong case. He's lucky New York State doesn't have the death penalty, if you ask me.'

'New York doesn't have it because of cases like this.'

'What do you mean?'

'What gets someone strapped into old Sparky, or a big syringe of potassium chloride these days?'

'How come I feel I'm about to be on the receiving end of one of your little lectures?'

'Humour me.'

'OK. A crime which horrifies. Child murder, abduction.'

'And in cases like that there's one hell of an amount of pressure on the authorities to bring someone before the courts.'

'Hey, it's not like they picked Cody Parker

from the phone book. They've got some pretty strong evidence.'

'And I'd bet all of it is circumstantial.'

'I can't believe you're standing up for this guy! You heard what I said a moment ago. He's sure as hell guilty of digging up a little old lady and dumping her body in the middle of Times Square.'

'And he should go to jail for that. For a long time. But what they're doing,' Lock said, glancing over at the Jacob K. Javits Federal Building, 'is railroading him for the kidnap.'

'So if Cody Parker didn't do it, who did?'

'Meditech.'

She burst out laughing. Lock held her gaze.

'Oh my God, you're being serious.'

'OK, it wasn't a collective effort. I'm guessing very few people even knew about it. I'm not even sure Nicholas Van Straten knew.'

'But he's the CEO.'

'Precisely. Look, Carrie, the reason people think you're nuts when you mention something like this is that they have a picture in their mind of some big boardroom meeting with Van Straten sitting in a high-backed chair stroking a white cat. Shit like this doesn't go down like that. The company needed Richard Hulme back at work for them.'

'So why not offer him, I dunno, ten million bucks?'

'Because someone like Richard is every company's worst nightmare.'

'And what's that?'

'A guy with principles who can't be

210

compromised by a big set of zeros.'

'So they kidnap his child?'

'In my opinion, yes. Hulme was a problem to be solved. Someone did some out-of-the-box thinking.'

'Don't you mean out-of-the-stratosphere?'

'The cover was already there. The kid goes missing, everyone's going to be looking at the animal rights people. After everything that had gone on, who wouldn't believe they'd be involved? Especially after their beloved leader got smoked right on the front steps of the company.'

'And Meditech did that too?'

'You're looking at it the wrong way. You think Nicholas Van Straten ordered Gray Stokes' assassination.'

'Isn't that what you're suggesting?' Carrie said.

Lock sighed. The truth was that it didn't make a whole lot of sense to him either. Yet neither did the official version. In fact, that made even less sense.

'The thing is that a big company like Meditech doesn't operate like the army. The way the army is, every task gets broken down into tiny little steps. That makes it idiot-proof, but it also means that no one can just go off and do their own thing. In a private company it's different. They don't give a shit about how something is achieved, all they care about is the bottom line. That's how you get guys with security companies out in Iraq smoking civilians left and right. They're all former soldiers but all of a sudden they don't have a command structure, no one to stick their ass in a sling if they do the right thing the wrong way.' He paused, rubbing at his stitches. 'Suppose Meditech has someone black-mailing them, and the wrong person gets hold of that information, and they decide to solve the problem directly. And as soon as that line's been crossed once . . . '

'So who was it who took Josh Hulme?' Carrie asked.

Lock looked straight at her. 'Someone with boardroom backing from Stafford. More than likely Brand.'

'Are you sure? You and he never saw eye to eye.'

'That's true, but that's not why I think he's involved.'

'Then why do you?'

'Because Brand was sleeping with Natalya Verovsky. But he told her his name was Cody Parker.'

43

Josh Hulme sat huddled next to his father as the cruiser surged its way towards the dock, churning foam in its wake. Ahead of them lay the old Brooklyn Naval Yard, home to Meditech's new research facility.

Richard gazed up at the hulking compound. A twenty-foot wall ran to the edges of his peripheral vision. Atop the wall, a solitary Stars and Stripes snapped tight in the wind. Beneath the flag two guards prowled a walkway. Both of them armed.

Richard pulled Josh in closer and kissed the top of his son's head. 'You OK, sport?' He reached into his pocket, pulled out a packet of Scopace tablets. 'If you're feeling seasick, I can give you one of these.'

Josh waved him away. 'Dad, when can we go home?'

'Daddy has some work to finish up first.'

'Today?'

'Maybe in a week or so.'

'But it's almost New Year.'

'I know, big guy, I know, but Daddy made a promise.'

In truth, Richard hated himself. Josh needed him. Needed him now more than ever. But without the undertaking he'd given Meditech, Josh wouldn't be here, might not even be alive, so what could he do?

Stafford clambered down into the cabin of the cruiser. 'Bit choppy out there.' He settled on the bench seat next to Richard, tousled Josh's hair. 'Don't worry, we'll be there in a minute or two.'

Josh stiffened and pushed away his hand.

'Listen, can I borrow your dad for a second there, sport?'

Richard followed Stafford out on to the deck as the boat ploughed onwards.

'Eighty million dollars. Beautiful, isn't it?'

All Richard could see was a blank wall which ran maybe a thousand feet along a parcel of land facing the dock. The only notable thing was its height. A solid twenty feet. Maybe more.

Stafford slapped Richard on the back. 'He'll be OK.'

'He's not your son. You can't possibly imagine what this has been like for us.'

'That's true. But the main thing is, he's safe now.'

Richard stared straight ahead.

Stafford looked at the wall too. 'Don't think we'll have too many whackos coming out here to protest, somehow.'

'You don't think all this security's overkill?'

'Jeez, Richard, I know you academic types sometimes don't see the big picture, but for crying out loud. We're going to be dealing with Level 4, Category A here. You could take out half the country with what we'll have inside.'

'But no animals?'

'Nothing with a tail, paws or fur. You made your case, Richard. And I for one agree with you.

214

What we were doing was bad science. Which made it bad business.'

The boat pulled in at one of the piers and tied up. Stafford clambered off. He stretched out a hand to Richard, who in turn helped Josh on to dry land.

They followed Stafford along a walkway and up on to a concrete apron, Josh struggling to keep up with Stafford's long strides. They then walked along to the very end of the wall and turned left.

Stafford glanced over his shoulder at Richard. 'Not far to go now. I thought the river approach was a better idea. Give you more of an idea of the size of the place.'

Four hundred yards further up, the wall was split by a driveway big enough to accommodate trucks passing either side with a metal drop-in booth manned by a middle-aged African American man dressed in a Meditech security uniform. They stopped at the booth and Stafford presented his laminated Meditech card. Richard followed suit. The guard checked them without saying a word, then matched their name against the visitors list.

'Could you folks look up for me, please?' he said, pointing to a spot behind him.

They did so, and there was a flash from a fixed point on the wall where a camera had been mounted.

The guard looked at a computer screen. 'That's fine, you can go through now.'

'Facial recognition software,' Stafford said, marching on through.

'The security here's like Fort Knox,' Richard said.

'Not like,' said Stafford. 'Better.'

Once through the gate they passed through a guardhouse manned by two guards, both armed. It was wide enough to obscure the view of the area behind it from anyone standing at the first checkpoint. They ran through the same rigmarole and stepped through into the body of the compound where Missy was waiting for them, stomping her feet to keep them from freezing but otherwise as perky as ever.

'Hey, Josh, let me show you where you're staying,' she chirped.

Stafford had, apparently, drafted her in as unofficial childcare.

They passed a series of single-storey white buildings, notable only for their uniformity. The sheer scale of the place was impressive, especially so close to the city.

Josh didn't release the grip on his father's hand.

'We've got a Christmas tree for you and everything,' Missy said.

'It's OK, Josh,' Richard reassured his son, 'you can go with her. I'll catch you up in a few minutes.'

Reluctantly, Josh let go of his father's hand and Missy led him away. Richard watched them go.

'This couldn't have waited until after the holidays?'

'Richard, we're on a deadline here. We wait, we lose our competitive advantage.' Stafford

216

slapped Richard on the back. 'Listen, the trial goes well and you can have three months' paid vacation. Hell, I might even come with you. Now, let me show you the research lab first. I think you're going to be pretty blown away.'

Stafford turned left, but Richard stayed where he was. His attention had been drawn to an area maybe two hundred feet away. A building the same as the others, it was surrounded by chain-link topped with razor wire. 'What's that?' he asked.

'It's an accommodation block. Don't worry, you won't have to go anywhere near it if you don't want to.'

'What are we accommodating?'

'The test subjects.'

'You lied to me.'

'Semantics, Richard. That's all.'

'And there's something else,' said Richard. He hadn't even thought of it until now. It was something that Lock had said to him back in his apartment that only now floated to the surface. Something about the presence of the abnormal, and the absence of the normal. The razor wire landed in the abnormal column, but there was something else about the place that was off. 'I've been here five minutes and the only people I've seen are guards. Where are the technicians?'

'We're running a skeleton staff through this phase.'

'So why do you even need me here for this?'

'Because you have to sign off on the data. Your name means a lot to the Food and Drug

Administration, not to mention the Department of Defense.'

'So do it and send me the clinical results. I can make a judgement based on — '

Stafford cut him off by grabbing his arm and squeezing hard. It hurt. 'We don't have room for any more ethical dilemmas, even after the trials have taken place. That's why we'd prefer it if you were as hands-on as possible.'

Richard felt a low terror start to form at the bottom of his stomach. 'So these test subjects. What are they exactly?'

'Think of them as higher-level primates.'

44

A fierce crosswind buffeted the Gulfstream as it began its final approach towards the airstrip, visibility severely hampered by the fierce rain which slammed into the side of the aircraft. The ski masks worn by the pilot and co-pilot didn't help either. Neither man knew the other's name, or who he worked for. The same held for the other eight members of the crew.

In the cabin, the plush leather seats, usually used to cushion the already well-upholstered buttocks of senior executives, had been replaced with six gurneys. On each gurney lay a person. Six in total. Five men and a woman.

Their heads were hooded, a slit cut in the cloth two thirds of the way down to allow breathing. Their hands were cuffed, each cuff attached to a welded bracket either side of the gurney. Their feet were similarly secured. Their clothes consisted of bright red T-shirts and pants. Underneath their pants they wore adult diapers. None of them had been unshackled during the flight for a trip to the bathroom.

Not that they had much interest in moving anyway. Before departure they'd each been injected with an amount of Haldol, a powerful anti-psychotic. Pills could be slipped under the tongue or spat out, so intravenous delivery was deemed the most effective way to ensure that the drugs made it into their system.

Mareta Yuzik, thick-tongued and groggy, opened her eyes to darkness. For a moment she wondered if she'd been blinded. Then she remembered the hood. She could feel the fabric of it against her face. She smiled with relief.

There was a searing pain in her left side. She tried to reach a hand down to touch where it was tender but her hand wouldn't move. The tightness around her wrists and ankles told her that she was shackled.

Not blind, only hooded. Not paralysed, merely shackled. And, miraculously, she could hear. Over the past few weeks, when she'd been moved from one location to another ear defenders had been placed on her head so she could only sense the loudest of noises, more through vibration than anything else. Being able to hear meant that she knew she was on an aircraft. It also meant she could hear the guards, even over the sound of the engines. She recognized their accents from the movies. They were American. She could hear two of them talking.

'Man, it's good to be home.'

'How long of a layover you have?'

'Week, maybe. Depends on how this goes. You?'

'About the same. Let me tell you, I'll be glad to get off this thing. These guys creep me out.'

'Relax, they've got enough shit in their system to flatten an elephant.'

'What're they being moved back here for, anyway?'

'Dunno. I heard something about a trial.'

'Good. Hope they smoke 'em.'

'I'd stick a bullet in them, save on the energy.'

The Gulfstream taxied to the end of the runway and turned right, heading for a remote hangar no more than five hundred yards away. The doors of the hangar were already open and more than a dozen men were inside, along with six SUVs. Like everyone onboard, all of the men were masked.

The aircraft inched its way inside the hangar and the vast metal doors were rolled closed behind it. A few seconds later the aircraft door opened and the steps were unfolded and lowered to the ground. One of the men walked up them and disappeared inside the aircraft.

Only one of the detainees had been unshackled. The woman. One of the guards unholstered his sidearm and passed it to his partner. He helped her off the gurney and on to her feet. She struggled to stand and it was as much as he could do to prevent her keeling over. They lumbered down the steps of the plane like lovers stumbling from a bar.

As she stepped on to the concrete, she sank down on to her knees.

'She OK?'

'Be careful, she might be faking it.'

'Dude, you've got an overactive imagination.'

'You read that bitch's file? She's snuffed more people than Bin Laden.'

45

'This is bullshit. I didn't take any kid!'

'Then what were you doing there, Cody?'

Frisk was facing Cody Parker and his court-appointed attorney, a Hispanic woman in her late twenties, across a table in an interrogation room on the third floor of Federal Plaza.

'I told you. I got a phone call.'

'That's very convenient. From who?'

'I don't know. They said they knew who killed Gray Stokes and that if I wanted to know I should meet them at that address.'

'They didn't give you a name? You didn't recognize the voice?'

'Nope. Look, if I kidnapped this kid then where's the money, huh? Or did you plant it in my truck?'

'Why don't you tell us where it is.'

'Someone set me up.'

Frisk rocked back in his seat, stretched out his arms and yawned. 'Go on, then, I'm prepared to explore alternative scenarios.'

'It was that company. They were looking to get back at me.'

Frisk laughed. Unprofessional, but he couldn't help it. 'They arranged a kidnapping of the child of one of their employees in order to exact some kind of revenge against you personally? OK, it's certainly an interesting hypothesis. But it still doesn't speak to motive. Why you?'

'What do you mean, 'why me'? I've been taking them on. And why aren't you out there trying to catch whoever killed my mom?'

'Because we don't have any evidence that she died from anything other than natural causes. But it does bring us neatly to another event. Digging up Eleanor Van Straten's corpse. That what you mean by 'taking them on'?'

Cody glanced up at the ceiling. 'I don't know what you're talking about.'

'Except we've found particles of soil on your boots which match the soil from Mrs Van Straten's grave.'

Cody's jaw tightened. He gave his attorney the briefest of looks. 'OK, so that was me.'

'Finally,' Frisk said. 'And who was with you?'

'I was alone.'

'Moving a body, even a little old lady, is a two-man job. Minimum.'

'I told you. I was alone.'

'So this friend of yours, he the one who blew up the car, get rid of any forensics?'

'You got me blowing shit up to get rid of forensics *and* sitting across the street from that boy?'

'Well, you have to concede you were there. I mean, no one teleported you or anything.'

'I was there. And I told you why. Check the phone records at the house if you don't believe me.'

'We already did.'

'And?'

'You received a call when you said you did.'

223

'Then I'm telling the truth.'

'Records don't say anything about what was being said. And as for telling the truth, how many times were you questioned about Mrs Van Straten?'

'Don't rightly remember.'

'Three times. And three times you denied having any involvement. So allow me some scepticism when it comes to your record on honesty.'

Cody stretched his arms towards the ceiling. 'So what happens now?'

'You're arraigned. You wait to go to trial. You'll have plenty of time to think about whether or not you want to plead guilty.'

'You can't put this on me. Or anyone in the movement.'

'That so?' Frisk said, getting up from his seat and crossing to a plastic storage box in the corner of the room. He removed the lid and pulled out a clear plastic evidence bag. Inside there was a photo album with a red spine and a plain grey cover. He brought it back to the table. 'Go ahead.'

Cody opened the bag like something might leap out from the album's pages and bite him. 'This is mine. So what?'

'Oh, we know it's yours. It's got your prints all over it.'

'So why are you asking me then?'

'Because it was with Josh Hulme when he was found. Someone dropped it at the exchange point. And it has your prints all over it as well as those of Josh Hulme.'

'I had a bunch of shit taken in a robbery,' Cody said flatly.

'You report it?'

'No,' Cody answered, shaking his head.

'Josh Hulme told us that this album was in the room where he was kept after he was abducted.'

Frisk reached over and opened the album to a random page. The eyes were big, brown and familiar to Frisk and Cody. So was the red raw flesh on top of the dog's skull.

The door opened and a uniformed officer walked in. He bent down next to Frisk, lowered his voice. 'There's a Ryan Lock demanding to speak to you.'

Frisk got up. He picked up the album and held it up to Cody's face. 'Pretty sick thing to expose a child to, wouldn't you agree, Mr Parker?'

46

'You want me to one-eighty this investigation on the word of a teenage hooker you found in a strip club? Which, incidentally, you entered carrying a firearm. You keep going the way you are, Lock, and we're gonna have to get some new felonies on the books just to keep up.'

'But you'll look into it?'

Lock had known Frisk would be a hard sell. Hell, he wasn't even sure that Carrie believed him. But here he was in Frisk's office asking the man for a favour.

'For what it's worth,' Frisk said.

'All I'm asking you to do is keep an open mind.'

'This wouldn't have anything to do with Brand replacing you as Meditech's head of security, would it?'

'I'm convalescing.'

'Most people do that at home in bed with a nice bowl of chicken soup.'

Lock smiled. 'I didn't say I was any good at it.'

Frisk opened the bottom drawer of his desk and dug out a plastic Tupperware container. 'The wife makes me lunch. You know, try to ensure I eat my greens.' He took the top off and held it up for Lock to inspect. 'I mean, seriously, would you eat this shit?'

Lock waved it away.

'You've had a boner for Brand since the first

time I met you,' Frisk continued.

'He's had a boner for me.'

'Volunteering to testify against one of your own guys? Wouldn't that usually get you fragged in the military?'

'Not where I served. Not if someone had crossed the line.'

'Oh yeah, I forgot you served with the Limeys. That why you and Brand don't get along?'

'Head over to Scotland. Try calling them Limeys and see what happens. I served in the same branch of the military as my father. I served his memory. Took a lot of shit from both sides for being a mutt while I was doing it. But I've never felt the need to wrap myself in any flag in order to prove my patriotism.'

'Nice speech,' Frisk said, putting the lid back on his lunch box. 'Look, I have a perp.'

'Who didn't do it.'

'There's evidence you're not aware of.'

'Such as?'

Frisk stood up. 'Who the hell are you anyway, Lock? Just some hired hand.'

'This case is bullshit, and you know it.'

'I know I've got a guy who's now admitted to digging up Eleanor Van Straten's body, and who was at the handover. All you've got is the fact that one of your co-workers was schtupping Richard Hulme's nanny.'

'Who had to have been involved in the kidnapping.'

'A few months earlier she'd been giving out handjobs in the back of a strip club, so how do you know she wasn't dropping her panties for more than one guy?'

Lock flashed back to the minutes he'd spent in Natalya's bedroom after Richard Hulme had tracked him down. It seemed like a lifetime ago, but he could still see in his mind's eye the photograph of the young girl with her family. All that optimism, all that promise. He clenched his right fist and started to draw it back, not even fully conscious that he was doing it.

Frisk watched the blood drain from Lock's knuckles as he took a step back. 'That would be an extremely bad idea.'

Lock was aware of a couple of agents at nearby desks watching him.

'Y'know, when I heard about you running *towards* that sniper, I thought you just might be crazy. But now I'm positive.'

Lock took a deep breath and counted to ten slowly.

'Are we done here?' Frisk asked him.

'Well, seeing as you brought it up. What about Gray Stokes? Anyone going to be charged with his murder?'

'It's ongoing.'

'What did forensics say about the rifle that killed Stokes?'

'An M-107 fifty cal sniper rifle.'

'Traceable?'

'Missing from a combat unit serving in Iraq.'

'So we're probably looking at ex-service personnel,' Lock stated flatly.

'I'd say that would be a fair assumption.'

'And that doesn't fit any of the animal rights people.'

'They're not all known to us,' Frisk objected. 'Hell, Cody Parker kept a pretty low profile, and look what he was capable of.'

'Listen, when I went in the back of that store, I knew straight off I was dealing with something more than a bunch of people who break out in a rash about a beagle being handed a pack of smokes. If someone was prepared to go to all the trouble of laying their hands on an M-107, and learning how to use it, you think they'd miss Van Straten and get the other guy?'

Frisk put on his coat and strode towards the door. 'For Christ's sake, Lock, next time bring me something more than a grudge.'

47

Brand stood outside the door with two other members of the team. All of them were dressed in full riot gear: visored helmets, body armour and heavy boots. Now that the Hulme situation was resolved satisfactorily, Brand would be taking personal charge of the day-to-day running of the isolation unit. In total they had twelve individuals to look after, brought in on two separate flights. Each of them deemed to be extremely dangerous.

In his hand, Brand held a small monitor which was receiving the live feed from the camera placed on the other side of the door. A peep hole, even one using glass or Perspex, would be far too dangerous.

The woman was lying on the bed, staring up at the ceiling. The other two men would go into the cell, shackle and cuff her, while he stayed on the other side of the door. Any more than two men in the cell along with the trial subject would make movement too difficult. They'd just end up getting in each other's way. For the same reason no firearms were allowed inside the cell, or the rest of the accommodation block for that matter.

'Ready?' Brand asked them.

The men made a final check on their equipment.

'I don't understand why they can't be doped,'

one of them said. 'It'd make this a whole lot easier.'

'Can't run trials on someone with all that shit in their system.'

'So what do we do if there's a problem with one of them?'

'What kind of a problem?'

'Like they jump us.'

Brand lifted his visor and pointed at the monitor. 'You're afraid of a woman?'

'I'm asking a question is all.'

'Procedure is you're on your own.'

Five minutes later, Mareta was led into the examination room, chained and shackled. She didn't look frightened. Or defiant for that matter. She looked blank.

Richard's stomach did a back flip. He'd known since his conversation with Stafford that they'd be using human test subjects and had rationalized that maybe they were volunteers. The payment for clinical trials could run into thousands. Lots of money to some people. But who would volunteer for this?

He knew too that research into vaccines against bio-weapons had a chequered history. From soldiers deliberately exposed to high doses of radiation during nuclear testing through civilian drug trials going horribly wrong, live trials were an ethical and legal minefield. Get them right and you could save thousands, sometimes millions of lives; get them wrong and the consequences lingered. Sometimes in the form of birth deformities, for generations.

This was why Stafford had been so keen to

231

have him on board, whatever it took. His best bet, maybe his only bet now, was to go along with what was happening.

'Why is she restrained like that?' he asked Brand.

'Don't worry, doc, it's for your safety more than anything.'

'Might I speak with you in private for a moment?'

'Sure thing, doc.'

Richard opened a door at the rear of the examination room and Brand followed him through into a small office space.

'What's going on?' he challenged.

'Hey, I'm just here to make sure everyone's safe.'

Yeah, right, thought Richard, noticing the look of enjoyment on Brand's face.

'You think we were going to put an ad in the *Village Voice* and get volunteers for this, doc?'

'Who is she?'

'Someone this planet won't miss if it all goes wrong. That's all you need to know.'

'That's not good enough. I refuse to conduct any tests until someone tells me what's going on here.'

'Then talk to Stafford. He'll be here later on.'

'And what if I'm not here?'

'That's up to you. But right now all you're being asked to do is check them over and make sure they're fit for purpose.'

The door connecting the two rooms was still half open, and Richard could see Mareta with her two guards. She looked tiny in comparison,

232

the difference accentuated by the body armour. Wearily, he walked back through to her, mindful that his son was in the compound.

Mareta's body was a tapestry of torture. Richard had guessed as much when he first saw her walking in. Her gait was slow, the length of her stride shorter than it should have been. She walked almost on tiptoes, reluctant to put her heels on the ground — the result of a technique known as falanga. In lay terms it meant the striking of the soles of the feet with a blunt instrument. Repeatedly.

'I can't examine her properly when she's restrained like that.'

Brand traded glances with his two men. 'She's too dangerous not to be.'

Richard had to suppress the urge to laugh. The woman was five feet six inches, no more than a hundred and five pounds, and seemed to be on the verge of collapse.

'She might not look much, doc, but it only takes one blow to your throat or a finger in the right place to snuff someone.'

Richard pulled the chair from behind his desk and put it down next to the examination couch. 'At least let her sit down.'

Mareta was prodded the few feet to the chair. One man supported her under each arm so she could sit down.

Richard knelt down in front of her so that he was at eye level. She seemed to study him.

'Hello, my name's Dr Hulme, what's yours?' Richard said, in a tone that suggested he was speaking to a child.

One of the guards snickered.

'No habla anglais, doc,' Brand volunteered.

'She speaks Spanish?'

Another snicker.

'No, we didn't kidnap any beaners,' Brand replied. 'Although I wish I'd have thought of it. Could have cut a deal with the Minutemen and saved a bundle on air transfers.'

'Look, I need a name for my file.'

'We have a number for you if that helps. Might make things simpler all round. Specially when it comes time to shoot her up with whatever you're testing.'

'Thanks, I'm familiar with the theory,' Richard replied.

After the first trial of the drug DH-741, a memo had been issued to all employees at Meditech involved in animal testing that all subjects were to be known by a number only, and that under absolutely no circumstances were they to be given a name or referred to by anything other than their number. Anyone referring to an animal by name was to be immediately reported to Human Resources. The ostensible reason was that it would reduce the likelihood of data from subjects being mixed up, but Richard suspected another reason. Give something a name and you give it an identity.

Very few of the scientists had bothered to name their subjects anyway. They sneered at any anthropomorphic tendencies among their colleagues, regarding the prescribing of human traits to animals as childish. However, Richard suspected that their attitude stemmed from a desire to close down their own feelings. At best the animals suffered discomfort, at worst an agonizing death.

Richard had looked at it differently. If two dozen primates had to go through hell to develop a treatment that could save thousands of lives, then the end justified the means. When his wife died from cancer it had only strengthened his belief. Now, standing in this room, it occurred to him that the means had just increased exponentially. And for him, so had the end. Refusal risked the termination of the thing he cared about more than anything in the world: Josh. Acceptance required him to cross into moral territory from which there was no return.

'OK, I'll put her down as subject zero one,' Richard said, swivelling his neck round to look up at Brand.

'Catchy,' Brand replied.

Richard turned back to Mareta, just as she puffed out her cheeks and launched a gob of spit straight at his face. It caught him just above the left eye and started to dribble down his cheek towards his mouth.

Trying not to look at her, he wiped it away with the sleeve of his lab coat. When he took bloods he'd ask the lab to run a check for hepatitis.

It was time to get to work.

48

When people imagined New York, they thought first of the skyline and then of the press of bodies. But on the right block, at the right time, you could be all alone, with not a soul around. That's where Carrie was now. Ten blocks from home. And the silence meant she could hear the scuff of footsteps behind her as clear as crystal.

The footsteps quickened. She glanced back but didn't see anyone. She could feel the presence of the person following her now. A man, almost definitely a man.

Her hand went into her pocket and she felt for the small canister of mace. It was a gift from Lock, accompanied by a lengthy explanation. A knife can be taken off you. Ditto a gun. A taser, the latest must-have for ladies who lunch, too tricky to deploy. Miss with the stinger and you have to get in close. A rape alarm? Someone had to make a decision to get involved, and this was New York. So he'd given her pepper spray and taught her a few moves: elbow strike, double-handed fend-off. All designed with only one end in mind: to give her enough time to get away. As he told it, that's all bodyguarding was anyway. Organized running away.

She felt for the red cap at the top of the canister and flicked it forward. Felt for the trigger just beneath that. Used her index finger to move round the cold metal and locate the nozzle. The last thing she wanted to do was spray herself.

She could feel the guy almost on her shoulder. She was sure it was a man by the sound of his steps.

Three more steps, and she turned and pulled out the mace at the same time.

'Whoa! Carrie, sorry, I wasn't sure it was you. I didn't want to go shouting after some stranger in the street and freak her out.'

'You asshole, Ryan.'

'I get that a lot.'

'I thought you were a mugger.'

'You might wish I was in a second.'

'Why's that?'

'I need one final favour.'

★ ★ ★

Her day had started at six with a trip to the gym and an hour of punishment on a Stair Master. Thousands of people in the city who lived in walk-ups dreamed of moving out so they could escape having to climb flights of stairs. Yet here she was, surrounded by women of her age and younger, paying for the privilege.

Men could get away with going to seed in front of camera. A few extra pounds and a face like a bloodhound lent them gravitas. For a woman it was a career-finisher. That was the reality of her business.

Now it was nine in the evening and she was standing in front of a camera outside Meditech headquarters. Three hours after she'd left work.

Two of those had been spent persuading Gail Reindl to agree to the story.

Through her earpiece, she could hear the voice of the anchor back in the studio: 'For another dramatic development in the abduction case of Josh Hulme, we cross to our correspondent who's live outside the head offices of Meditech Corporation for an exclusive update. Carrie, what's this new information that's come to light?'

Like a golfer, Carrie had a routine every time she went live. She took a deep breath that lasted to the count of three. This time it lasted to the count of five.

'Thanks, Mike. As those of us who have been following this story already know, an arrest has been made, and the FBI have informed news sources that they are not looking for anyone else in connection with this crime. However, earlier today I spoke off record to a source close to Meditech Corporation who is claiming that Josh's au pair at the time, a young Russian woman who was found dead shortly after the abduction, was having a relationship with a member of the company's security personnel.'

The anchor came back in. 'And why is that a particularly significant development, Carrie?'

'Well, Rob, if you recall, Josh Hulme was last seen with the au pair getting into a town car outside an Upper East Side apartment block, leading many to conclude that this young woman was in some way involved in the kidnapping.'

'And what are the FBI saying about this?'

'So far not very much, although it is believed that this new information has been brought to their attention before now.'

As she finished up, Lock led the applause. Angel joined in, barking her approval as she rubbed against his leg.

'You want to get something to eat?' Carrie asked him.

'What about Paul?'

She was quiet for a moment, then sighed. 'We broke up.'

Lock did his best not to show his delight. 'That was sudden.'

'Yes, it was.'

'Who had the change of heart?'

'Does it matter?'

Lock hesitated. 'If it's the person who's asking me out to dinner then maybe it does.'

Behind them, the camera guy took time out from eavesdropping to clear his throat loudly.

Lock turned to him. 'You got something you want to say?'

'Only that if it was me, I wouldn't need asking twice.'

★　★　★

They dropped Angel back at the apartment and headed downstairs to Carrie's neighbourhood Italian. Red and white chequered table cloths, vampire-dark lighting — the place had stayed unchanged for so long it was now considered retro. They both ordered pasta and split a bottle of red wine.

'More ripples in the pond?' Carrie asked Lock as a single candle flickered between them. 'Is that why you asked me to do that piece?'

'No, insurance.'

'Against?'

'Life insurance.'

'For who?'

'Me.'

'And how does that work?'

'Well, assuming it's the same people, someone who's prepared to kidnap a minor and assassinate someone in the middle of the day in Midtown isn't going to think twice about snuffing me.'

'But if you're the accuser . . . '

'Starts to look bad if I have an accident. Doesn't make me safe, but sure as hell gives them something to think about.'

'And where does that leave me?'

'They won't touch you.'

'Glad you're so confident.'

'If journalists were fair game you'd be an endangered species by now. Anyway, there are better ways to manipulate a story than killing the messenger. They're counting on the fact that given enough time all this will go away.'

'And will it?'

'Everything does in time.'

'So why keep pressing?'

Lock smiled, reached over and refilled both their glasses. 'Because I'm an asshole like that.'

She reached down into her bag and pulled out a bulging manila envelope. 'I know. Which is why I've brought you everything I've managed to gather on Meditech. And the retired Colonel Brand.'

He took the envelope. 'You mind me reading at the table?'

'If you can in this light.'

He flipped to the stuff on Brand, and two words caught his eye. Abu Ghraib.

'He was there when Lindy King and her boyfriend were keeping prisoners on a short leash,' Carrie said.

'So how come no one ever heard of him?' Lock asked as he read on.

As soon as the photographs from Abu Ghraib came to light, Brand had been offered, and accepted, an honourable discharge. If he had known what was going on there he'd been savvy enough to keep his face out of the frame.

'Meditech did a full service check when they took me on. Spoke to a bunch of people. They must have done the same for Brand.'

'Maybe that's *why* they took him on,' said Carrie.

★ ★ ★

Later that evening, they made love at Carrie's apartment. It wasn't like it had been before. It was slower, with more of a connection. Before it had been recreational. This felt like the prelude to something that went deeper.

Afterwards, Carrie snuggled up next to him, her head on his chest. She drifted off to sleep, still cradled in Lock's arms. No *Harry Met Sally* quandary for Lock. It felt good. They lay like that for a long time.

When she woke, it was still dark and he wasn't there any more. Angel must have snuck in and was asleep at the foot of the bed. Carrie got up and put on her robe. She walked through into the living room.

Lock was standing by the window, putting on his jacket while staring down at the empty street below. 'It's early, go back to bed.'

She yawned, stretching her arms above her head. 'I get up early.'

'Not this early.'

'Why? What time is it?'

'Four.'

'Where are you going?'

'Brooklyn.'

'At four in the morning?'

He walked over to her and kissed her softly on the lips. 'Best time to see Brooklyn. When it's pitch-black.'

49

Sunrise was still a distant threat as Lock and Ty, dressed in full black-out gear, made a dash for the secondary perimeter fence of the Meditech complex.

Lock wet his finger and jabbed it at the fence to see if it was electrified.

'I bet you shoved forks into power sockets when you were a kid just to see what would happen, didn't you?' Ty asked.

'A blue flash and you get thrown halfway across the room.'

'And you know not to do it again,' Ty said.

'Nope, did it again a year later. Wanted to make sure it hadn't been a one-off.'

Lock stopped, took the entire inner area of the compound in with one sweeping look. His eyes settled on the accommodation block.

'OK,' Ty said, 'so we've looked. Now let's get the hell out of here.'

'What's that over there?'

'I don't know, man. This is as far as I've been.'

'Then what does it look like?'

Ty scanned the same fence as Lock had, picked out the same razor wire, noted the way it curved back in on itself. The curve of the top of a fence could tell you a lot. Most crucially, was it there to keep someone out or keep someone in?

'Looks like a brig,' Ty said.

'So what's a scale model of Guantanamo Bay

243

doing in the middle of a research complex?'

Ty looked skywards. 'How should I know?'

'You go back. I'm going to take more of a look around.'

'OK, I'll meet you out front,' said Ty reluctantly.

Lock tossed him his keys and watched him disappear into the gloom. Then, putting down the black knapsack, he took out a pair of wire cutters and set to work in an area where the surveillance camera was directed across a broad sweep of open ground beyond the fence.

In less than two minutes there were two slits in the fence, far enough apart that he could slip through. Safely on the other side, he rolled the fence back down so that, at least from a distance, it looked intact. Then he quickly paced out the distance from the nearest metal fence pole to his ready-made escape hatch.

As Lock put the wire cutters back in his knapsack, he felt the barrel of an M-16 press into the small of his back.

'You know, Lock, if you wanted the grand tour, you only had to ask.'

50

Lock lay face down on the ground while they searched him, taking his wallet, cell phone and Gerber. His 226, thankfully, was back in his car.

Brand scrolled down the names on Lock's cell. He stopped at Ty, held up the display so Lock could see it. 'He's still outside waiting for you. Better tell him you'll find your own way back, that you didn't find what you were looking for and that you're going out of town for a while.'

'And why would I want to do that?'

'I thought he was your buddy. You wouldn't want to drag him into this any further than you already have, would you?'

Brand hit the green call button and handed the cell back to Lock. He then took an M-16 from one of the two men with him, tucked the stock into his shoulder and pressed the business end into the centre of Lock's forehead.

'Ty? Yeah, listen, no need to hang around . . . No, I found a different exit. Listen, I have a few things to do. I'll catch up with you in a few days.' He paused. 'No, man, I'm fine.'

He ended the call and Brand snatched the cell back from him, powered it down and jammed it into his pocket.

'Now, you want that tour or not?'

'Do I have a choice?'

'Nope. It's like the old Chink curse. Be careful what you wish for, because you might just get it.'

They reached what Lock guessed was the main entrance to what Ty thought had looked like a brig. There was no handle or external lock. It simply clicked open.

'No expense spared, huh?' he asked Brand.

'Not when you see what we have inside.'

'Oh, I'm as giddy as a kid at Christmas,' Lock shot back.

Inside there was a hallway. It was about six feet wide, and extended about thirty feet, ending in a door of a similar type to the one they'd just come through. The walls were bare whitewashed concrete.

'This where you kept the kid?' Lock asked Brand.

'Just keep walking.'

They reached the next door and stopped. Brand pushed past Lock and went ahead. 'I'm going to prepare your room.'

The door clicked open and Brand walked through it, leaving Lock with the two guards. On the other side, Brand called for another two-man team to join him at the door into one of the cells. They were instructed to bring his riot gear down with them.

Five minutes passed. Then ten.

Finally, Lock could hear heavy boots and a door being opened followed by the sound of a brief but violent struggle. Then the door facing him opened again and Brand stepped through, removing his helmet. He had deep scratch marks running down one side of his face, but he was smiling. 'Wanna meet your new roomie?'

Lock was led through. They stopped outside

Mareta's cell. There was a smear of blood on the wall next to the door. Lock counted off six doors on each side. Banging noises and shouts were coming from behind all but one of them. The one they were standing in front of.

Brand produced Lock's cell phone again. Flipped it open. 'Anyone you want to say goodbye to?'

Lock stood where he was and said nothing.

Brand started to scroll down through the numbers. 'Here's one. How about Carrie?' Then he stopped and slapped his head with the palm of his hand in a mock show of embarrassment. 'Silly me. Should have told you earlier. There wouldn't be any point calling her.' Brand held the phone up so Lock could see him deleting her number. 'Hit-and-run accident. Driver didn't even stop. Some asshole in a Hummer.'

Lock lunged at him. The open palm of his right hand came up at an angle into Brand's chin, snapping his neck back and sending him stumbling backwards. The shouting from the other cells intensified.

A baton smacked into the back of Lock's knees, and his legs folded underneath him. Black shapes swam in front of him as he took a second blow to the back of the head. Then he heard the door being opened and he was hauled to his feet and thrown inside.

He landed a couple of feet clear of the door, and heard it slam shut. Then came the sound of something metal skittering across the floor. He blinked a few times to try to clear his vision.

His Gerber lay on the floor of the cell, the

blade extended. A woman's hand reached down and picked it up. He lifted his head. She stood over him. The fingers of her right hand formed a tight fist around the handle in a hammer grip.

Lock stared into her eyes and braced himself for the blow.

51

Carrie slept late. Her late unscheduled appearance the previous evening meant she wasn't due in to work until lunch. Usually she jumped straight into the shower but this morning she could smell Lock on her skin and she didn't want to lose that. In the kitchen, she made breakfast for herself and Angel. They both cleared their plates in record time.

She wandered through into the living room and flicked on the TV. A few of the other networks had picked up the Meditech story. They were following in her wake, and had been since Gray Stokes' assassination. The next month would be a good time to ask for a move into the studio. She liked the buzz of chasing stories, but she also knew that people doing her job were likened to sharks for a reason: you kept moving forward or you died.

On the kitchen counter her PDA blinked red. She picked it up and scrolled through the emails. There was a fresh one from Gail Reindl giving her the overnights. Gail wanted to congratulate her in person when she got into the office. That anchor job was getting closer.

Angel had taken up position at the door and was barking. Carrie went back into the bedroom, threw on some sweats and tied her hair back in a ponytail. She grabbed Angel's leash from the closet next to the door, along with a jacket, and

249

headed downstairs. In the lobby, the doorman greeted them both.

Outside it was still cold, but the sky was bright blue and the sun was shining. The weather reflected Carrie's mood. She half walked, half jogged to the end of the block. Angel trotted alongside her, occasionally outpacing her and straining on the leash, desperate to get to the park.

Carrie gave the leash a sharp tug as they reached the crosswalk. 'Hey, easy there.'

The dog stopped and looked up at her. The sign flashed WALK.

'Now we can go.'

Carrie stepped off the sidewalk. She didn't even see the Hummer as it ran the light and barrelled straight towards her, ten thousand pounds of chaos doing forty miles an hour and picking up speed with every foot of blacktop rolling beneath it. She looked up at the last minute, and hauled herself and the dog back up on to the sidewalk as the vehicle's rims scraped the concrete at the top of a drainage hole.

An old man in his sixties, milk-bottle-thick glasses, touched her arm. 'Are you OK?'

Her heart was drumming against her chest. Her whole body seemed to be vibrating. *It was coming straight for me!* she thought.

'Those damn things don't belong on the roads!' the old man shouted after the receding Hummer as it ran the next lights, slowed, and swung left out of sight.

52

'Man, we should have popcorn for this.'

Brand was like a guy who has to go to work at the start of the fourth quarter of the Super Bowl and decides to TIVO the whole game to watch later. As soon as Lock was inside the cell he'd radioed the CCTV operator to make sure to dump the footage from Mareta's cell on to hard drive.

'You got it cued up?'

The operator nodded. 'All ready to go. This one here,' he said, pointing to the centre screen in a bank of monitors.

The image was frozen: Mareta, the grieving widow, staring down at the wounded soldier as he crawled his way towards her.

'Man, when this is over, I'm uploading this shit on to Live Leak. Come on, lemme see.'

The operator hit play, and Brand leaned forward to enjoy the action.

* * *

Lock had had a few things already worked out before the door into the cell had opened. It was clear that Brand was enjoying himself immensely and in a manner that went way beyond the satisfaction he would have gotten from just locking him up. Something lay on the other side of the door that was giving

251

Brand one hell of a woody.

From the design of the building, both inside and out, Lock was clear it hadn't been built just to prevent escape, but also to limit and contain movement to the nth degree. That meant the occupants were deemed dangerous to staff.

Lock had readied himself for a fight. To the death, if necessary. His or the other guy's. Then Brand had dropped the bomb about Carrie. Brand had obviously expected the news to cut Lock off at the knees, but it had had the opposite effect. He'd felt a surge of energy, and with it a surge of adrenalin. Even in his diminished physical state he'd felt that the raw anger would carry him through.

When he looked up from the floor of the cell to see a woman, the decision had been simple. Natalya dumped in the East River with her brains blown out. Carrie, the victim of an unfortunate 'accident'. Two dead women was enough.

He lay still and waited.

★ ★ ★

'You sure this thing's working?' Brand asked, slamming a meaty hand down next to the keyboard.

Lock and the detainee had hardly moved on the tape. Just remained where they were, watching each other in some goddamn Mexican stand-off.

'Yes, sir,' the operator replied.

'Move it on. Let's get to the action.'

The operator moved his mouse, pulling the slider along. The woman jerked forward as Lock lay on the floor.

'OK. There.'

On screen, Mareta laid the knife down on the floor. Still within reach should she need it. Then she knelt down next to Lock and helped him to his feet.

'What the hell?' Brand exploded. He'd got halfway through the first quarter only to find one of the defensive linesmen break through and start waltzing with the opposition quarterback.

* * *

Mareta had heard the men approaching. Even after all this time she hadn't been able to escape the low dread that clouded her mind as the cell door opened. She'd tensed and then relaxed each part of her body. Less chance of breaking a bone if you were relaxed. Bruises and lacerations were one thing, but she'd spent three months in a prison in Moscow with a fractured fibula and no medical attention. The bone had healed on its own but left her with a limp and the memory of the intense pain.

They'd rushed in, one at a time. The biggest of them had dragged her off the bed and pinned her shoulders against the wall. The other man had reached down to her waist and grabbed her wrists with one hand while his other hand fumbled in his pocket. There was a click and one of her hands was free. She'd waited for him to uncuff her other hand and scratched at his face.

She'd felt his skin wedging in a strip under her nails. She'd tried to get hold of his hair but it was too short. He'd shouted at her, calling her a bitch, and punched her in the face.

She'd gone down under the force of that punch. One man had sat on her chest and the other on her legs, sending a shard of pain shooting up her left leg, the one that had been broken back in Moscow. She'd heard the shackles clanking against the concrete as they too were taken off.

The men had then retreated from the cell, and she'd run at the door as it closed. Slamming her fists against the steel. She'd heard a door open and slam shut. Then they'd come back, her cell door opened again, and another man was thrown inside.

He was dressed normally. He looked American, or at least how she imagined Americans looked when they weren't in uniform. His hair was shorter than the guards' and he had a fresh scar that ran along the top of his head. He'd looked from the knife to her but made no move towards it, not even when she bent down to pick it up.

His gaze had met hers. There was no fear in his eyes. She'd held the knife in a hammer grip like she'd been taught by her husband. Still he hadn't moved. They'd stayed that way for what seemed like an eternity. She'd sensed he was conscious of the knife but he never looked at it. Not once.

Then, finally, he'd spoken. 'I'm not going to

fight you. So if you're going to do it, then let's get it done.'

She'd looked from the man to the unblinking eye of the camera mounted in the corner, put down the knife, and put out her hand. He'd taken it, and she'd helped him on to his feet.

★   ★   ★

Back in the control room, Brand had tired of the love-in. 'OK, go live.'

The operator punched a key. The screen went blank. The operator hit it again.

'What is it? What's the problem?' Brand asked, agitated.

'We're not getting any signal from that camera.'

'Try again.'

'I just did.'

Brand kicked out at the wall in frustration. Half an hour ago the cell had been occupied by a solitary woman, cuffed and shackled. Now it was her, Lock and a knife. What the hell had gone wrong?

53

Lock handed the knife back to Mareta — a calculated show of trust he hoped he wouldn't have cause to regret. If he was going to get out of here he'd need her cooperation.

An alarm that had been shrieking in the background for the past five minutes fell silent. Lock prowled the cell, examining its construction from every angle. Mareta watched him.

'The only way out is through the door,' she said.

'You speak English? Sorry, stupid question.'

'They don't know I understand them,' she said, nodding to the disembowelled camera which lay on the bed.

'Who are you? Why are you here?'

'My name is Mareta Yuzik.'

That piece of information alone went most of the way to answering both questions. Lock wouldn't have recognized her face, because very few people had seen it. And most of those who had were dead. But he sure as hell knew the name. In fact, it sent an involuntary shudder all the way from the base of his spine to the back of his neck.

Mareta was the most infamous of Chechnya's black widows, women whose husbands had been killed by the Russians and who operated as suicide bombers in the Chechens' bloody guerrilla war to win independence from the motherland. Mareta's husband had been a notorious Chechen warlord. But that wasn't what had made her exceptional. What made her stand out was the fact that she'd disavowed martyrdom to assume command of her former husband's group of fighters.

Mareta's band had spent the last few years on a murderous rampage. Lowlights included the wholesale slaughter of some of Moscow's prime movers and shakers during a performance by the Bolshoi. Demonstrating a horrifyingly accurate understanding of the theatricality required to get yourself noticed as a terrorist in the modern world, Mareta had kicked off proceedings by personally beheading the lead ballerina live on stage. Of course, where the newly rich Russians were, so were their bodyguards. A firefight had taken place during which the respective close protection teams took out more of each other's clients in the crossfire than the Chechens managed. The finale had been a huge explosion.

In that particular puff of smoke, Mareta and her comrades had disappeared, leading to speculation that the whole thing was a put-up job by the Kremlin, who'd seen one of their main political rivals taken out during the outrage. The apparatchiks had seen it as a happy coincidence.

Mareta's follow-up was no less demanding of world headlines. Her fighters entered a kinder-garten just over the border from Chechnya and held two dozen infants hostage before slaughtering them in cold blood, taping events for posterity. Once again, Mareta slipped into the night before the building was overrun and most of her fighters were killed by Russian special forces.

It was this second escape which had earned her the nickname of the Ghost in the Russian media. There had been numerous sightings of her since then, including in northern Iraq, Pakistan and Helmand Province. Her popping up here beat them all.

Lock decided to follow Mareta's lead and play dumb. 'Do you know why you're here?'

'To die,' she said, matter of factly.

'Are the other people they brought here also from your country?'

'Some. Some from other places.' She picked at a hang nail with the tip of the Gerber. 'Now, let me ask you the same question you asked me. Why are you here?'

'It's a long story.'

Mareta glanced around the cell. 'Maybe we have a long time.'

Lock trusted his new cellmate about as much as Brand, so he gave her an edited version of events, telling her he was an investigative journalist looking into the activities of a drug company.

'You have investigative journalists, right?'

'Investigative?' She rolled the word around in her mouth like it was the funniest thing she'd heard. 'Yes, we have these people. The government kills them.'

She was clearly a glass-half-empty kind of a gal.

'So when I was looking around this place,'

Lock continued, 'they found me, beat me up. I guess they threw me in here hoping you'd finish me off.'

Mareta listened calmly. She paced to the door and back again, making shapes in the air with the blade of the knife. 'So why do you think I'm here?'

'You mean, what would a drug company want with you?'

'Yes.'

'I think you're a guinea pig.'

'Guinea pig?'

'Yes. They're going to use you to see if something they're developing is safe to use on humans.'

'What?'

'That, I don't know.'

In fact, he had a couple of ideas. Mareta's presence here had to have been sanctioned at the highest level. Maybe a private deal between governments. Maybe Meditech was developing something which the Russians thought could open her up for interrogation. Both the CIA and KGB had chased down so-called 'truth' drugs during the Cold War, everything from sodium pentathol to a more orthodox tongue loosener like whisky, or a picture of the target in a compromising position. In a world where quality intelligence could save thousands of lives, something surefire would be worth more than its weight in gold.

'So, which paper do you work for?' Mareta asked.

'I'm freelance,' Lock said. It was only half a lie, but Mareta's expression told him that she didn't buy it — and neither did he for that

259

matter. It wasn't such a bad thing to be crap at playing dumb, he supposed.

Mareta stopped pacing the cell and approached Lock. She held the point of the knife about a foot from his right eye — not close enough for him to take it from her. 'And say I don't believe you.'

Lock did his best not to blink. He knew that arguing would make him seem even more suspicious. 'Not much I can do about that.'

She kept the tip of the blade where it was. 'They tried this once before. In Moscow. They put me in a cell with another woman. I made sure she would never have children. And that time, I had no knife.'

'You were captured?'

'Twice. Twice I escaped.'

Lock glanced at the knife, then shifted his gaze back to Mareta. 'So if you think I'm a spy, why haven't you killed me already?'

'Getting information from someone can go two ways. I have learned more from my interrogators over the years than they ever learned from me.'

'No shit.'

'Please don't use such words.'

Lock made a mental note. *Likes: public decapitation. Dislikes: Inappropriate language.*

'Maybe I make sure you won't be able to make any children either.'

She moved the knife slowly down from his face, letting it come to rest level with his crotch.

54

Lock sat on the floor with his back against the cell wall. All he was missing to complete the Steve McQueen look was a baseball.

'So, what do you think we should call the kids?'

Mareta, who was on the bed, pointed the knife in the direction of his face again. 'You talk too much.'

'Just trying to pass the time.'

'You should be thinking of how we get out of here.'

'I thought you'd have that covered.'

She looked straight at him. 'And why would that be?'

Damn. Nothing Lock had said since he'd entered the cell had in any way suggested that he knew her by reputation, and that was too close. 'You said you'd escaped twice after being captured, didn't you?' he countered, thinking quickly.

She sneered, swung her legs over the edge of the bed frame. Jabbed the point of the knife gently against his arm, like a housewife checking the chicken to see if the juices are running clear.

'You're not a journalist,' she said.

'And why do you say that?'

'I've met many of them.'

Lock flashed back to another story that Mareta had reputedly featured heavily in. Six pro-Kremlin reporters dispatched from Moscow to show how well the war effort was going in Chechnya. The first head arrived back in their Moscow office in a large brown box a week later. A day later, a second head. Within the week all the heads had been returned. Then the hands started to arrive. That took two weeks. In all, it was a three-month process. A constant drip of gruesome detail. Only their hearts didn't make it back. Presumably they left them in Chechnya.

'Most journalists are fat,' Mareta continued. 'From sitting on their backsides and sticking their noses in the government trough.'

'Not here they ain't, lady,' Lock said. 'We have freedom of the press.'

'So does Russia. They're free to say or write whatever they like. But somehow what they write is what the people who pay them want to hear. Big coincidence.' She kept staring at him. 'So, who are you?'

She didn't look like she was about to give up this line of questioning any time soon.

'I told you already.'

'You mean you lied already.'

'Listen, if we're going to get out of here in one piece, we're going to have to trust each other.'

'Trust requires honesty.'

Lock conceded that point. He was about to break the primary rule of capture: pick a cover story and stick to it. But this wasn't a regular situation. For one thing, Brand wouldn't hesitate to break his cover, especially if he thought it would get him killed.

He examined Mareta. In a straight fight it

would be no contest, despite her reputation. But she had the knife. Guys who watched the Ultimate Fighting Championship might talk about knife 'fighting', but in reality there was no such thing. There was only getting stabbed. Quickly followed by bleeding to death.

'OK, you're right,' he said.

She listened calmly as he told her about working for Meditech and filled in the details leading up to his being taken prisoner at the facility. She said nothing, remained resolutely expressionless, only occasionally stopping him to seek clarification of a word or phrase she didn't understand. The only time she reacted to Lock's story was when he mentioned the animal rights activists and their cause. The very idea seemed absurd to her. Lock understood her scepticism. For someone who'd witnessed and enacted the slaughter of human beings, it must have seemed a foreign concept. He considered repeating the Gandhi quote that Janice had fired at him from her hospital bed, but thought better of it.

He finished, and waited for Mareta to say something. Silence filled the space between them. Normally he would have been content with that, but what was needed now was rapport. Storytelling was about as good a way to establish that as he knew.

'So, what about you? Why are you here?'

'You already know who I am,' Mareta replied.

'Yes, I do.'

'But you don't seem scared.'

'Should I be?'

'Everyone's afraid of ghosts.'

263

Lock mulled it over. 'Maybe I'm different.'

Mareta studied the walls of the cell, equally reflective. 'That's true,' she replied. 'You're still alive. And if you want to stay that way you might want to think about how we can get out of here.'

55

Lock was the first to hear the door being opened at the far end of the corridor. He waved Mareta to her feet. They flattened themselves either side of the cell door as two sets of footsteps made their approach, accompanied by the rattle of a metal trolley. There was more clanking of metal, followed by a man shouting something in a language that Lock didn't understand.

'What's he saying?'

'He's asking who else is here.'

Mareta pressed her face to the cell door and shouted something back. Lock picked out that it was her name. In her own language it sounded more guttural, and laden with threat.

'Proper little reunion you got going on,' Lock noted.

Mareta shouted something else, this time maybe in Chechen. He could hear the man laugh at whatever it was she'd said.

'What did you just say?'

'I told him that we would wash in the blood of our captors.'

'No wonder we don't get any Chechen stand-ups playing the clubs here. Why don't you try asking him how many of you there are?'

She shouted something else, and the man roared a reply.

'Ten. Maybe more.'

'What's happening now?'

265

Mareta pressed her face to the access panel at the bottom of the door. Lock grabbed her by the shoulder and pulled her back. She glared at him.

'Get too close and they might open that thing and give you a good dose of mace,' he warned.

Another shouted exchange.

'It's feeding time,' Mareta told Lock.

Sure enough, a few moments later the flap opened and a tray was shoved inside — metal, so it would be difficult to break to form a weapon. Filling the tray's ridged compartments was what Lock imagined to be standard-issue prison food. Two slices of bread. Orange juice. Some kind of a stew with rice. A square of low-grade cooking chocolate, and a banana. Not bad. Better than economy in most airlines he'd flown.

He took a slice of bread, handed the other one to Mareta.

She pushed it away, wrinkling her nose. 'You eat first.'

He was guessing this wasn't a sign of hospitality on her part. 'You're not hungry?'

'I don't know what's in it.'

'So if it's rat poison you'd like me to find out first?'

'Exactly,' she said.

Lock put the bread back down on the tray.

'You don't think about these things,' Mareta observed with a sneer.

She was right. Lock hadn't.

She picked the bread back off the tray, tore off a hunk and handed it to Lock. 'They didn't bring me here to poison me. But there could be something in it to make us sleep.'

266

'So why do you still want me to taste it?'

'You'll see.'

Lock took the bread and popped it in his mouth. As he chewed tentatively, it turned sweet in his mouth. He swallowed. Took a tiny sip of orange juice to wash it down. It tasted funky. He poured the rest of the juice into the tray compartment. A gritty residue floated at the bottom. He swirled it round with one finger.

'They could at least have sprung for some Rohypnol. Least that dissolves.'

He sat on the floor, his head resting against the cold concrete.

'So, what's a nice girl like you doing in a place like this?' Lock asked her, the question designed to kickstart some more conversation and stave off the frustration that he could feel creeping into his bones.

'You're not interested.'

'That's where you're wrong. I mean, I'm presuming you weren't *born* an evil bitch who thinks it's acceptable to brutally slaughter civilians.'

'You want to know why I cut the head off Anya Versokovich?'

Lock shrugged.

'I did it because . . . she was there.'

Lock was feeling tired, more likely as a result of the hectic week he'd had and the after-effects of repeated adrenalin dumps than anything surging through his bloodstream from the tiny sip of juice. 'That's it? That's your big reason for beheading the Bolshoi's prima ballerina?'

'It's the same reason the Russians gave me.'

'Gave you for what?'

'What they did to me. You want me to tell you?'

Lock laid his head back against the wall of the cell and closed his eyes. 'Sure.'

'You know of my dead husband?'

'I know of his reputation.'

'I was bathing my two children when they came. My son was four. My daughter was three. When the commander of the Russians couldn't find my husband, he left two of his soldiers in the room with us. He didn't want anyone to say later that he was there.'

With a grim predictability, Mareta went on. Lock kept his eyes shut. He wasn't sure he wanted to be looking at her as she finished her story.

'While one of the soldiers raped me, the other put a knife to my children's throat. Forced them to watch. When the first man was finished, the other took his turn. Then they tied my hands behind my back and made me watch. They drowned my son first. And then his sister. Afterwards, I was taken downstairs to speak to the commander. My husband had killed Russians, but what had I done? So I asked him, 'Why did you do this?' And he told me, 'Because you were here.' '

Lock opened his eyes. Mareta's face was set. Expressionless. Only her eyes betrayed any feeling. His voice broke a little as he spoke. 'What happened after that?'

'They left me, but I followed.'

'You killed them?'

'Every last one.'

'So where does it end, Mareta?'

'It doesn't.'

'You know there's no way out this time.'

'There's always a way out,' she said, staring off into the middle distance.

'Always?'

'Death is a way out.'

'True, but what I don't understand is how come you were always the only one to make it out before?'

'It's simple. The harder someone looks, the less they see.'

More riddles. 'And what does that mean?'

'When they look high, I stay low. They look low, I stay high.'

'You want to try it in English?'

The same wafer of a smile. 'You'll work it out.'

56

'Why don't we just roll a grenade in there, frag the whole lot and let God do the sorting?' Brand asked.

Stafford rounded on him. 'Because twelve's the clinical minimum for Phase One.'

'So we find one other person,' Brand countered.

'And where do you suggest we do that, Colonel? Craigslist?' Stafford pointed a finger at the blank screen. 'Take me down there. I'll talk to them.'

Brand snorted. 'She doesn't speak English, and there's no way Lock's dumb enough to walk out of there with us waiting for him. Don't have time to starve them out either.'

'Then we'll find some other way.'

Brand shrugged as Stafford marched out of the control room. 'Can't wait to see that.'

'Bring your weapon with you,' Stafford called back as he strode ahead.

'Firearms aren't allowed in the accommodation block,' Brand reminded him, grabbing his Glock and following him down the corridor.

'Make an exception.'

'I really don't think it's a good idea.'

'They have a knife. You said so yourself.'

'And what if they get hold of a gun?'

'It won't come to that.'

A few minutes later they arrived at the door of

Mareta's cell. Brand stood one side of the door, Stafford on the other.

'Give me your weapon,' Stafford said.

Brand unholstered the Glock, pulled back the slide to chamber a round, and handed it, handle first, to Stafford.

'You're not going in there, are you?'

'No,' said Stafford, taking the Glock and pointing it at his head of security. 'You are.'

Brand kept cool. 'You don't have it in you.'

'Had it in me when I killed Stokes,' Stafford said.

'That was different. Everything was set up for you. All you had to do was pull the trigger.'

The pad of Stafford's index finger bulged as he applied pressure to the trigger. 'Which makes it different how?'

Brand raised his hands in surrender. 'OK, OK.'

'Look at it this way,' said Stafford. 'You were always telling me how Lock was a grandstander and you were the real deal. Now's your chance to prove it.'

57

'You OK?'

Carrie hadn't even noticed Gail Reindl getting into the elevator.

'Fine. Why?'

'Your hands are shaking.'

Carrie faked a smile. 'Over-caffeinated.'

Gail seemed to search Carrie's face. 'Sure that's all?'

'Some jerk in a Hummer ran a stop sign when I was crossing the street. Almost took me out. Shook me up a little. I'll be fine in a second.'

Gail made a *whaddaya gonna do, this city's crazy* face. The doors opened and she stepped out, much to Carrie's relief.

What else was she going to say? That it was a Hummer just like the one that had run down Gray Stokes' wife, except this one had been black rather than red. That she didn't think it was an accident. That someone was trying to kill her. That just because you're paranoid doesn't mean they're not out to get you. Ever since the movie *Network* got a release, complete with barking mad anchorman, the one surefire way to get canned as an anchor was to show any sign of mental instability. And Carrie hadn't even made it there yet. No, if she was going to talk to anyone, it'd be Lock.

Carrie stopped at the water cooler. One of the producers was there filling his coffee mug.

272

'You got a guest,' he said, nodding towards her desk.

The first thing Carrie saw was the wheelchair, then Janice Stokes. Before she could censor her next thought it had already flashed into her mind. *She looks like death.*

Carrie sat down, shifting her chair so she was side on to Janice.

'They've arrested my brother.'

'What's the charge?'

'Aiding in the abduction of a minor. Lock promised us that if we helped him he'd keep us out of this. Don wouldn't cope with being in jail.'

'Did he do it?'

'No. And I need to get him out of Rikers before something bad happens to him.'

'Wouldn't you be better off talking to a lawyer?'

'I already did.'

'And what did they say?'

'That I'd have to wait until it comes to trial.'

'Your brother could ask to be placed in protective custody.'

'Which would make him look even more guilty.'

'Sorry, I don't mean to seem unkind, but what do you think I can do?'

'I thought you might know where Ryan Lock is, for a start. I've tried calling him, but his cell's switched off. Can't get hold of his buddy Ty either.'

Carrie believed her. She'd called Lock straight after the incident with the Hummer and left a voicemail. 'It's not unusual for Lock to go off the radar. Believe me, I know.'

Janice paused, like she was making a decision. Then she reached down the side of her chair and pulled out a manila envelope. 'Some friends helped me sort through my parents' stuff. I couldn't face it until yesterday.' She handed the envelope to Carrie. 'Ryan asked if my dad had something on Meditech. You know, to make them change their mind about animal testing.'

Carrie put her hand in the envelope and came out with a single sheet of paper. Printed at the top was a web link: www.uploader.tv/Meditech.

58

The food tray lay empty by the door, Mareta next to it, curled up in a fetal position. Knees hugged to the chest, eyes closed. Her right hand tucked under her body to conceal the knife.

Lock lay next to her, similarly stricken. His legs were stretched out so that one of them was almost touching the door. That way, even if he did doze off, he'd know when someone walked in.

It had been deathly quiet for the past hour. Then there were footsteps in the corridor directly outside. A single person, moving slowly, betrayed only by the acoustics, which seemed designed to betray the slightest sound.

The footsteps stopped. A dribble of saliva trailed from the corner of Lock's mouth to the floor.

The door slammed into Lock's leg. He stirred, but kept his eyes closed.

'OK,' he heard Brand whisper.

Two more sets of boots double-timed it down the corridor. Lock opened both eyes a fraction. Out of his left he could see Brand's boot as he went to step over him.

Lock darted out a hand to grab Brand's ankle. Brand struggled to keep his balance but timbered to the floor. He landed on top of Lock, his knee smashing into Lock's left eye socket.

The knife came down in an arc, slipping down

275

the inside of Brand's helmet and slicing into his ear. He screamed, and wrenched at the helmet. His ear lobe flapped from the side of his head like a decked fish.

Brand drew his arm forward, towards Lock. Lock tried to grasp it at the wrist but wasn't fast enough. Brand accelerated his arm backwards into Mareta's face, the rear elbow strike sending her spinning back on to the bed. The shift of Brand's weight allowed Lock to squirm out from under the heavier man.

The other two guards were almost at the door now. In a second they'd be coming through it. Then it would be a lottery as to who lived and who died. And someone was definitely going to die.

Lock pushed past Brand and threw himself at the door. Mareta lunged at Brand, the knife embedding itself in his groin protector. Mareta pulled it back out but not before catching another elbow strike to the face. One of Mareta's front teeth flew out of her mouth, and landed on the floor.

Brand's body armour was throwing her off. His head was covered by a Kevlar reinforced helmet. Neck and throat protector panels transitioned to the main vest. Armoured sleeves transitioned to anti-slash gloves. Below the waist, the protection was similarly complete. All the way down.

Brand swung at her again. She ducked the blow and dived for his feet. His knee caught her on the side of the face, cracking her cheekbone. She jabbed the knife as hard as she could through the tongue of his right boot, piercing the soft leather and wedging the blade down and into his foot. It was Brand's turn to scream.

The noise from the other cells was reaching critical mass. What Lock guessed were exhortations to victory, and Godly praise, made for a surreal background.

Mareta skittered around Brand's back, her hand twisting as she kept a firm grip on the handle of the knife protruding from Brand's foot. Then she let go and put her forearm around his neck, choking him out. This time she was too close in for his elbows to reach her.

Brand flailed as Lock struggled to be heard above the noise. The door was being forced open and his strength was draining by the second. 'You come in, he's dead!' he yelled.

The pushing stopped.

Lock glanced back to where Brand stood, Mareta behind him, right forearm tourniqueting his neck, left hand up at the chin end of his helmet. Lock knew she was ready to swivel his head past the point of no return for his top cervical vertebrae as soon as the door opened.

'Hold your positions!' Brand shouted, in a half-strangulated voice.

'Tell them to withdraw.'

'You heard him. Fall back.'

Lock stayed at the door. 'If I see *anyone*, he's dead.' He counted to ten and opened the door. He took a quick peek. Clear. Empty corridor all the way to the security gate at the far end, which was closed.

He stepped back inside the cell and stripped

Brand of his baton, radio, taser and the pepper spray he'd never had a chance to deploy. The problem with just about every single non-fatal weapon was that cramped spaces rendered them useless. No room to swing a baton, pepper spray was non-selective, only the taser was an option, but once that was in hand it was easily taken.

Lock pressed the taser into the small of Brand's back, finding the crack between his vest and his groin protector. Mareta released her hold, then Lock pressed the button.

Brand's body jolted. 'Shit. What was that for?'

'My own personal satisfaction, asshole.'

Lock popped out the earpiece and microphone connector from Brand's radio. 'OK, so what's your back-up channel?'

'Three,' Brand grunted.

Lock knew that there was always an alternative broadcast channel for comms in case the original was compromised. It was something agreed beforehand. Sometimes it went down in predetermined increments, twos or threes. Usually the patterns were easy to crack, as they had to be kept as simple as the simplest guy out there.

'I'd better hear some chatter or I'm going to strip off that armour and let Mareta have at it with that Gerber,' Lock said as he surfed down to three.

Sure enough, a full-blown Chinese parliament was in effect. Transmissions cut across each other, punctuated by bursts of static. Lock turned the volume down.

'There's no way you're walking out of here, Lock.'

Lock buzzed Brand with the taser again. He yelped.

'When I want your opinion, I'll give it to you,' Lock told him.

'Can't you at least get that freakin' knife out of my foot?' Brand gasped.

'Sure thing.'

Lock knelt down and pulled it from Brand's boot. It came out with a sucking noise and a pulse of blood. He wiped down the blade and kept it in his hand.

There were a number of questions that had been nagging away at Lock. Not just about Josh — he'd figured most of those out for himself — but about the presence of Mareta and her colleagues.

'What's she doing here?' Lock asked Brand with a jerk of his head.

'Test subject. They need to try it out on human beings and she was the closest we could get.'

The smartass answer earned Brand another high-voltage pulse from the taser.

'That why she's still alive?'

'Pretty much.'

'And you took Hulme's son to make him think it was the animal rights people? Scare him back on board.'

'Not my idea.'

'What about Stokes?'

'He got wind of the human trials. Some upstanding citizen in the company must have leaked it. He used it as leverage to broker the deal, but you know how much the company likes *loose ends*.'

'Hulme know any of this?' asked Lock.

'Doubt it. He seemed pretty shocked when he figured who was replacing the monkeys.' Brand glanced at Mareta, who was standing with her head tilted back, pinching her nose to staunch the bleeding.

'So why a Chechen?'

'Search me. Probably got scooped up in the Middle East. I thought we'd be getting mostly ragheads or Guantanamo Bay's leavings, but the bleeding hearts have most of them accounted for.'

'OK, Brand. How do we get out?'

'I told you, Lock, you don't. Right now, this place is locked down tighter than a gnat's asshole. You get past our guys, there'll be army on the perimeter.'

'We have you.'

'Big whoop. I'm as dispensable as you are. Soon as they get a look, they'll light you up like a Christmas tree.'

'Better take off that body armour then.'

Mareta and Lock watched Brand closely as he stripped off. Lock, feeling slightly ungallant, took the extra padding of Brand's clothes and put them over his own before slipping on the body armour, leaving the helmet off for now. He comforted himself with the fact that Mareta was the safest person among the three of them. Her status as a trial subject ensured that.

The radio chatter had fallen away. Lock

turned up the volume and waited. Just as he was wondering if there'd been another change of channels there was a burst of static and Stafford's voice crackled over the speaker. 'Lock? You there?'

Lock raised the walkie-talkie to his lips. 'I'm here.'

'Is Brand alive?'

'Everyone's alive. For now.'

'In five minutes the military will be here.'

'The military?'

'That's right.'

'Don't drag them into this, Stafford. If anyone in the military knew what you've been doing, they'd drop you out of a helicopter over Tehran with a signed photo of Dick Cheney pinned to your shorts.'

'Five minutes, Lock. I'll kill everyone in that cell if I have to.'

'Bullshit. You need the woman to make up the numbers.'

Stafford didn't reply, which said a whole lot.

Lock turned to Mareta. 'You're the escape expert. What do we do now?'

'We do this,' said Mareta, slashing Brand's throat.

59

Stafford stood at the end of the corridor, Brand's Glock warm in his hand. Three doors down, Lock's cell door opened and a broadly spherical object rolled out. It took a second for him to register what it was. The eyes blindfolded. The scalp shaved. A jagged wound snaking down the skull. It was Lock's head. That crazy bitch had butchered Lock and tossed his head out into the corridor like a bowling ball.

Stafford's stomach lurched, and a two-hundred-dollar dinner spattered over five-hundred-dollar split-toe Harris brogues.

A figure stepped from the cell, face obscured by his riot visor, pushing Mareta forward at knife point. Her face was a mess, her own hair matted slick with blood.

'Well, screw me,' Stafford said, gesturing for the two guards with him to open the door. 'He did it.'

The figure gave Mareta another shove. Hard. The momentum carried her through the open door and into the two guards. They scrambled to get a grip of her.

As they did so, the figure reached out a hand and took the Glock from Stafford. Awed, Stafford didn't even try to stop him.

'You did it, Brand! You did it!'

The figure pointed the gun at his head.

Stafford stumbled over his words. 'Listen,

there's no need to be sore. I knew you would. Lock was never any match for you.'

The visor tilted up.

'That so?' said Lock, grabbing Stafford and pressing the barrel of the Glock into his temple.

A scream went up from one of the two guards as Mareta fastened on to him, trying to prise away his throat protector. He raised his hand to ward her off and she bit down on it. As his sidearm clattered to the floor, Mareta's other hand, which held the knife, crept towards the man's face, ferreting out a gap in his body armour and driving home the point of the knife straight into his carotid artery. A jet of blood pulsed out irregularly and ran thick down the wall as his partner tried to wrestle her off.

Lock shoved Stafford out of the way, levelled the Glock downwards, and picked his spot as best he could using iron sights at close range. He squeezed off a single round into Mareta's leg. She released her grip, her hand reaching down to where she'd been shot. The uninjured guard pulled her to the floor, wresting the knife from her and jamming his knee into her back.

A second too late, Lock caught sight of Stafford reaching down to retrieve the dying guard's sidearm. He spun round, levelled his Glock at Stafford, but not before the guard kneeling on top of Mareta had managed to point his weapon straight at Lock's unprotected face.

He sensed the red dot of a laser sight tracing a pattern from his mouth to his face and up to a spot directly between his eyes. Slowly, he took his finger from the trigger of the Glock and laid it gently on the floor.

60

In the hospital block, Lock was staked out on a gurney. Across the room, Mareta was similarly restrained, her left leg a bloodied mess. Richard Hulme, who'd been drafted in as a surrogate ER physician, stood over her.

'How'd this happen?' he asked Stafford, who was pacing the room.

'Ask the Lone Ranger over there,' Stafford said, gesturing towards Lock.

Lock rested his chin on his chest. His only real injuries were cuts and bruises sustained during the beating he'd taken after he'd put down the Glock. All the guards had been members of Brand's detail. Grief, in this case, manifested itself in the form of kicking and punching Lock all the way to the medical block.

But, Lock had noted as he was taking his beating, they hadn't laid a finger on Mareta. She was a woman. She was injured. But he didn't think that would have stopped them. They needed her. And now, he hoped, they'd need him just enough to keep him alive for a while longer.

'Well, the good news is I doubt it'll require amputation,' Richard said. 'But we need to get her to a proper emergency facility as soon as we can.'

'No can do,' Stafford said. 'You'll have to patch her up here. We can get you whatever you need.'

'It's been twenty years since I went near anything like this.'

'Good opportunity to brush up on your skills then.'

'Dad!'

Josh stood in the doorway of the room, flanked by two guards.

'Sorry,' one of them said as the other tried to hustle Josh back out of the room. 'All we heard was that Dr Hulme was in here.'

Josh broke away from their grip and rushed to his father. 'What's wrong with those people?' he asked, staring at Lock and Mareta over his father's shoulder.

'They had an accident. But don't worry, Daddy's going to make it all better. Now, why don't you go back to your room?'

One of the guards came over to lead him out. 'Come on, son.'

'No, let him stay,' Stafford interrupted.

Lock watched as Josh shuttled his gaze between his father and Stafford, unsure who to obey. It was the first time he had seen the boy in anything other than photographs. The anger he felt that he'd been used as a pawn in this whole thing by Stafford acted like an opiate to dull his pain. Damn. He should have shot him when he had the chance and been done with it.

Stafford turned his attention back to Mareta, and grimaced at her leg wound. 'She still good to go for the trial?' he asked Richard.

'Are you out of your mind? Of course not.'

'You couldn't juggle the results?'

'Wait a second. One minute you want me to

sign off, now you want me to fake them?'

'You're right. But it still leaves us one short. We'll have to find someone else to take her place.'

Lock watched as Stafford's gaze settled on Josh.

'I wonder if there'd be any clinical benefit in seeing how effective the vaccine is with a different age group?' Stafford mused.

Richard placed himself between Stafford and his son. 'You can go to hell, Stafford.'

Lock strained to lift his head. 'You can use me.'

61

Carrie full-screened the RealPlayer window on her computer. The screen was black, save for a time/date stamp in the lower left corner. If it was accurate, the tape had been shot at ten minutes to midnight, a month before Gray Stokes had been shot outside Meditech.

White text rolled up the screen. Someone had taken their time putting this together. Carrie pulled a yellow legal pad from a drawer and jotted down what it said.

1st PHASE TRIAL OF DH-741
MEDITECH ANIMAL TESTING ROOM
ANIMAL TRIAL SUBJECT REACTION
POST-VACCINATION FILOVIRUS EXPOSURE

As the text scrolled off screen there was an abrupt cut to video footage — shaky, handheld, snatched. Grey metal filled the frame. A slow zoom out revealed the grey as the bar of a cage. It was joined by another bar, then Carrie could make out a brown rhesus monkey staring out. The monkey's hands gripped the bars, its mouth opened wider than seemed possible. It screamed. Blood-red tears seeped from its eyes. It shook the bars of the cage.

The camera panned across, picking up its neighbour banging its head against the bars, simultaneously clawing at its eyes with its

288

fingers. Screams came from all sides.

In the cage next to that another rhesus writhed. Its back arched and fell, as if a strong electric current was being passed through it. Near-human features contorted in pain. Then it arched once more, fell back, and didn't move.

The person shooting the footage moved along the line. One dead or dying animal after another.

There was the clank of a heavy door closing and someone walking in.

'Dr Hulme?'

Then the screen went black.

62

Back in the cell, Lock tried to doze, but sleep was made all but impossible by leg irons, cuffs, an aching body and a bad case of buyer's remorse.

He'd made the decision to shoot Mareta in the heat of the moment, rationalizing that she wasn't the best thing to be unleashed on an unsuspecting American public, but not having the guts or the heart to kill a woman. Shooting her kept them both alive, and bought him time, although for what? It had been his best, probably only chance of escape, and he'd screwed it up royally. The monkey might be dead, but the organ grinder was very much alive. And he guessed Mareta wasn't best pleased either.

The cell door opened unexpectedly and two guards in riot gear stepped inside.

'Relax. I'm not about to throw down,' Lock said, rolling over on to his side. 'Although I may throw up.'

They pulled him to his feet and dragged him from the cell. He waited for the punches and kicks to start again but none came.

The gate slid open at the end of the corridor and they marched him through and out of the building. The watery low winter sun hurt his eyes as they led him across open ground to the medical block. Here there were more gates, more security points to pass through.

Eventually, they reached a room that Lock vaguely remembered passing on his way with Mareta to the medical area a few hours earlier. There were no gurneys inside, just an examination couch, a desk and a chair. Richard Hulme sat behind the desk.

The guards lifted Lock up on to the couch.

'I'll be quite safe,' said Richard.

The guards didn't budge. 'Sorry, Dr Hulme, we have our orders.'

Lock wondered how much either guard knew about what had happened in the lead-up to his appearance in Mareta's cell. He doubted Brand would have trusted all but his closest confidants with the knowledge of Josh's kidnapping, or Lock's role in trying to track him down.

'He's fully restrained,' Richard shot back.

'Like we just said, we're here to ensure your safety,' the second guard replied.

'And I appreciate it. And if you get your rocks off seeing me giving a grown man a full medical, including a prostate check, that's your business.'

'Prostate?' said the first guard.

'He's going to shove his finger up my ass,' replied Lock.

The two guards traded a look.

'He *is* in restraints,' the second guard said, not relishing the thought of what was going to be happening in the room. 'OK, we'll be right outside, but leave the door open. If it closes we'll be coming through it.'

Once they were alone, Richard began the examination, starting with a visual assessment. 'You took a real beating.'

'I've taken worse,' Lock lied.

Richard leaned in closer as he checked Lock's ears for signs of bleeding. 'You think there's a camera on us?' he whispered. Then he drew back. 'Are you experiencing any pain?'

'I think that's safe to assume,' Lock said. 'But as long as it's low level, I think I'll be OK.'

Richard took the hint and dropped his voice as he continued the examination. 'Listen, do you know the procedure for this test?'

Lock shrugged. 'Does it matter?'

'In your case, yes. I'm going to give you a placebo but I want you to act as if you're having a violent reaction right after I give it to you.' He raised his voice again. 'Could you raise your arms for me?'

'What about the others? Are you going to test them too?' Lock asked as Richard placed a stethoscope against his back.

'I'm hoping to test you first.'

'It's too risky. Especially now they've got Josh here.'

'They can't blame me if the vaccine doesn't work.'

'You don't think it'll work?'

'No, I think it will, but I'm not going to play God with these people no matter who they are.'

'You might not have a choice, Dr Hulme.'

63

Josh lay on the bed reading a comic, one for boys his age. Not like that horrible album. He'd already worked out that if he looked at enough other stuff he could push those pictures out of his brain. But he couldn't seem to get rid of the smell of the place where he'd been kept. It was everywhere.

He glanced up as his dad walked into the room. 'What was wrong with that lady?'

'She got hurt in an accident.'

'It looked like she'd been shot.'

'She had. But like I said, it was an accident. That's why you should never pick up a gun if you see one.'

'Had she been bad?'

'Yes, but that's not why she got shot.'

'Was Natalya bad?'

'No, not really.'

'A little bit?' Josh looked up at his father, registering how tired he looked.

'She trusted the wrong person, that's all.'

★ ★ ★

Mareta was sleeping when Richard arrived to check on her, her breathing slow but insistent. He reached out for her hand, shackled to the bed. Her fingers folded into his as she woke. Her hand felt soft and warm.

'How are you feeling?'

Her pupils dilated and contracted, struggling to find focus through a curtain of morphine. 'Yani?'

Was Yani her husband? Her son?

'No, it's Dr Hulme. I came to check on you.'

'My leg, did you save it?'

'Yes, but we need to get you to a proper hospital.'

'You know what I did to that man?'

Richard had caught snatches from the guards of how Brand met his end. Each retelling was more gruesome than the last. 'It's not my job to judge you,' he said.

'I had to do it,' she whispered. 'He was going to kill me. I had no choice.'

He studied her face, the olive skin, the calm brown eyes, the high cheekbones. 'Are you comfortable? Is there anything I can get you?'

'Maybe some water.'

Richard crossed to a sink at the far end of the room and filled a beaker from the tap. He helped her sit up and put the beaker to her lips. She took tiny sips then sank back into the pillows.

'Thank you.'

Then she tried to reach out for his hand, the cuffs rattling against the bed frame. The tips of her fingers traced a circle on his palm.

'Help me. If I stay here, I'll die.'

64

Cuffed and shackled, Lock was wheeled through an airlock and into the testing room. Red air hoses hung from the ceiling at intervals of six feet. The two bio-suited guards who'd brought him in made a final check on the restraints.

Lock lifted his head in time to see them go back through into the airlock. Another man in a bio-suit was coming the other way. On his back was a respirator. Richard Hulme looked like the world's most unlikely astronaut.

Lock noticed that Richard's hands were shaking as he laid out everything he would need on the bench. Swabs. Sterilized syringes. He crossed the room to something that looked to Lock like a super-charged temperature-controlled beer cooler which was plugged into the wall.

Richard opened it, took out the first of twelve aluminium vials, then closed the lid again. Lock knew that the vaccine had to be kept at a constant temperature. Richard had told him that. A tiny red heat marker on the label turned blue as soon as it moved more than three degrees above. On this vial there were two heat markers. The second had been placed there by Richard to denote that the contents were saline solution.

Richard rolled up Lock's sleeve. Lock had attended enough executions in his life to know that the person about to die rarely exhibited any great hysteria, either because their mind was already gone or because they'd received a little something to level off their mood before they got into the chamber.

Lock didn't like needles. Never had. So he looked the other way as Richard dabbed at a vein on his arm with a sterile swab. A near comical precaution, given the circumstances. If Lock was going to die he doubted a lack of hygiene would play any part.

A clear screen ran the length of one wall. He could see Stafford watching him. As the needle slid in, Lock gave him the finger. It was what Stafford would expect. And if Stafford was looking at him he wouldn't be too focused on Richard.

It seemed to be working. With Lock strapped down and plenty of firepower between the two men, Stafford smiled, waving four fingers in a goodbye gesture.

Richard finished filling the syringe. He tapped the barrel to force out any tiny bubbles of air.

As the needle pressed against Lock's skin, Stafford stepped forward and pressed a button on the console in front of him. He leaned forward to speak into a microphone. A speaker on the wall inside the testing room relayed his voice. 'Change of plan.'

'But . . . ' Richard started to object.

The airlock hissed open and the two guards rolled another gurney in. The man on it was of indeterminate age, his skin weatherbeaten, the rest of his face almost entirely obscured by a bushy beard. He was muttering to himself. The guards pushed the man's gurney level with Lock and left. Richard shrugged his annoyance and reached for a new needle.

Stafford got back on the Tannoy. 'Shouldn't you use the syringe that's already filled, Dr Hulme?'

Richard picked up the syringe intended for Lock and pressed the needle into the man's arm. The man closed his eyes with a look of serenity worthy of a junkie. Maybe he was dreaming of all those virgins, Lock thought.

Richard pressed down on the plunger, emptied the contents of the barrel, withdrew the needle from the man's arm and swabbed it down again.

The man's eyes opened. A look of vague disappointment crossed his face.

'Now Lock,' Stafford ordered.

Richard opened the cooler again, broke out a fresh syringe from its pack and filled it with a batch of live vaccine.

A thin film of sweat settled on Lock's palms. His mouth was dry and tasted of copper.

On the other side of the screen, Stafford's face remained neutral. 'Just think, Lock. You're making history here.'

Lock flipped him the bird for a second time. This time he meant it.

Preparations complete, Lock stared stoically at the ceiling. The last thing he wanted to see of this world was Stafford's smug features.

The jab of the needle barely registered against the background of pain his body was already experiencing on an ongoing basis. He felt a warm sensation spreading across his forearm. Too late now to do anything, except wait. He'd thought about sticking to the original plan and feigning a fit, but Stafford wouldn't buy it, even if everyone else did. Plus, he didn't rate his acting skills.

The next thing he knew Richard was dabbing at the puncture point, a tiny blush of blood spreading across the swab. Richard secured it with some surgical tape.

'How do you feel?' Richard asked him.

'As bad as I did before.'

'OK, contestant number three,' Stafford said, with all the gaiety of a gameshow host.

'What happens now?' Lock asked Richard.

'We give it twenty-four hours and then you're exposed to the live agent.'

'And then?'

'We wait to see if the vaccine's effective,' said Richard.

'And if it's not?'

Richard broke eye contact. 'You'll die.'

65

The procession of trial subjects took over an hour to work through. Led in two by two, to save time, most of them proved compliant. Some less so. In one case, a lot less so: subject number eleven laid out one of the guards cold with a devastating head butt, the default method of attack for someone whose arms and legs are bound. Richard had to inject the man in the leg. None of the subjects showed any reaction to the vaccine.

When it was over, Richard joined Stafford in the observation room.

'Good job.'

'A charge nurse could have done that,' said Richard, stepping out of his bio-safety suit.

'They could have, but it's important that you feel part of the team,' Stafford said.

This hadn't occurred to Richard until now. By making him perform the menial task of actually injecting the trial subjects, he was complicit. He'd breached their human rights as much as anyone else. He could claim duress, but what had Meditech done bar 'rescue' Josh from the animal rights people and then keep him safe? Any claims he made would now look like special pleading. Stafford had played his hand beautifully.

'Don't look so downcast, Richard,' Stafford went on. 'If this does work, think of the lives that could be saved.'

'And the money you'll make.'

'The money *we'll* make. This is a collaborative venture, which is why we all have share options.'

'Am I done here?' Richard asked.

'For the time being.'

Richard walked back, unescorted, to see Josh. There was a tangible air of relief to the place now. A collective tension that had built in the lead-up to the initiation of the trial seemed to have dissipated. Even the guards, who'd been hyper-vigilant bordering on trigger-happy since the incident with Brand, appeared to have taken it down a notch. One of them even managed a mumbled acknowledgement as Richard passed.

Maybe it would all turn out OK, he told himself. If the vaccine worked, Stafford would be appeased. Richard could leave. Forget it ever happened.

Clinging to those thoughts, he opened the door into his room. Josh was snuggled under the duvet. He sat on the edge of the bed and reached out a hand to stroke his son's head.

But his fingers found only pillow. Frantically, he pulled it out, tossing the duvet on to the floor at the same time.

The bed was empty.

66

A light above the bed spotlighted Mareta. Beyond that was semi-darkness. The guard detailed to look after her was gone. From what she'd noticed of his breath and the pallor of his skin she guessed that he'd stepped outside for a cigarette.

But she wasn't alone. Next to the bed, Josh perched on a seat.

'What happened to your leg?' he asked. 'I mean, what really happened?'

'A man shot me.'

Josh didn't react. 'That's what I thought. Why'd he shoot you?'

'To save himself.' She paused. 'And perhaps to save me.'

Josh's brow creased as he tried to follow the logic and came up blank. 'Do you get bored lying here all the time?'

'Very,' Mareta said.

'Me too.'

Mareta turned her head and smiled at him. 'Maybe we could play a game.'

★ ★ ★

Richard rushed from the accommodation block, a guard at his side struggling to keep up.

'Don't worry, Dr Hulme, we'll find him. He probably just wandered off.'

Richard spotted Stafford getting into his car. He raced over to him. The guard stepped between them.

'What have you done with him?' Richard demanded.

'What the hell are you talking about?'

'Josh has gone.'

★ ★ ★

'This game sounds difficult,' Josh said, counting off the things he had to do on the fingers of one hand.

'I thought you were good at games?'

'I am.'

'OK, so prove it to me.'

Josh's chin jutted out. 'OK then, I will.'

'So I'll count to two hundred,' Mareta said, and closed her eyes.

'A thousand.'

'OK, a thousand. One. Two. Three . . . '

Josh turned and ran out of the room.

★ ★ ★

Having reassured Richard that he'd help with the search for Josh, Stafford ducked into his car and put in a call to his father. 'It's going like a dream,' he told him.

'Stage one's complete?'

'Vaccine's eliciting no adverse reactions so far.'

'It didn't in the animals either,' Nicholas Van Straten said coolly.

'But it's been tweaked since then.'

'What about Brand?'

'What about him?'

'You think word wouldn't reach me, Stafford?'

'We had a security situation. It's been resolved now.'

'Let's make sure we keep it that way. I've been catching a world of shit from the media over this footage.'

'What footage?'

*　*　*

Josh had been on scavenger hunts before, but not ones where he'd had to try not to be seen. It was hard. Especially as there were so many people rushing around. The good thing was that he only really had to find one item, although how he was going to get to it he didn't know. All he could do was try his best.

As he ducked into a recess in the corridor, one of the guards passed him. He had it, right there on his belt. That was no good. He had to find someone who didn't have it on their belt. He knew where the guards slept when they weren't on duty. Missy had shown him when he'd first arrived. Maybe he could try there.

*　*　*

The guard stubbed out his cigarette as the man in the white lab coat ran towards him. One of the science guys, a pretty senior one if he remembered rightly.

'I was just heading back inside, sir.'

303

'Inside where? Where were you supposed to be?'

'The medical block.'

Richard grabbed at the guard's sleeve. 'Show me.'

* * *

Josh handed the keys to Mareta. 'What number were you up to?'

'Nine hundred and ninety nine,' Mareta said, palming the keys into the folds of the sheet.

'Wow, I made it just in time.'

'You did really good.'

The door burst open and Richard rushed in, flanked by two guards. He snatched up Josh into his arms, pressed his son's head into his shoulder.

'He OK?' asked one of the guards.

'Why wouldn't he be?' Mareta said.

'We were just playing a game. Am I in trouble?' Josh's voice was shrill with worry.

'Just don't do that ever again, do you hear me?' Richard scolded him.

'What did you think I was going to do?' Mareta asked, the tiny set of cuff keys clutched tightly in her hand.

* * *

She waited an hour before calling over the guard.

'May I have some water?' she asked, her voice rasping.

'Sure.'

He brought over a glass. She struggled to sit up. As he put his arm behind her back to help her, she brought her free hand up and jabbed two fingers as hard as she could into his eyes. Her other hand grabbed the hair at the back of his head, pulling his face so close that she could smell the tobacco smoke on his collar. Then she bit down as hard as she could on his nose, taking off the fleshy tip and a strip of cartilage with her front teeth.

Too close to get a punch in at her, he flailed his arms. Quietly, deliberately, Mareta balled up a corner of blood-soaked sheet and forced it into his mouth to muffle the screams.

67

Lock snapped awake, surprised by two things. He was alive, and his cell door was wide open. He struggled to his feet and made it out into the corridor. Empty. No guards in sight.

He stood there for a moment, trying to orient himself. He'd had his best sleep in weeks, even if it was for only a couple of hours. The coppery taste was still in his mouth, but otherwise, beyond the usual aches and pains, he felt fine.

There was a click, and the cell door next to his opened. Like the external doors, it must have had some kind of remote override. A man stepped out, the man who'd been injected with the placebo intended for Lock. He blinked his eyes and reached out to pat Lock on the shoulder, as if physical contact would reassure him that this wasn't a dream.

There was another click. Another cell door opened. Then another. And another. In under two minutes all the trial subjects had emerged. All of them looked well.

They gathered in small groups, some of them talking in urgent whispers. One of them crossed over to Lock, squaring up to him. Placebo guy stepped in between them, talked to the aggressor. He backed off.

The gate at the far end swung back on its hinges. Tentatively they started towards it.

One of the men said something and some of

the others laughed. Placebo guy raised cuffed hands to his face and hushed them.

Lock brought up the rear as they walked towards the open gate. As he passed through it, the gate closed behind him. The men at the rear started as it clanked shut. At the far end of the corridor the door clicked open. They pushed through it and out into the darkness.

All twelve of them were still cuffed, and made for a surreal sight as they shuffled forward in the moonlight, a chain gang on evening manoeuvres. Placebo guy seemed to be assuming some kind of leadership role. He hissed at them to spread out, directing them to back into the shadows.

Lock picked his moment and filtered away from the group. He had as much idea about what was going on as they did — none. But he knew that with the amount of firepower in the vicinity; being out in open ground was about the worst idea possible.

Placebo guy waved at two of the men to go ahead on point. They did so, creeping forward to the edge of the building. Then they stopped, suddenly.

Lock could hear the guard coming round the corner, not because of footfall, but because he was on his radio letting the control room know that he'd cleared one sector and was about to move into the next. Standard procedure for non-static security. Clear and confirm. Clear and confirm. Repeat till dead. Almost certainly literally in the case of this poor chump.

'Base from Leech. Yellow clear, moving to red.'

There was a pause.

'Base? Can you acknowledge?'

It made sense that the guard wasn't getting a reply. The cells had been remotely opened, and the only way to do that was from the control room.

There were twelve of them here. Which left only one person unaccounted for.

68

The room was empty when Lock got there. There were some books, some of the boy's clothes, but no Josh. The thought that the escapees had already reached him first flitted briefly through his mind, although there was no blood or sign of a struggle.

He picked up one of the boy's sweaters and stood there for a second. Then he walked back out, and straight down the barrel of an M-16 wielded by a white-faced Hizzard.

'Get down on your hands and knees.'

'Hizzard, we don't have time for this bullshit.'

Fear seemed to have defaulted Hizzard to auto-pilot. 'How did you escape the accom block?'

'I teleported.'

Hizzard jabbed the gun at him. 'Get down on the ground.'

Lock waved a hand in front of his face. 'Hizzard, it's me, Lock. Remember?'

'You're a detainee. I'm tasked with apprehending and returning all detainees to the accom block.'

'Well, good luck with that. You've got twelve pissed-off Chechens, or Iraqis, or Pakistanis, or whatever the hell they are, on the loose right now, and we don't have much time to contain them.'

A burst of small-arms fire neatly punctuated

Lock's condensed rundown.

'How do I know you ain't lying?'

'Who gives a damn if I'm lying or not? Didn't you understand what I just said? This is a level four bio-research facility which is in the process of being taken over by terrorists. We act *now* or we all die.'

Hizzard reached for his radio.

'That's not going to do you much good either. I'm guessing the ops room's been breached. You won't get any sense from anyone up there.'

Doubt flickered in Hizzard's eyes. 'Base from Hizzard.'

The response was the empty crackle of static, then a voice, female, with an accent. 'Hizzard from Base. Go outside and lay your weapon on the ground.'

Under other circumstances, Lock might have allowed himself a smile as he watched the *oh shit* expression seep across Hizzard's face. Instead he grabbed the M-16 from him.

'You have a sidearm?'

Hizzard lifted the flap of his jacket. 'Glock.'

'Better than nothing, I guess,' Lock said, setting the M-16 to single shot and heading back outside, Hizzard trailing reluctantly in his wake. 'How many guards you guys have on duty?'

'Round about a dozen.'

'Round about?'

'I think.'

A classic Brand-run operation, thought Lock. 'And what about weapons? M-16s and Glocks?'

'There's other stuff in the armoury.'

'Whoa there, soldier, what armoury?' Lock

asked, looking around for the door back to his own universe.

'That building over there.'

Hizzard pointed through the gloom to a small squat building about four hundred yards away placed between two other blocks. Lock had assumed it was some kind of boiler room or back-up generator facility.

'You have access to it?'

Hizzard reached down to his belt. 'Sure, got the key right here.'

'Terrific.'

'What?'

'Well, if you have the key I'm assuming the other 'dozen or so' guards have one as well.'

'I dunno.'

'Come on then, Einstein, let's go take a look.'

The main door was wide open when they got there, reinforced steel rendered useless by a profusion of keys. Amateur didn't even begin to describe the place. Lock let Hizzard step through first, then followed him inside.

A few boxes of assorted shells lay scattered on the ground, but judging by the empty shelves and gun racks, the place looked to have been pretty much picked clean.

The distorted lid of a large grey metal chest stuck up at forty-five degrees. Hizzard yanked it open and peered inside. 'Oh shit.'

'What was in there? Rocket launchers?' Lock asked.

'No, that was where Brand kept the plastic explosives.'

69

Lock and Hizzard inched their way out of the armoury. Bursts of small-arms fire punctuated the silence.

They rounded a corner, Lock wheeling wide in case the escapees were right there, Hizzard providing cover, the Glock extending from his right hand.

'Clear,' whispered Lock, a second before one of the detainees shuffled into view.

Lock started to raise his requisitioned M-16. But too late. The detainee already had Lock sighted. Time slowed for Lock. Hizzard spun round, but he was going to be too late.

Then, as the detainee offered a broken-toothed smile and his finger began the millimetre-by-millimetre journey on the trigger, a round smacked into the middle of his forehead. He slumped forward, his round catching dirt rather than Lock, as Ty stepped from cover to their left. 'One down, eleven to go,' he said, moving towards the detainee.

Lock stared across at his second-in-command. 'You were standing there the whole time, weren't you?'

Ty grinned. 'Yup.'

'You're a big-timing asshole sometimes, Tyrone, you know that?'

'What can I tell you, man? I learned from the best.' He turned towards Hizzard, who still had his Glock trained on the dead detainee. 'How you holding up there, Hizzard?'

Lock answered for him. 'Bottle of Jack, tube of Anusol, and homeboy'll be good to go.'

Ty turned the detainee over with his boot. 'Yup. Very dead.' He let the man slump back, face down, and gave Hizzard a playful punch on the shoulder. 'In't this fun?'

In the distance they could hear distant sirens, and some more small-arms fire from contact near the perimeter. They continued towards their goal, the control room, the entrance to which lay five hundred feet ahead of them.

The final approach to the doorway was over open ground. Lock couldn't see any escapees, or guards for that matter. Presumably the escapees were at the edge of the complex engaged in contact, while Brand's guards were hunkered down somewhere trying to figure out just what had gone so badly wrong, so fast.

Lock left Ty and Hizzard to lay down cover and readied himself to make the dash. Like stepping off a high board, he knew not to dwell on it. The secret, like most things in life, was to put one foot in front of the other. In this case, as quickly as possible.

Go. He took off towards the entrance, aware only of his own breathing and his feet jolting against the ground. The M-16 he held in both hands. He waited to hear covering fire from Hizzard and Ty but none came.

He made it to the door, stopped to suck air into his lungs in three big draughts, knelt down and levelled the M-16, sighting to a point in the middle of the nearest building. He signalled for the other two to make their dash.

Watching Ty run over was worse than doing it himself. He kept waiting for the fizz of tracers or crack of a single shot. None came.

Ty and Hizzard bumped fists, Death at their heels making for instant esprit de corps.

Inside, all was quiet. A sporadic trail of blood splashes marked the path to the ops room. Lock and Ty followed it all the way, leaving Hizzard to secure the entrance.

The control room was reinforced glass on three sides. Mareta barely acknowledged them as they approached. Lock could also see Richard. Josh was cradled in his arms, asleep.

He had a clear shot at Mareta. He doubted the first round would penetrate, but a second might, or a third. But she remained unperturbed. Then she got to her feet. Ty lowered his gun. As she turned to face them, Lock saw why. Around her chest was a hastily assembled explosives belt. Strips of C4 with what looked like nails all wrapped in gaffer tape and web-linked at one-inch intervals, a detonator clipped at waist level.

Lock had seen suicide belts before, but this one differed from the common-or-garden variety in one chilling respect. Explosive, especially something like C4, was hard to come by, and was therefore used as sparingly as possible. What did the damage was the packing material buffered around the charges — ball bearings, nails, screws, bolts. What made this device different was the amount of explosive. Easily four or five pounds. Mareta wouldn't just explode, she'd evaporate into a fine mist. And so, most likely, would everyone else in the room.

70

Frisk stood fifty yards back from the perimeter of the compound and watched as, on the other side of the wall, dark shapes flitted between the buildings. He looked around at the groups of law enforcement clustered in small huddles. FBI. ATF. SWAT. They were all here, and they all had a different plan as to how to proceed. Although the Joint Terrorism Task Force of which he was a part had been designed to establish clear chain of command, old habits were dying hard.

Frisk glanced up to see a lone figure stepping into a patch of light thrown by floodlights erected by the SWAT team at the main gate. The figure held up his hands in a gesture of surrender. He strained his eyes to get a better look.

The figure was soon close enough for Frisk to identify him. 'Son of a bitch.' He should have guessed.

A couple of SWAT officers in bio-suits dashed towards Ty, ballistic shields held up in front of them, handguns wedged around the sides. 'Get down on the ground!' one of them shouted.

Ty waved them away. 'Listen, I wasn't exposed. But I need to speak to someone, like right now.'

'Get down on the ground now or you *will* be shot!' the SWAT officer warned, gesturing with his gun.

Frisk watched as Ty assumed the position, and cuffs were snapped around his wrist. They shuffled him back to the perimeter. Men and women who'd spent a lifetime facing down the worst the human race had to offer backed away.

Frisk followed as Ty was led to a white Winnebago. Three steps and he was inside. It was kitted out as a mobile lab. Two more people in bio-suits greeted him.

'I told you, I'm clear.'

'We need to make sure.'

Ty offered his arm. 'How long will this take?'

'Thirty minutes.'

One of the bio-suits took a blood sample. 'This will tell us if you have one of the ten main viral haemorrhagic diseases.'

'And what if I do?'

'You'll be quarantined and treated.'

'You can treat this stuff?'

'Most of it. Apart from the Ebola variant. We don't have a vaccine for that yet.'

Ten minutes later, Frisk stepped into the trailer, also in a bio-suit.

Ty greeted him with a nod of the head. 'Pretty fly for a white guy,' he said, 'although you might want to think about getting the pants taken up an inch or two.'

'Might have known you and Lock would be in the middle of this. What the hell's going on in there?'

'Short version or long version?'

'Short.'

Ty told him. With each new piece of information, Frisk grew paler. All he'd known

317

was that a major firefight had broken out at a Level 4 Bio Facility.

'So why'd they send you out?' he asked Ty.

'Messenger boy.'

'And what's the message? What do they want?'

'A signed undertaking from the President guaranteeing their status as prisoners of war under the Geneva Convention, along with an undertaking that they won't be deported. Oh yeah, and a signed picture of Will Smith.'

'That all, huh?' Frisk asked.

'The last part's negotiable. I think they'd settle for Eddie Murphy at a pinch.'

'Nice to see you find this all so amusing, but I'm about six levels down from being able to start offering signed executive undertakings.'

'Then you'd better start moving it up the chain.'

'Even if we get agreement, they'll all be going to jail for the rest of their natural lives.'

'They know that.'

'OK, I'll pass it on,' said Frisk, stepping back out of the Winnebago. 'But that's it, right? There's nothing else.'

'That's it.'

Ty watched Frisk exit the trailer. He uncrossed his fingers and let out a sigh. Mareta had had one other demand but Lock had told him not to mention it, although Ty hadn't needed telling. Soon as he had the all clear, Ty was going to take care of it himself. In fact, he was looking forward to it.

71

Ty found Carrie among the lines of news trucks which had been pushed to the very edge of a service road. The good news was he was clear of any infection. The bad news was that he was going to have to convince her to assist in something that could see them both spend the rest of their lives behind bars.

As soon as she spotted him, she rushed over. 'Where's Ryan? What's going on in there?'

'You're slipping, girl. Aren't you supposed to reverse the order of those questions? With you being a member of the press 'n' all.'

'Just tell me.'

'He's inside. I wouldn't say he's safe exactly, but he's in fair shape considering.'

'Considering what?'

Ty pulled her to the rear of the truck. 'He needs our help.'

Carrie took a breath and centred herself. 'OK. What kind of help?'

Ty had already decided to feed it to her piece by piece. 'You have a car here?'

'No.'

He produced a set of keys. 'Damn, have to use Lock's then.'

'Ty, what's going on?'

'Where's the dumb dog he left you with?'

'In the truck, asleep.'

'We'll need to take her with us.'

'Where? Where are we going?' She glanced back at the news truck. 'I'm on duty here. I can't just pick up and leave.'

'Ryan needs you to do this.'

'You still haven't told me what it is he wants me to do. And I'm not going anywhere until you do.'

Ty rested his hand against the spare tyre on the back of the news station's RV. 'Second thoughts, we can use this too. Kill two birds with one stone. You can get your story while I make my pick-up.'

'Are you deaf? I'm not going anywhere until someone tells me why.'

'Then a lot of people are gonna get killed.'

'Fine, but you at least have to tell me where we're going.'

Ty waved over Carrie's camera guy. 'Saddle up.' Then he turned back to Carrie. 'We're going to enforce some corporate accountability.'

72

Mareta watched the dark shapes flitting periodically across the wall of monitors with about as much interest as a retired cop relegated to the graveyard shift at an out-of-town mall. She palmed some painkillers, checked the time-code running at the bottom left of the nearest screen, swivelled on her chair, and shot the guard nearest to her in the face.

Josh stirred in his sleep as Richard handed him to Lock and rushed towards the dying man. A spurt of blood covered Richard's face — unfair reward for an act of compassion.

Lock put his hand behind Josh's head and pressed the little boy's face tight to his chest. Even with children's seemingly endless capacity for absorption, there were some things better left unseen.

Lock could feel Josh's arms and legs stiffening as he watched Richard tend to the dying guard. He stretched out as best he could, catching Richard's eye as he did so.

'Let the kid go, Mareta. He's been used enough already.'

'I won't harm the boy.' Mareta paused. 'So long as my demands are met.'

'This country doesn't negotiate with terrorists.'

'Correction. It's not seen to. There's a difference.'

'Look, you have me, you have him,' said Lock, indicating Richard.

She swivelled round on the chair, the suddenness of the movement leaving Lock's heart in his mouth. 'This situation is not of my making,' she said.

There was movement outside the control room. One of the detainees, a young Pakistani the others called Khalid, led in three of Meditech's guards at gunpoint. Their uniforms were torn, and one of the men's eyes were closing from the beating he'd taken. Mareta buzzed the door open and they were pushed inside, forced to sit on the floor.

'OK, I make you a deal,' Mareta said. 'Once your friend delivers his cargo to us, the boy can leave. But in the meantime, for every hour that passes, one of these men will die.'

Lock knew that arguing would get him nowhere. 'I already explained to you that this would take at least two hours. The travel time alone will be that, never mind the actual extraction.'

Mareta seemed to mull it over. 'Then only two of these men will die.'

73

Two German Shepherds prowled the fence surrounding Nicholas Van Straten's Shinnecock Bay estate, white teeth bared. Ty reached down into a brown paper bag, came up with half a dozen hamburger patties they'd picked up on the way from a bemused fast-food operative, stepped back and lobbed them over the fence. The dogs sniffed at them suspiciously. Then one of them, presumably the alpha male, cocked his leg and took a leak on them. The other one followed suit a second later.

So the dogs had been trained to eat only what they were given by their owner, usually achieved by a rather crude form of aversion therapy involving beating them with a stick any time they got close to food not delivered by him.

'Plan B it is then,' Ty said, walking back to the car. He opened the back door and Angel bounded out.

Carrie followed. 'Whoa, where are you taking her?'

'Oldest trick in the book. Don't worry,' he said, patting Angel on the head, 'she likes bad boys.'

Carrie folded her arms. 'How do you know that?'

'Well, she followed Ryan, didn't she?'

Carrie looked around. 'I shouldn't even be here.'

'Price of getting the scoop of the century.'

He took Angel off her leash and she wandered over to the fence. 'Go on,' Ty whispered, before turning back to Carrie. 'What's the way to a man's heart if not through his stomach?'

'That's so disgusting.'

'Hey, it was your boyfriend's idea, not mine.'

The Shepherds were frantic now, wet black noses pressed against the fence. Bared teeth and barking had given way to quivering tails and yelps of desire. Much to Ty's relief, Angel reciprocated, seemingly pleased with the attention from not one but two strapping Germans. One of the Shepherds began to paw at the ground near the fence, clods of earth flying up. The other joined it, and soon both dogs were engaged in a race to see who could tunnel their way to Angel first.

It took the two dogs just under ten minutes to dig a hole under the fence big enough so that they could squeeze through to the other side. They didn't even give Ty or Carrie a second look as they sniffed around Angel.

Ty set to work cutting a hole in the fence with a pair of wire cutters, then turned back to Carrie. 'You clear on what you have to do now?'

Carrie started the walk back to where the news truck was parked short of the compound's gates. 'It's hardly rocket science,' she said.

The two dogs snarled and Ty glanced over his shoulder, worried that they'd lost interest in Angel. He was relieved to see that they were facing off at each other, presumably to see who got the first shot. Angel sat watching them, wagging her tail. Ty left Carrie to enjoy the live show and slipped out of sight into the undergrowth.

As he made his way towards the mansion, he ran through in his head the security systems in place. The dogs were the most noticeable and in all likelihood the most effective deterrent, especially to the casual intruder. Mounted on the exterior of the house were motion sensors. Infrared lights and CCTV cams allowed a three-sixty view of the area surrounding the house to the member of the security detail in the ops room, a converted space next to the utility on the ground floor. Anyone escaping detection on their approach would then face wireless contacts on all points of entry, and further motion sensors in every room, except the four bedroom suites and hallways. No one wanted Van Straten getting up to take a leak in the middle of the night to the whoop of a hundred-fifty-decibel alarm.

Ty got within fifty yards of the front of the house and stopped. Lights were on in two of the rooms. He made a quick mental adjustment about the time he'd have once he was in place.

He skirted the motion sensors and headed for the garage. It was adjacent to but separate from the house. No cameras here. No motion sensors either. He forced open the side door and stepped inside. The place smelled of motor oil and detergent. There were three cars parked inside a space which could easily accommodate twice that number. The first was a Mercedes 500 SLK, a smooth ride. Ty immediately discounted it. The second was Stafford's. This just got better and better. But he wouldn't be using that one either.

Next to Stafford's vehicle squatted the up-armoured Hummer. It was black rather than the fire engine red he'd seen previously. With fresh paintwork. He guessed this had to be the one they'd used to try to clip Carrie with. She'd told him all about it on the drive over.

He dug out his cell and texted four letters to Carrie's number: C-A-L-L. Then he climbed under the Hummer and set to work.

★ ★ ★

'It's that dumb bitch from NBC,' said Stafford, holding up the phone for his father, who was already deep into his third Scotch on the rocks.

'What does she want?'

'Something about a breach of security at the naval yard site.'

Van Straten snatched the handset from his son's grasp. 'This is Nicholas Van Straten.'

'Mr Van Straten, where are you?'

'Why?'

'Have the FBI spoken to you?'

'No, why would they have?'

'Because wherever you are, you have to leave there, immediately. There's a grave threat to your life and that of your son.'

'Ms Delaney, I can assure you that we're quite safe where we are.'

'Mr Van Straten, do you have a television in the room?'

'Yes.'

326

'Then switch it on to NBC.'

Nicholas clicked his fingers towards the remote on the bed. Stafford picked it up and tossed it to his father, who caught it and thumbed down to the channel. The screen was split. On the right side was a mass of emergency response vehicles shot from a distance but recognizably parked near to the Meditech facility. On the left side of the screen was a static shot of the front gate of their house.

'Mr Van Straten?'

'I'm here.'

'And Ryan Lock will be joining you shortly. I received a call from him an hour ago to say that he was on his way to speak with you. He sounded pretty angry — '

Carrie didn't get to finish the sentence before Nicholas Van Straten hung up. Satisfied that she hadn't told a single lie, she turned back to her cameraman. 'OK, let's get back to the naval yard.'

'He won't do an interview?' asked her cameraman.

'He's not even there,' she lied.

The guy shrugged and began hastily packing up his gear as Angel trotted back to them, covered in dirt and wagging her tail.

'Slut,' said Carrie, reaching over to open the rear door of the truck for her.

★ ★ ★

Ty tensed as the side door into the garage opened. A pair of boots made their way across to

327

the Hummer. They stopped at the driver's door, right next to where Ty's head was. Ty could have reached out and touched them.

He waited for the boots to walk round to the other side and start the vehicle inspection. Or for the driver's face to appear at his eye level so he could shove a gun in his face. Or for the mounted mirror to appear so he could grab it, drag the guy under and choke him out with the rag tucked into his shirt.

But none of this happened. Things had gotten sloppy real fast since he and Lock had been relieved of their duty. Or the driver was in one holy hell of a rush. Maybe both.

The Hummer chirped as the driver hit the clicker, disabling the alarm and unlocking all four doors. Ty watched as a boot lifted on to the running board, the door opened and the other boot followed. The driver's door thunked shut.

Ty pushed back with his hands, crawling backwards, emerging just to the right of the Hummer's tailgate. He unholstered the Glock, ready to go, and hunkered down, duck-walking the few steps round to the right rear passenger door. His next action called for one solid component: speed.

He reached up and gripped the handle, opened the door and flung himself inside. The interior of the Hummer was big enough that he could extend his arm without the driver being able to reach it.

He held the gun to the driver's head. 'You even breathe wrong, asshole, and you're history.'

74

Croft reached slowly under his shoulder and came up with his weapon, a Sig 226. He handed it, butt first, to Ty. Ty switched it with the Glock, jamming that into his holster as back-up.

'Leave the keys in the ignition and step out of the vehicle.' Once Croft had done that, Ty threw him a rag. 'Put that in the big hole in the middle of your face and turn round.'

Croft caught the rag and stuffed it into his mouth. Then he turned round. Ty dug around in Croft's pockets for the keys to the Mercedes, using them to open the trunk. He shoved Croft towards it. Croft got in, still at gunpoint.

'Soon as I get some distance I'll call the local PD and send someone to get you out.'

Ty slammed the trunk shut and got into the driver's seat of the Hummer. He took the Glock back out of the holster and stowed it in the compartment between the front seats; the Sig he left on his lap. He then reached up, hit the button on the garage opener and drove out, closing the door again as soon as the Hummer was clear.

He swung the monster vehicle around in front of the house. The door opened and a guard appeared. That made sense. He'd been expecting a three-man team: one to drive, one to act as BG, and one to stay behind and act as residential security in case they had to come back in a hurry.

The guard was followed by Nicholas Van Straten. Then came Stafford. In the darkness and through tinted glass, Ty knew that none of them would be able to see him.

As per standard procedure, the guard opened the door and stepped back. Van Straten and Stafford were too busy talking to look in Ty's direction. Plus the interior dome light had long since been disabled — standard procedure to mitigate against sniper attack. Nothing a shooter liked better than a nice big shaft of light to spotlight their target.

The Van Stratens took their seats. Stafford was yakking away like he was on speed. In the rear-view Ty could see his father doing his best to tune him out. Still neither man had looked at him. Staff were like so much background scenery to guys like them.

The guard closed the door and started round the vehicle to get into the front passenger seat. Ty clicked the button on the console to his left which locked all the doors and accelerated away, leaving the guard standing where the Hummer had been.

The gates were open, and he sped through.

'Where to, gentlemen?' he asked, swivelling round, and savouring their expression of shock. 'Or I could stop somewhere quiet, pull the two of you out, make you kneel over a ditch and shoot you in the back of the head.'

Stafford spoke up. 'Listen, Tyrone, if this is about my terminating your contract — '

'Oh yeah, cos this is how I usually respond to being laid off.'

'Turn this vehicle around immediately!' said Stafford, his voice shrill and unconvincing.

One eye on the road, Ty took his right hand off the wheel and pointed the 226 at him. 'Shut the hell up.'

'Yes,' said Nicholas Van Straten. 'Shut the hell up, Stafford.'

Ty noticed Stafford's hand sliding down to the door handle, about as casually as a fourteen-year-old trying to cop a handful in a darkened movie theatre. 'It's locked. But if you want to take your chances, at least wait until I hit the freeway.'

'Where are you taking us?' Nicholas asked.

'Don't worry, you'll recognize it when we get there.'

75

Josh stirred in his father's arms as Mareta made the guard kneel on the floor with his face to the wall. In her right hand she held a Glock; in her left, two pieces of metal linked to the detonator, contact guaranteeing everyone's death. Lock wanted the kid out of there, and here was his chance.

'Hasn't he seen enough killing?' Lock asked her.

'Then take him outside.'

'I'll do it,' said Richard.

'Go on, then,' Mareta said, as if the desire to spare a child from seeing cold-blooded murder was a clear sign of weakness.

Lock watched as Khalid escorted them both out. 'Thank you.'

The guard facing the wall began to break down. 'Please, don't let her do this. I have a wife and kids.'

Mareta swiped at the back of his head with the Glock, leaving a gash across the top of his skull. 'Then why do you take this job?'

'Five minutes. Give him another five minutes, Mareta,' said Lock.

'Then at the end of those five minutes, you ask for another five. I know these games.'

That was something Lock hoped Frisk and the rest of the JTTF were also factoring in. Most terrorists didn't survive their first siege; Mareta attended them with about the same frequency that newly married women out on Long Island attended baby showers. By now she must know the hostage negotiator's playbook better than they did.

'How's your leg?' Lock asked, hoping to distract her.

'Wonderful.'

She checked the screens. More vehicles massing outside the perimeter. Most of them clustered either side of the gate.

'No sign of your friend,' she said.

'He'll be here.'

Mareta lowered the gun. 'OK, have your five minutes. But after that, it's half an hour until I kill the next one.'

'You said every hour.'

Mareta sighed. 'We negotiate. I give you something, you give me something back in return. That's how it works, no?'

76

Twenty miles short of the naval yard, the empty tank light on the Hummer's console pinged on. Ty groaned. The fuel consumption on a Hummer wasn't great at the best of times, but throw on close to a ton of B-7 armour and it practically required its own oil field.

'Problem?' asked Stafford from the back seat.

'Nothing I can't handle,' Ty responded with a grimace.

Three miles down the road, he found a gas station. His plan was simple. Threaten the living shit out of his cargo. Get fifty bucks of gas. Throw a Lincoln through the slot and get back on the road.

Ty pulled in and swivelled round. 'I'll be gone less than two minutes. You'll be in my sight the whole time. If I see you move in any way, shape or form that makes me uncomfortable, I'll kill you faster than David Duke at a Nation of Islam cookout.'

He turned off the ignition, took the keys with him, got out and locked up. He then grabbed the nozzle and jammed it into the gas tank. His eyes flitted between the dollars and cents ticking over on the display and the doors of the Hummer. He stared at the point where Stafford and Van Straten would be. He couldn't see a damn through the tint, but he didn't want them to think that.

334

These days when he bought gas, the numbers flicked past like a slot machine, but this pump seemed near glacial. Fifty dollars up, he placed the nozzle back in the pump, closed the flap and went to pay, looking back at the Hummer every few yards.

He pushed the money through the tray in the bandit screen and jogged back.

As he went to open the driver's door, he remembered. Damn. The Glock. He'd left it in the front compartment.

He glanced back. The gas attendant, a young Hispanic kid in his early twenties, was perched on a stool watching whatever crap they threw on TV at this hour.

Ty drew his own weapon, yanked open the door and stepped back behind it, bracing himself for the first flash of movement.

Nothing.

From the angle he was at he could see only Nicholas Van Straten's shoulder. But Pops wasn't the one he was worried about.

'Step out of the car. One at a time. You first, Stafford.'

'Stay in the car. Get out of the car. Which one is it?'

'Be quiet, Stafford,' Ty heard Van Straten mumble.

'Could you at least open the door, then?' Stafford asked, tetchily.

Ty slammed shut the driver's door, moved up the side of the vehicle, reached over and opened the passenger door, making sure to keep the armoured plate between him and Stafford.

Stafford stepped out, hands held high in the air.

Ty glanced over his shoulder to see the gas attendant staring at them, no doubt trying to work out what kind of special-needs criminal brings his victims to a gas station to rob them.

Nothing else for Ty to do now but get on with it. He patted Stafford down. Clean.

'OK, now you.'

Nicholas Van Straten stepped out and Ty repeated the procedure. Nothing on him either.

'Stay there,' he told them.

Clambering into the front seat, he opened the compartment. The gun was gone. He stepped back to see Stafford waving frantically to the attendant, miming someone making a phone call.

'OK, where is it?' he asked Stafford.

'Don't know what you're talking about.'

Stafford was doing exactly what Ty would have done in this situation. Stall. The gas attendant was already on the phone, one eye on what was unfolding outside, spitting his words out as fast as he could into the handset.

Stafford must have known that Ty had some purpose for them. Otherwise he would have killed them both at the house. Or pulled off the road back in Shinnecock Bay and done it.

'I don't need both of you,' Ty said. 'So who's it to be?'

'I think if you took a vote, it would end in stalemate,' Nicholas Van Straten said drily.

'Hmm,' Ty said, mulling it over. 'Guess that leaves me the casting vote then.'

He levelled the gun at Nicholas Van Straten's head.

'Go ahead,' said Stafford.

'It's tucked into the back seat,' Nicholas said.

'So much for family unity,' Ty said, reaching back into the vehicle and securing the weapon.

He hustled them back inside the Hummer, just as the police cruiser pulled in.

A single-officer patrol. More units presumably on the way. Judging from the rapid gesticulations of the attendant, who'd been busy on the phone trying to explain a robbery when he wasn't being robbed, Ty guessed that the call had been put down as a roll by and report. Still, if he let the situation develop it could go only one way.

He waited for the cop to step out of the cruiser, then he shifted the Hummer into reverse and hit the gas. The rear of the hulking SUV concertinaed the engine block of the Chrysler.

Smiling for the first time since he'd turned into the gas station, Ty took off, leaving behind a very pissed-off cop scrambling for his radio.

77

The Hummer inched between a Nomad Command Post trailer and an up-armoured NYPD Bomb Squad forklift. Van Straten and Stafford could only stare out in bewilderment as more than a hundred men and women, many of them heavily armed, moved carefully between the perimeter and the vehicles.

'Here we are, boys,' Ty offered. 'All ashore that's going ashore.'

He slowed the Hummer. Over to his left, two regular NYPD cops were taking a good look at him. One of them was on the radio, the other talking out of the side of his mouth to his partner. As they started towards the Hummer, Ty eased down the window to hear what they were saying.

'Hey. Stop that vehicle.'

Yup, that's what he thought they were saying.

He closed the window, shifted the transmission into low and aimed straight at the gate. The trick was to hit it at ramming speed, approximately twenty miles an hour, then push on through the very centre. The mistake most people made when ramming, say, a roadblock was to get up as much speed as possible and go straight for it. In close protection circles that was known as 'crashing'. Very different to what he was about to do.

Ty didn't look back as he got to the gate. He

didn't have to because he was pretty certain no one would be following him in. The perimeter was more psychological now than physical.

The fence shook on the initial impact. That was followed by the grinding of metal on metal.

By now Stafford, at least, realized what was going on. They were ransom payment, in human form. Next to him, his father sat ramrod straight, tapping into some long-lost patrician fortitude.

As the Hummer breached the fence, the couple of cops who'd been running alongside, banging on the doors like demented groupies chasing a limo, fell away.

The Hummer forged ahead, straight for the building holding the control room. A couple of rounds zinged off the roof, the first metal raindrops of a fast gathering storm.

Ty pulled the Hummer up to the entrance of the main building, got out and opened the rear passenger door on the driver's side as cover. 'OK, ladies, end of the line. Better get inside before some over-eager ATF boy scout uses your bony white asses for target practice.'

Van Straten and Stafford scuttled out and inside the building, followed by Ty, all three men met by Mareta's honour guard. One of them reached for Ty's gun but he pushed him off. Stafford and Van Straten were led down the long corridor towards the control room.

The door clicked open, and Ty ushered them inside.

Mareta looked the Van Stratens up and down with all the professional detachment of a hangman shaking a man's hand to calculate his weight.

'OK, so we've delivered what you asked for, the boy and the doctor come with me now,' Lock said.

Ty stayed by the door, his hand on the butt of his gun. The Glock was tucked uncomfortably into the small of his back.

'This isn't all I asked for,' said Mareta after an uncomfortable silence.

'Listen, if it's money . . . ' Nicholas Van Straten spluttered.

Mareta ignored him. 'The boy can go, but the doctor I need.'

Josh rushed to his father and snaked his arms around his waist.

'Why is he here, anyway?' asked Nicholas.

'Ask your son,' said Lock, gesturing towards Stafford. He then bent down so he was eye level with Josh. 'How about if I drop you off and then I come back to look after your dad? Would that make you feel better?'

Josh's head whipped a 'no' back and forth.

It was Richard's turn. 'Please, Josh. I'll be fine — really.'

Lock prised Josh from his father, finger by tiny finger.

'OK?' he said, finally.

Josh rushed back to give his dad a hug.

'Ready?' Lock asked, one hand on the boy's shoulder.

Josh swallowed hard. Nodded. His hand slipped into Lock's and they started out of the control room.

Nicholas Van Straten rounded on Stafford. 'You're a disgrace!'

'I did what I had to do. Mother would have understood.'

'Your mother was a cold-hearted bitch.'

'Better that than a wimp.'

Mareta eyed the exchange with contempt. 'I'll give you both the chance to prove your manhood soon enough,' she told them.

Stafford and his father stopped arguing and exchanged a worried look.

'You don't think I brought you here simply to kill you, do you?'

78

Silhouetted by the spotlight from an NYPD chopper, a piece of white cloth fluttered from Lock's hand. His other hand clasped Josh's as he led him to the perimeter gate, one section of which was hanging from a single hinge. He counted at least two sharpshooters with scopes sighted on them. Given the recent terrorist penchant for using both themselves and, in some cases, civilians as body-borne IEDs, it was hardly surprising.

'Josh, can you take off your jacket for me?'

'But, it's cold.'

'Just for a moment.'

'Why?'

He could see in the kid's eyes that he wasn't doing it without getting a reason first. 'Because you might have a bomb under it.'

'Don't be silly. Little boys don't carry bombs.'

'Not usually, no.'

'But sometimes?' Josh asked him.

Lock had once seen a twelve-year-old girl with Down's Syndrome walk up to a Marine manning a checkpoint on Route Irish in Baghdad, shake the soldier's hand, then blow herself up.

'Not really,' he said, 'but I'd still like you to.'

Josh struggled out of his jacket. Lock lifted up Josh's top for a moment so that his stomach was visible.

'OK, you can put it back on.'

The snipers re-sighted fractionally. He guessed

they were now both on him. One head. One torso.

Lock opened his jacket and lifted his shirt, giving a full three-sixty twirl, arms spread out to his sides. The snipers stayed sighted on him.

Twenty yards from the gate, he let go his grip on Josh's hand. 'Go on.'

The little boy stepped forward, then turned to look at Lock.

'I'm going back, Josh. I have to go take care of your dad, remember?'

Josh almost managed a smile before taking to his heels and rushing towards a JTTF agent in a bio-suit posted on what was left of the gate. The agent approached the boy tentatively, put his arms around him, patting him down in the process.

'Lock!'

Lock glanced over his shoulder to see Frisk. He was waving him forward. Lock raised a thumb back towards the complex.

Frisk broke from the ranks and darted into no-man's land. Lock moved quickly to stay between him and the buildings. A shot from the detainees at Frisk and they'd both be toast.

'What's going on in there?' he said, winded after the brief sprint.

'They wouldn't release Hulme.'

'How about Van Straten and Stafford?'

'You saw them, huh?'

'They were reported missing about a half-hour after your buddy picked them up.'

Good, Lock thought. Croft must have decided to gift Ty a proper start.

'I gave the detainees what they want.'

'Which was?'

'The people responsible for this mess.'

'You mean the Van Stratens?'

Lock nodded.

'And what do we get?' Frisk asked him.

'Everyone out alive.'

'And you believe that crazy bitch?'

'Look, Frisk, we don't have much of a choice right now.'

'And while you're here, what's with your girlfriend showing up?'

Lock scanned the circus on the perimeter, taking in the press and emergency personnel drawn in like moths. 'Incidentally, what are you telling the media?'

'Non-specific security breach.'

'That should stand up for all of two seconds.'

'Which is why it's important we get this resolved as soon as possible,' Frisk said. 'One way or another.'

'No argument from me.'

Just before he turned back towards the building, Lock glimpsed Josh, covered in the kind of foil blanket usually handed out at the end of a marathon, being helped into the back of an ambulance by two people in bio-suits. At least he's safe, he told himself. That had to count for something.

'Hold up. You're not going back in there?' Frisk asked, screwing up his face.

Lock kept walking. He waited for Frisk to start after him. For someone to try to stop him. But no one did.

79

Stripped to the waist, cuffed and in leg chains, Nicholas and Stafford Van Straten, along with the remaining guards captured by the escapees, stood to attention. Mareta hobbled along the line, a black Sharpie in her right hand. She stopped at Nicholas and drew the number one on his chest with the marker. Stafford was marked number two. Just like cattle.

As she reached the third man, one of the guards, Lock spoke up. 'This is bullshit. They're hired hands. And what you're doing is no better than what they were going to do to you.'

'Except we're not terrorists,' Stafford chipped in.

She ignored them both, etched the number three on the man's chest. Once all the men were numbered, Mareta stepped back to admire her handiwork. 'Now, let's begin.'

Two of the escapees stepped either side of Nicholas Van Straten and ushered him out of the room.

They gathered behind the glass partition, Mareta, Lock, Ty, the remaining terrorists and guards and, standing in the centre, with the same look of interest he'd reserved for Lock, Stafford. 'Finally, someone's found an actual use for the old man,' he observed.

Lock glanced over at him as Richard, now clad in a bio-suit, emerged on the other side of the partition and walked towards Nicholas. 'Don't worry, Stafford,' he said, 'your turn's coming real soon.'

'Do I look worried?'

Lock had to concede that Stafford was a whole lot more composed than he'd imagined. Certainly more than when Lock had led him up on to the roof that night.

'I've seen all the data, remember,' Stafford continued. 'The vaccine'll work.'

'Makes for a pretty damn solid endorsement if it does work,' said Ty as on the other side of the screen Richard gingerly opened the container and filled a syringe from one of the vials. His hands were shaking.

'I want you to know that I am administering this entirely against my will,' he said as he pressed down on the plunger and forced the liquid into Nicholas Van Straten's bloodstream.

A few minutes later, as Van Straten was led out, Stafford was led in. Nicholas looked straight past his son. His face was pale, his lips were edged white.

'For God's sake, it's only vaccine,' Stafford said. 'It's already been given to the trial subjects and they've shown no ill effects.' He rolled his neck, as if working out some kinks left by a particularly strenuous set of tennis as two of Mareta's men pushed him down on to the gurney. 'I'll stand, thanks.'

The two men forced him down on to the gurney and strapped him in as Lock and Ty shared a look of surprise.

'Hey, could be worse,' said Ty, 'least he ain't

346

face down. Then he'd really be screaming for mommy.'

'Not a show I'd be buying a ticket for,' Lock said.

Behind Stafford, Richard walked over to a large refrigerator, opened the door and retrieved a stainless-steel vial with a rubber stopper from a large white cooler on the second shelf. His hands were steady now as he popped a fresh syringe from its sterile packet.

'Come on, Hulme, let's get this over with,' Stafford taunted.

'Yes, let's,' said Richard from behind the helmet of the bio-suit, filling the barrel.

Stafford raised his head as far as he could and stared, defiant, at the screen. 'I mean, they've all had the vaccine, and they've suffered no ill effects.'

'That's correct,' said Richard, emptying the contents into Stafford's bloodstream.

'So what do I have to worry about? Nothing, right?'

Richard paused. 'Nothing at all, apart from the fact that I've just injected you with live Ebola variant.'

80

Stafford's stomach lurched with fear. He knew that the Ebola virus emptied your body from both ends. And when you had no more vomit or faeces left to expel, and you felt like things couldn't get any worse, that was when the bleeding started. Ears, nose, mouth, anus. When multiple organ failure or hypovolemic shock showed up to put you out of your misery, it came as a relief.

But the process wasn't instantaneous. Far from it. The virus took its time to take up residence in your body, secreting itself in your cells, lying in wait, giving you plenty of time to think about what lay ahead. And, as he stared at Richard's upside-down features, unyielding behind the bio-suit, Stafford swore he could feel the Ebola variant dispersing through his body, hunkering down before it began its assault.

'Give me the vaccine, Richard,' he begged.

'Give me one good reason why I should.'

'You're a doctor. You've taken an oath!'

'That's true. I did. But I need something from you in return.'

'Anything. Name it. Listen, if this works, Meditech could be the first trillion-dollar biotechnology company. I'll double your stock options. Treble them. Just name a figure.'

'I don't want money. I want you to go public on how you brought these people' — he gestured round the room at Mareta and her companions — 'into our country to use them like animals, and put the lives of millions of Americans in jeopardy, all so you could step out of your family's shadow.'

'Of course, of course. That won't be a problem. Soon as I get that vaccine.'

'No. Confession first, then absolution.'

'But this stuff is already in me! The longer it takes for the vaccine to be administered the less likely my chances of recovery! You know that!'

'Then we'd better move fast, hadn't we?'

★ ★ ★

Behind the screen, Mareta was getting twitchy. Since she was wired to enough explosives to take them all with her, Lock figured twitchy was bad.

'What are they talking about?' she asked.

'I'll go find out.'

When he was halfway to the door it opened, and Richard emerged. He took off the helmet section of the bio-suit. Face flushed, he swiped at a curl of hair pinned flat to his forehead by sweat. 'I've given him an ultimatum. He's going to confess on live television.'

'What was the ultimatum?' Lock asked.

'I just injected him with the Ebola virus. He keeps his part of the deal and he gets the vaccine.'

'And how do you propose we get someone who's a live carrier on the tube?'

'Your friend's a reporter.'

349

'No chance. Way too risky. Carrie's not setting foot in here.'

'But this way people will know the truth.'

'The truth? The truth is that someone importing terrorists to use as guinea pigs in a drugs trial aimed at neutralizing their biological capabilities would get a ticker-tape parade in every state in the nation.'

'Excepting maybe Vermont,' interjected Ty. 'They're commies.'

Mareta clapped her hands together. 'Enough. I didn't ask to plead for my life. But this new method' — she turned to Richard — 'this I like. Bring in the next test subject, give him the live agent too. Then we see if this vaccine really works.'

81

Mareta sat in a chair, her bad leg propped up on the control desk. Both the Van Stratens and all the former guards who remained had been given the Ebola variant and returned to their cells. Mareta had decreed that an hour should elapse before they were given the vaccine. Nicholas Van Straten, having received both vaccine and agent, would act as some kind of mid-point control, with Lock and the former detainees at the other end of the spectrum. Only Richard, Ty and Mareta were wholly unsullied.

'Should have brought some playing cards,' Ty said, to no one in particular, as they watched the security monitors suddenly go blank.

Khalid, who was sat next to the control desk, experimentally tapped one of the screens, first with his hand and then with the business end of an M-16.

'Hey, Fonzarelli, that won't work. They've cut the power,' said Lock.

Mareta shrugged, unfazed. A second later, the lights went out. The darkness was total. Then the beam of a Maglite search lit everyone's face, bar Mareta's.

There was a staccato exchange between Mareta and Khalid, then the light went out again and the door slammed.

'Who's here?' Lock asked, moving two paces right.

'Yo!' Ty shouted.

'I am,' said Richard.

'OK, Ty and Richard. Anyone else?'

Nothing. He listened again, the darkness blanketing them in paranoia.

'Have they gone?' It was Richard asking.

The answer came as another flashlight beam emanated from the control desk. Khalid was shining the light straight at Lock.

'Listen, we can't stay here. You understand?'

Khalid didn't answer. He probably didn't speak English, although given Mareta's record Lock was taking no chances.

'If you understand us, Khalid, say something, you dumb-ass mother-loving camel molester,' Ty said.

Nope. Not even a guy who'd picked up a few key phrases from rap records.

'Don't think he speaks English, Ryan.'

'Thanks for clarifying that for me, Tyrone.'

'Welcome. You still armed?'

'Yeah.'

'Me too. Homeboy's outnumbered.'

'That's what I was thinking. Richard?'

'Yes?'

'You ever play murder in the dark when you were a kid?'

'Sometimes with my cousins. They always won.'

Great, Lock thought.

'OK, in a moment I need you to move. Make some noise doing it. And stay low.'

'I can't.'

'How come?'

'I'm scared.'

'Would it help if I told you I am too?'

'Not really.'

The chatter of light-arms fire struck up outside. Then the boom of what Lock guessed was a thunder flash going off. Or some spare C4. Whatever it was, it sure as hell wasn't the sound of the President putting pen to paper on any guarantees.

Richard's voice: 'Lock?'

'Yeah?'

'I'm ready now.'

'OK, in your own time.'

Richard's chair skittered across the floor. The beam snapped from Lock's face and to his right. Where Khalid should have found Richard, there was only glass.

Lock made his move, launching himself across the room on the line Khalid had established a moment ago with the Mini-Mag. It was as existential a moment as stepping off a cliff.

Lock caught the butt of the M-16 with his stomach, but his momentum carried him forward, tipping Khalid from his chair. A starburst of light broke in front of him as he caught the butt again, this time on the face. He tried not to fall back, to stay as close as he could. He drew back his right hand and short-punched Khalid, glancing off a jut of bone and finding what he guessed from the sudden wheezing was windpipe. Then he did it again, and again, until the wheezing gave way entirely.

He rolled off Khalid's limp body, and grabbed the Maglite. He used it to locate the M-16,

353

which had spun away a short distance. He kept the light moving, finding Ty gun-facing him and Richard huddled into a ball in the corner of the room.

Richard peered out from between his fingers as the wave of a blast rolled through the room from outside. Mareta? Lock doubted it. You didn't walk out of all the situations she had just to go meekly to God when there was a chance of escape.

Lock crossed the room and helped Richard to his feet. He clapped him on the back. 'You did good. Now, let's get out of here.'

'Wait.' Richard crossed to where Lock was. 'Give me that,' he said, taking the flashlight. He shone it on Khalid, who was laid out on the floor. 'Is he dead?'

'I very much hope so,' said Lock. 'Now, let's move.'

82

Too soon. The words had clambered into his mind and refused to vacate. It wasn't that he'd die alone. Or in agony. No, the worst thing about how this had turned out, the ultimate ignominy, was that he'd die a footnote.

Then, with a loud thump that shook the walls either side of him, he was given a sign that maybe all was not lost. The light went out. A puff of dust caught at the back of his throat, and he coughed. More powder sucked into his nostrils.

He lowered himself down on to the floor and crawled to where he thought the door might be as another explosion shook the concrete floor. His hand slid out from under him and he fell, face first.

He took a moment to right himself, then started to edge along again, using his fingertips to navigate. Cold metal. The door.

He felt his way to its edge. It was at an angle. He could get his hand round the side of it. More than his hand. His arm. Both arms.

He squeezed his way through and into the corridor. The dust had begun to settle back to ground level. The door at the far end was open, light seeping in.

Tentatively, he got to his feet. The door next to his cell had been damaged too, wrenched away from its frame. He pushed at it, and it fell in. He almost fell in after it.

He could make out a man lying on the bed. Stafford Van Straten stepped through and stared down at his father. Two deep cuts bisected the old man's face in a bloody cross.

'Stafford?'

His father reached out a hand, but Stafford chose not to see it.

'The vaccine. You have to find the vaccine,' he whispered.

'And then what?'

Nicholas tried to raise his head, but the effort was too much. 'If you don't, you'll die.'

'Die in prison, don't you mean?'

He watched as his father tried to wipe away the blood seeping down into his right eye. 'Then get out of here.'

'Like a coward?' Stafford spat. 'Prove once and for all what a screw-up I am?'

'What are you talking about?'

'You'll never understand, will you? This isn't about money. It was never about money.' Stafford fell to his knees so that he was at eye level with his father. Outside, he could hear small-arms fire still echoing round the compound. 'This is about history, and our family's place in it. *My* place in it.'

83

Caffrey had just dug a plastic fork into his Holy Molē burrito when he saw the woman struggling towards him, a crutch under one arm, a cooler in her other hand. 'Shit.'

He stepped from his cruiser, drew his weapon, an old-school stainless-steel Smith and Wesson 64 revolver, and levelled it at the centre of her chest. 'Stop right there.'

She kept coming.

He'd heard something at one of the briefings about a woman. He knew she was foreign. Someone had said something about her not speaking English. Or was it that she could speak it? Damn. He should have been paying more attention, instead of texting one of his patrol guys to swing by Burritoville.

'Lady, stop right there.'

He looked around for back-up but everyone seemed to be pouring, like flies to shit, through the gates towards the buildings.

Still she kept coming. Utterly calm. No sign on her face that she even saw his gun.

A woman. Fresh off the boat. Who maybe didn't understand what he was saying.

Then she stopped. Maybe ten feet from him. Maybe less. Never breaking eye contact. Never looking at his gun. Tuning it out.

'OK, that's good. Now, stay there and don't move.'

But move she did, placing the cooler on the ground. One hand reaching across her chest.

'I said, don't move.'

She was wearing a padded man's ski jacket, or at least that was what it looked like to Caffrey. Her hand wrenched at the zipper.

He'd have to wait to see a weapon. Couldn't shoot someone for unzipping their jacket.

'OK, that's far enough.'

She kept going, yanking the zipper free at the bottom.

'Lady, I don't have time for games.'

'Neither do we.' A man stepped from the shadows. White. A young guy. Covered in a thin layer of grey dust that made him look like one of those human statue guys who hung out in Midtown making money from tourists. 'Go ahead,' he said. 'Show him.'

Slowly, deliberately, the woman pulled the jacket to one side, and the hand holding Caffrey's gun stopped working. The Smith and Wesson tumbled to the ground.

Twenty-four years of jumpers, jackers, slashers, stoners, rapists, recidivists, baby killers and crackheads. Twenty-four years of witnessing what was very often the lowest point in someone's life. Over and over again. A never-ending loop of human failing, which occasionally seeped into evil. Caffrey was sure he had seen, smelled, tasted, heard, touched and, yeah, even sensed it all. But this, this went way further.

She held the jacket open with a stage magician's flourish and Caffrey stood there, half expecting her to take a bow. But all that happened was that the guy who was standing behind her ran forward to retrieve Caffrey's service revolver.

Still transfixed, Caffrey didn't try to stop him.

'You have a cell phone?'

'What?' said Caffrey.

The guy pointed the gun at Caffrey. Caffrey barely registered it.

'Do you have a cell phone?' the guy asked again.

'In the car.'

'Go get it,' he instructed. 'I need the number.'

84

Smoke rose from every building in the compound. In two, fires still burned, the foam pumped into them by fire crews wearing respirators and bio-suits seemingly doing little to dampen the flames. Between buildings, bodies lay scattered. The detainees had put in a good shift resisting the assault, taking with them at least half a dozen JTTF and other personnel.

In the Center for Disease Control trailer, Lock was losing patience as he waited for his test results. 'How many times? Right now I might be one of the safest people in America.'

His pleas cut no ice. There was procedure, and it was going to be followed. Outside he could hear the chatter on the radios was accelerating rather than diminishing. Not a good sign after an assault. Then, as one of the CDC techs made her final checks, he heard Ty giving someone some serious shit right outside the door.

'You lost her? You assholes!'

That was it. Lock was on his feet and out, brushing aside the thick-necked twat on the door with an open palm.

The guy followed him out, drawing his weapon. 'Sir, step back inside.'

'I've met meter maids that were more intimidating than you, bud, so put away the pistol while your hands still work.'

The confrontation was cut short by the CDC

360

tech. 'It's OK, Brad, he's clear.'

Lock joined Ty. 'The Ghost done it again?'

'Looking that way.'

Lock glanced back to the smouldering ruins as an NYPD Bomb Squad bulldozer trundled past them. 'Hell, she's probably halfway to South America with what's left of the family fortune by now. What about everyone else?'

'Richard's safe, back with his boy. Hey, we did what we set out to. Just have to tie up the loose end.'

'I'd say that crazy bitch rigged to two kilos of C4 is more than a loose end.'

'She's Chechen. Thought they had a beef with the Russians, not us.'

'They didn't, until now,' said Frisk, coming up fast behind them. 'And she's not the only thing that's unaccounted for.'

'Care to elaborate?'

'The entire stock of Ebola variant's gone too.'

85

High above the Manhattan skyline, night-time and a set of rolling winter clouds rendered four Air Force F-15s invisible as they threw a wide loop around the island. Below, the skies were empty, save for the NYPD's fleet of seven choppers which buzzed briskly around Midtown. All other commercial aircraft had been grounded, Kennedy closed; ditto La Guardia and Newark.

Beneath them, the chopper pilots could trace a red pulse of brake lights snaking along the full length of the Brooklyn, Manhattan and Williamsburg Bridges. Sitting next to the pilots, sharpshooters, ready to dispense retribution from on high, checked and re-checked their weapons, waiting for the call.

The same red points could be glimpsed in the far distance on the Queensboro Bridge, and at the entrance to the Queens Midtown Tunnel. On the other side of the island the traffic waiting to enter the Lincoln Tunnel seemed to back up all the way to some distant New Jersey exit ramp even Springsteen hadn't heard of.

From up in the gods, the city seemed to be enjoying a sudden spike in popularity at the very moment it had finally maxed out its capacity to contain any more human beings. The sky, finally, appeared to have a limit.

Underground was a different reality. Four

362

hundred passengers sat in the carriages of the A-Train, and didn't move. Tense. Silent. Further down the track, people being ushered from the platforms and back out on to the street. Iron grilles being pulled across. The city's veins snapping shut one by one.

It was the same story with the Holland Tunnel. Same story with every tunnel leading into the city. Car engines switched off. Angry drivers exchanging less than pleasantries with stony-faced cops.

'I got my daughter to pick up from a party. She called an hour ago. She was crying.'

'But my apartment's flooded. The super called me. I've had to drive here all the way from Maine.'

'What difference is it gonna make letting one car through, officer?'

Every plea, exhortation and bribe met with the same response. No dice. The city's closed. No one's getting in, and no one's getting out.

Manhattan's locked down.

86

'So who d'you think's gonna take the bragging rights?' asked Ty as the chopper cut low and left across the East River towards Manhattan.

'What the hell are you talking about? What bragging rights?' Lock asked, struggling to be heard above the thud of the rotor blades.

'Judgement Day, fool. The Jews think they're the lost tribe, right? And then you got the Protestants. They're the elect. Ditto the Catholics. Mormons think it's them. Muslims. Damn, wouldn't that be a kick in the nuts after all the shit they've pulled recently? Hindus? Can't see it myself. Jehovah's Witnesses? Hmm, done some hard lobbying. Gotta factor that in. Buddhists think they're gonna be coming back as butterflies or some shit. But it stands to reason, they can't all be right. Wanna know who my money's on?'

'Nation of Islam?'

'Nah, the hell with them, never been the same since they lost Farrakhan. My money's on the Irish.'

'Being Irish isn't a religion.'

'You try telling them that. No, something big as Judgement Day is gonna come down to dumb luck. And you don't get any dumber or luckier than the Irish.'

Ty sat back, apparently content with having slammed the world's main religions and the homeland of at least a tenth of the country's population in one burst.

Frisk swivelled round in his seat. 'Is he always like this?' he shouted to Lock.

'Unfortunately, yes. You get used to it.'

'Don't you think it's just a little disrespectful?'

Ty looked hurt. 'You think of a more appropriate time to ask this stuff, let me know. Oh, and before you get into any 9/11 guilt trip bullshit, I lost a brother in Tower Two.'

Ty's brother had been in the Fire Department, one of the guys who was walking up when everyone else was walking down. He and Ty had been close. Ty had joined the Marines in response, judging action more productive than mourning. Now, in the back of a chopper, flying into a city where any sensible person would have been flying out, Lock hoped history wasn't about to repeat itself.

'So can we return to the matter at hand?' Frisk said as the copter made its final approach to the landing pad.

'Let's,' said Lock, the pilot signalling for them to stay put for the next few seconds.

'If your hunch is right, and we haven't stopped her getting inside the cordon, she's going to head for where she can do the most collateral damage.'

'Which, in her head, is going to be here,' said Lock as they unbuckled, got out, and two JTTF snipers took their place.

Lock started towards the edge of the building, Ty on his shoulder, both clicking back into their respective roles of team leader and second-in-command.

'So how many people we got down there?' Lock asked, reaching a three-foot-high concrete plinth which demarcated roof from air.

'I'd ball-park it around eight hundred thousand.'

'No, not in the city, down in the square,' snapped Lock.

'Look for yourself if you don't believe me.'

Lock peered over, a sudden heart jolt almost taking him, head swimming, over the lip. Ty grabbed at Lock's jacket, pulling him back. Still Lock stared. Frisk wasn't lying. Times Square was crammed with a mass of humanity that stretched as far as the eye could see.

'What the hell are all these people doing here?'

Times Square was busy late at night, always had been, even after its sleazier residents had been pushed out, but this was insane. It wasn't just the sidewalks, every single inch was occupied.

Frisk gave him a puzzled look. 'You don't know?'

'That's why I'm asking.'

'You don't know what date it is?'

Lock didn't. And then, as he stared across at the gigantic crystal ball standing ready to descend from atop the One Times Square building, and the television gantries with their brown dots of celebrity presenters, alien from the masses even at this height, he did. He knew exactly what day it was. Or rather, what night.

'It's New Year's Eve.'

87

'How many people did you say again?'

The three men were standing on the concrete plinth, Ty with his hand poised behind Lock's back lest his friend suffer a blackout.

'In this immediate vicinity, we estimate eight hundred thousand,' said Frisk.

'Evacuation?' asked Ty.

'Not an option.'

'Why not?'

'You want to tell just short of a million folks we have one of the world's most notorious terrorists on the loose with a bunch of explosives strapped to her chest, go right ahead. We'd probably lose a few thousand in the crush alone.'

Lock knew that Frisk was right. This was every jihadist's wet dream made flesh. Perfect for a suicide attack. Lots and lots of people crammed into a small space. Beyond that there was infinite scope for the creation of panic. And, as Frisk had already pointed out, panic might just take out more people than the bomb. Although if Mareta was here somewhere and she did detonate the device, panic would prove an ideal secondary device.

'People are used to seeing this kind of law enforcement presence on New Year's Eve,' Frisk pointed out.

'What about closing the bridges and tunnels?'

'We've been as non-specific as possible and so

far the news people are helping us out with the embargo.'

Lock thought suddenly of Carrie. He flashed back to what Brand had said, how she'd been hit by an SUV, and how relieved he'd been when Ty told him that she was alive and well.

'You think Mareta's here?' Frisk asked.

Lock climbed back down off the plinth, then leaned over for one final look at the huddled masses below. 'Yeah, she's here,' he said, turning for the stairwell.

88

Soaked in sweat, Stafford clambered from the police cruiser, moved to the rear of the vehicle and flipped the trunk. He stepped back, Caffrey's revolver in hand, and waved for Mareta to get out.

She climbed out stiffly, her jacket riding up to reveal a cell phone clipped like a radio microphone to the back of her belt. Wires trailed from the phone up her back and out of sight.

'Date with destiny time, sweet cheeks.'

'I'm ready,' she told him.

'Say it with a bit more conviction, then. You sound like you don't want to cement your place in the history books. I thought that's what you people were all about.'

When he came across Mareta in the smoking ruins of the compound, having shaken off his armed escort, Stafford had quickly realized the secret of Mareta's success. She possessed the ability to embrace martyrdom in others, without welcoming the opportunity itself. The Ghost. Yeah, right. The Mother of all Cowards would have been more apt. Shock with none of the awe. This time, though, he was going to make sure that the Ghost went out with a bang.

Having somehow missed out on 'The Construction of Body-Borne IEDs 101' when he was at Dartmouth, Stafford was happy when he realized that Mareta had already done most of the hard work on his behalf. All that had remained for him to do was ice the cake and light the candles.

'You think your kids'll be waiting for you when you make it up there, Mareta?'

'Don't talk about my children,' she said, taking a step towards him.

He allowed the gun to drop to his side, moved back and pulled his BlackBerry from his pocket. A number was pre-dialled on the screen. His thumb hovered over the call button. 'Now, now, let's not be premature, shall we?'

He prodded her forward. Behind them, Caffrey lay slumped in the back seat of the cruiser, his mouth open, blood seeping from his eyes.

89

Lock had never known the members of the Fourth Estate so subdued. Even in the middle of a war zone the media could be relied on to leaven the darkest moments with a gallows humour to make the most cynical special ops soldier discover his inner sense of political correctness. This was different, though.

They'd convened in a broadcast unit, rigged to take up every separate camera feed. On air, the folks at home were viewing crowd shots from the previous year's festivities with colour commentary to match. No one had called in to complain. Either America was too toasted or the networks needed to find a new angle.

Lock sat next to Carrie and scanned the screens, occasionally prompting her to ask if a camera operator could take a closer look at an area of the crowd. Other than that, Lock was silent, focused. Concentrating on seeing rather than just looking. Men who did his job, and did it well, knew that most people walked around eyes open, wide asleep. They also knew it wasn't a luxury afforded to them.

Carrie reached over and touched his hand. He withdrew it with a word: 'Later.' Then, to soften the blow, 'OK?'

She sighed. 'OK.'

Down the gallery, Ty was taking a more robust approach with his supervising producer. 'No, that one, asshole. That one!'

Even a short time with Ty had left the producer, a man clearly more accustomed to being barker than barkee, watery-eyed and with a distinct quiver in his lower lip.

'Now, go in. Zoom, baby. Zoom.'

A moment later the subject of his interest turned to reveal a thick goatee perched above a prominent Adam's apple.

'Damn,' he groaned.

Frisk paced the length of carpet behind them. 'Any luck?'

Lock shook his head. 'At least when you're looking for a needle in a haystack, the haystack doesn't keep moving.'

A voice from further down the gallery: 'Those assholes.'

Heads rotated and eyes swivelled to a monitor at the far end, live feed of the revelry in Times Square. In the foreground the same frat boy correspondent whom Carrie had jousted with back at the Stokes/Van Straten press conference was on camera. At chest height a rolling banner of bad tidings: Major Security Breach at Bio-Terror Facility . . . Ebola Virus Missing . . . Times Square Believed Target.

The door opened, and a wall of perfume with more knock-down power than any bio-weapon preceded Gail Reindl into the trailer as cell phones chirped to life. 'OK, Carrie, cat's out of the bag, let's get you in front of that camera.'

As the TV people headed out, Lock's gaze fixed on the monitors as, slowly, the news began to filter through to the vast crowd. Cell phones jammed to their heads, some people were already on the move, heading out of the square, pushing their way if they had to. The collective result of so many individuals trying to break away from the crowd was to channel it in great funnels of humanity. They looked like plankton surging in every direction to escape an unseen predator.

Frisk stood behind him. 'Ah, shit.'

Then Lock spotted something. A closer shot of a small section of the crowd. A few isolated figures. Maybe two dozen. He got to his feet, trigger finger pressed to the screen. 'There. Top left edge of the frame. Get closer on her.'

One of the remaining techs whispered into his microphone, and the image reframed.

A few seconds later, the woman was caught in the centre of the frame. She was wearing a heavily padded ski jacket. Her hair was pulled back in a ponytail.

'Closer. The face. The face.'

The woman half turned, and from the screen, Mareta Yuzik stared back at them.

90

'Southeast corner of 41st and Broadway,' Frisk shouted as they bolted down Broadway, knocking aside anyone who didn't get out of their way fast enough.

Two blocks.

'We have men there now.'

'OK,' shouted Lock, already out of breath. 'They know the drill?'

Dealing with what was known in the trade as a BBIED, or body-borne improvised explosive device, was the same as dealing with a regular IED or any other type of bomb. Confirm. Clear. Cordon. Control. Except, with a bomb strapped to a human being, there was one hugely unpredictable variable involved: the human being.

The closer they got to the location, the stronger the current of people rushing in the other direction. From the snatched comments, it seemed like most of them didn't even know why they were running, except that everyone else was. Herd instinct kicking in.

A man was pushing his ten-year-old daughter in front of him. Ty saw her trip and go down under a flurry of feet. No one even looked down to see what or who they were standing on. Her father was dragged past her. Ty, with a Marine's determination, forced his way to her, elbows prominent. He pulled her back on to her feet, battered and bruised. She was crying. Shouting for her father to follow, he pulled her into a storefront doorway where they were reunited, and then ran on.

Lock had lost sight of Ty. And Frisk. But he was almost there. Not that he had to check any signs or get on his radio. He knew because the crowd was thinning out. And then, as if he'd pushed through a paper wall, he was standing in the middle of clear street.

The woman stood with her back to him. A blue line encircled her, weapons drawn. A couple had ballistic shields, most didn't.

'Mareta?'

The woman turned round. It was her. She stared at Lock with a look that betrayed nothing. Not even whether she recognized him or not.

One of the men behind the shields shouted over to her. 'OK, hands up, where we can see them!'

Mareta complied, stretching her arms out, crucifix wide.

'OK, with your right hand, I want you to open your jacket.'

Slowly, taking her time, and with no sudden movements, her hand fell to the zipper and she started to lower it.

'What the hell is that?'

Ty and Frisk had caught up and were standing next to Lock. They could see the suicide belt, but at the front, tucked in among the shrapnel, were six stainless-steel vials. Whether they literally did or not, Lock could sense everyone around her taking one very big step back.

'You thinking what I'm thinking?' said Ty.

'Could be a bluff,' said Frisk, clutching.

'It's no bluff,' said Lock. 'How many people did Richard think that amount of bio-material could take out?'

'The whole city.'

The Bomb Squad officer continued with his instructions, only the occasional crack in his voice betraying him. 'OK, keep lowering that zipper. One hand. No sudden moves.'

The slider caught on one of the teeth. Mareta tugged down, freeing it, and pulled the slider all the way down to the box at the bottom. The jacket was open all the way.

'OK, now shrug the jacket off,' said the officer, stepping from behind his shield for a moment to mime what he wanted her to do.

She mirrored him perfectly. The jacket tumbled to the ground.

'Why's she cooperating?' asked Frisk.

'I don't know,' was all Lock could say.

Then his eyes fell to her waist.

'That's not good,' he said.

'What?' Frisk asked.

Clipped to her waist, and gaffer-taped in place, wires snaking up from it into the explosive charges, was a cell phone.

'The phone. Last time I saw her she had hand-held contact wires. Now there's a cell phone.'

'Which means — '

Lock hushed Ty with a raised hand. 'Frisk, who else was missing when you did your final tally back at the research facility?'

'We had one of the other detainees still outstanding, but we've located him.'

'Anyone else missing? Think.'

'Only Stafford Van Straten.'

91

Stafford pulled the BlackBerry from his pocket, thumbed across the screen to his address book, clicked it open and thumbed down again to a single name: Mareta.

Below it was another single-word entry: Nicholas. He thought about giving his father a final call. But what did he have to say to him other than goodbye? So the dark band on the screen stayed where it was, a click on the wheel away from history.

A call to the phone clipped to Mareta's belt and everyone within a half-block radius would be toast. Those not killed by blast wave or shrapnel would be the lucky ones. The vials packed round her would spread the Ebola variant far and wide, open wounds ensuring effective and deadly transfer of the virus into the survivors. Who knew how many might die in the end? Ten thousand? A hundred thousand? A cool million? He smiled. Enough for him to be remembered.

Stafford was steeling himself, his thumb a tenth of an inch from pressing down on the wheel of the BlackBerry, when the screen lit up with an incoming call.

'Yo, Staff. It's Tyrone.'

'I can just hang up on you, Tyrone.'

'I know you can, Staff. But it's only going to take one clean shot for us to end you.'

'Good luck with that. If you knew where I was, you'd have taken it already.'

'Good point. One more thing though, Staff. Lock and I never got a chance to discuss our severance package with the company.'

'Don't worry, I'll take care of that now,' said Stafford, terminating the call.

★ ★ ★

Lock was on the move, one hand on Mareta's shoulder, hustling her down the street towards the entrance of the subway a half block away. A small crowd of people were gathered at the top of the steps. Some moved, others just stared as Lock barrelled towards them, pushing Mareta ahead of him.

Some assumed she was injured and he was trying to get her to safety, but one woman caught sight of the rig around Mareta's chest and started screaming. 'Oh my God! It's a bomb! She has a bomb!'

Lock shut out all of them, his vision blurred and narrow. He was way too tired to breathe it clear. A jolt, a fall, and the belt could detonate. No need for the cell to trigger it.

'Get out of the way!'

★ ★ ★

Stafford speed-walked parallel to the subway, people running past him in the opposite direction, no one sure of where they should be,

379

the situation unfolding fast enough to make panic total.

He could see Lock pushing through the people clustered near the entrance to the subway. Maybe a hundred of them, the timing perfect.

Stafford had the BlackBerry in the palm of his hand. The whole city, for that matter.

'Coming through!'

Stafford looked up a second too late to avoid being shouldered out of the way by a thick-necked Guido in a satin Giants jacket with matching ball cap.

He regained his balance, clicked down on the wheel. A second for the screen to read *Calling Mareta*.

* * *

Lock raised his Sig, and pushed Mareta behind him. Wrenching open the shutter blocking the turnstiles, he pushed Mareta on and through the safety barrier, a lone transit worker's complaints quelled by the sight of the gun.

Down some steps. Towards the platform. Each step taking them deeper into the earth. Deeper and, he hoped, safer.

* * *

Caller is out of coverage area.

Stafford resisted the temptation to dash the BlackBerry on the sidewalk. Instead, he took off for the subway entrance.

On to the platform. Lock stopped to catch his breath. The irony suddenly hit him. He was now the bodyguard of a suicide bomber. That was one for the résumé. If he lived.

A tunnel either end of the platform. Deeper into the bowels. Safer. No coverage in the tunnels. He took a big gulp of air and propelled Mareta down the platform towards it, away from the steps.

★ ★ ★

Stafford had it figured. Plan B. He didn't need to call the cell. They needed one clear shot? So did he. A single round to anywhere on Mareta's chest would do the trick.

He was at the top of the steps now. A middle-aged woman in a Transit Authority uniform stood at the bottom, unbelievably having to repel a knot of people headed down into the subway, New Yorkers' sense of entitlement and an open gate having done the trick. 'Folks, step back. The subway isn't open.'

A fat man in a suit asking, 'So why's the gate like that?'

Stafford edged his way through the crowd.

The woman lowered her arm across his chest. 'Subway's closed.'

Stafford produced Caffrey's revolver, shot her in the head at point-blank range, then vaulted the turnstile. Screams filled the air, followed by a mad rush to regain the street. Looking back,

Stafford saw Ty taking the main entrance steps three at a time, gun drawn, looking ready to dish out his very own severance package. Stafford kept running.

* * *

The end of the platform for Lock and Mareta. The reek of stale urine and a single rat splayed dead between the rails.

'What happens if I live?' Mareta asked.

Lock had no energy to lie. 'You die in jail.'

Mareta's hand went up and she broke free, jumping down on to the track. The electrified rail was inches from her feet. Lock's heart shuddered almost to a halt as she reached down, half lifted her injured leg over it and kept going.

Lock jumped down after her, losing his footing in a slick brown puddle of water. By now Mareta was pulling herself up on to the other side with a grunt. Stranded between the uptown and downtown tracks, Lock heard a clatter of feet down the steps at the far end of the platform. Then Stafford Van Straten appeared.

Hidden from Ty but visible to Lock, Stafford ducked behind one of the grimy white-tiled pillars.

Stafford saw Mareta on the other side of the platform and raised the stainless-steel revolver, tracking her with metal sights. Best shot in the ROTC. Four years straight.

Lock raised his Sig, punched it out with his right hand towards Stafford. He didn't track. He didn't have to. All he had to do was pull the trigger.

The round caught Stafford in the face, pulling up through his right cheek before carrying on through his back teeth, splintering enamel and root, then moving up through his cheekbone and out.

Before Stafford hit the ground, before the revolver clattered on to the platform, Lock gave him the good news twice more.

Tap. One in the throat — a hint of luck to that shot. Lock in the zone.

Tap. A final round in the sternum.

As Ty's boots hit the platform, Stafford Van Straten's dead body met concrete.

Mareta had taken off, running back towards the steps. Lock made to go after her, signalling to Ty to go the other way and catch her coming out the other side.

As Lock struggled to climb up off the tracks there was suddenly a hundred yards of platform between them, Mareta limping the whole way but somehow finding speed. The air ahead raged black in Lock's eyes. His body calling time. Too much time spent on red alert.

Ty shouting his name from what seemed like a million miles away. Confusion. His mind willing his body to work. Willing itself to explain what was happening to him. The vaccine. The bomb. A flip book of possibilities.

Then, a sudden change of direction from Mareta. Away from the steps. Away from the light. Towards the tunnel at the other end of the platform. Lock snapping back inside himself, inside the zone, as Mareta disappeared into the maw of darkness.

Determined to stop the Ghost from performing one last vanishing act, Lock ran down the track.

92

A hand clamped down on to Lock's shoulder. He spun round.

'Chill,' said Ty. 'It's me.'

'You see her?'

'Can't see shit down here. Got some good news, though.'

'Oh yeah?'

'They've switched off the juice to the third rail and we've got JTTF making a push on up from 34th Street. She's got nowhere to go.'

'Remember who we're dealing with here. You got a flashlight?'

'Yeah. Hang on.'

Ty pulled a Mini-Mag from his belt and rotated the end ring. He shone it down the tunnel, but the beam died ten yards out.

'Have to do,' said Lock, with a complete lack of conviction.

Ty lowered the beam so the light pooled at their feet, just enough so they could pick their way over the rails and assorted debris.

Lock glanced back over his shoulder as voices echoed behind them. Reinforcements. Four Transit Authority cops. No bio-suits. Their courage not in question, their judgement less so.

The beam from one of their flashlights caught Lock flush in the eyes. He put his hand up. The cop on point motioned to his colleague to lower it. 'Jesus, put that damn thing down.'

Ty jogged back to liaise. 'You guys should have bio-suits on if you're gonna be down here.'

'Yours must be invisible,' said the cop with the flashlight.

'Our situation's a little different.'

'How so?'

'We've both already been exposed,' Ty told them.

Two of the cops took a step back. The cop with the flashlight made a point of standing his ground. 'We had a fellow officer killed tonight,' he said, his voice cracking.

'All the more reason to let us do this right,' Ty responded.

One of the flashlight cop's colleagues started to pull him away. 'Let's go.'

The flashlight cop shrugged him off, slowly raising the beam of light and angling it past Lock. 'So if everyone down here should be in bio-suits, maybe you and your buddy should tell all those people.'

Ty spun back round and tracked the light all the way to where it dead-ended, illuminating a subway train packed with people.

93

Six cars. Each with a total capacity of two hundred and forty-six people. Plus a driver. Even allowing for it being two-thirds full, a low-ball figure on New Year's Eve, that made a thousand people. All underground, in the dark, with Mareta lurking in the shadows giving a whole new meaning to the term Ghost Train.

Lock inched his way towards the side of the first car. It was crammed. Faces distorted against the glass of the carriage window; some terrified, others expectant, most stoic. Lock figured the stoic ones as native New Yorkers. The four cops Lock had asked to hang back and establish a cordon in case Mareta tried to slip past them edged their way up again as Lock reached the rear car.

'We need to get these people out of here,' said one of them.

'No shit, Sherlock,' muttered Lock, waving Ty round to join him from the other side of the final car.

'She's deep in the cut, if she's even in there at all,' said Ty.

Lock looked from the cars back to the Transit cops. 'We got any more trains on this stretch?'

'Just this one.'

He closed his eyes for a moment, thought back to what Mareta had told him in the cell when he'd probed her about her ability to escape

387

detection, even when the odds seemed impossible. She couldn't walk through walls, he knew that. But somehow she did.

When they look low, I stay high.

She hadn't meant it literally, he was sure of that. She'd worked out one simple fact: the art of escape lay in first understanding where your enemy would look.

'You OK?'

Ty's voice snapped Lock back into the present. The Transit cops were inspecting the train now. He let them get on with it and pulled Ty to one side. He lowered his voice so no one could hear. A moment later they broke their two-man huddle.

Lock walked back to the cops. 'Can I borrow your flashlight for a moment?' The Maglite Nazi handed it over like it was his firstborn, and Lock turned to the officer in charge. When he spoke he made sure it was loud enough that they could all hear. 'You're right, let's get the juice back on and move this puppy up back to the platform. But tell the driver to take it slow. She's in there somewhere. Has to be.'

As the lead cop jogged down to speak to the driver, Lock stayed close to Ty. 'Soon as it's stopped at 42nd Street, get the power shut down again.'

'Roger that.'

Lock directed Ty to walk alongside the lead car while he crouched down next to the southbound tracks. From there he'd get a good view of the underside of the cars as they rolled past.

A few minutes later six hundred volts of direct current passed back through the third rail with a fizz, and the lights inside the cars flickered to life.

As soon as the last car had trundled slowly past, Lock made a point of following it back in the direction of the platform, catching up so that he was parallel with the third car. Two hundred yards up the track he switched off the Maglite. A hundred yards after that, he stepped into a service alcove abutting the tunnel wall, out of sight. Then he waited.

Hours of boredom, moments of terror. That was the job. But where bad bodyguards focused only on what to do during the moments of terror, a good bodyguard realized the real work was done during the hours of boredom. Lock cultivated the ability to stay switched on. To look and see. Not just to listen, but also to hear.

Up the tracks he could hear the passengers disembarking the train and the orders from a swarm of JTTF agents who'd joined the Transit Authority.

'Stay where you are.'

'Place your hands above your heads.'

'OK, now you can move forward.'

That's what he could hear. But it wasn't what he was listening for.

Ten minutes passed. His eyes began to adjust to the darkness as the molecules of rhodopsin in the rods of his eyes metamorphosed, allowing him to discern the space around him.

Then came Ty's voice. Plenty loud so Lock could hear it: 'Hey, Frisk, the juice off now?'

Frisk exasperated: 'I just told you it was.'

'Didn't hear you.'

Lock's right hand tightened round the butt of his Sig. Soon she'd make her move. She had to. Once all the cars were searched and they realized she wasn't there, they'd come pouring down the tunnel. More men. Dozens of them. Hundreds, maybe.

Lock moved carefully, crossed his left hand across his body so that the Maglite rested on top of the barrel of his Sig. He pushed away thoughts of what was at stake. The lives that could be lost. Hundreds of thousands, potentially. Dismissing it from his mind proved a whole lot easier than he would have thought.

One guy jumping to his death from a burning skyscraper horrifies. A million people starving to death seems like what it is, a number.

The only number that mattered now was two. Him. And her.

He settled his breathing. Filtered out the noise from the platform. Stopped listening. Tried to hear.

And then it came. A scraping sound. A rat, perhaps. Again, this time louder, more distinct, more like someone hauling a garbage bag through a pile of wet leaves. Mareta. He closed his eyes, focused on the direction.

It sounded close. He could hear her breathing. She must have been no further than fifty feet from him this whole time.

He swivelled round in one movement. The noise came again. Far as he could tell she was moving down the tunnel, away from 42nd Street.

He centred himself, and clicked on the torch, catching wet, grey-black wall. He lowered the beam to what he guessed would be head height and swept left.

Mareta blinked back at him.

'It's over, Mareta,' said Lock.

Her pupils fell away to dots. She managed a smile. Weak and unconvincing. 'It's never over.'

'This time it is,' he said, stepping out towards her, the cone of light spreading to the edge of her face as he got closer.

'Don't you remember what I said?'

'All of it.'

'And about death being an escape?'

A rustle of fabric. He didn't need to lower the beam to her hands to know she was reaching down for the metal contacts which would trigger the explosive bound around her torso. She'd used her time in the tunnel well, re-rigging the detonator attached to the cell phone so that it once again linked to those hand-held contacts.

'There's no escape this time, Mareta.'

He lowered the beam of the torch to her stomach. Her left hand was rigid by her side, the contact wire pinched between index finger and thumb. Her right hand was clenched into a fist, inching its way down to retrieve the other contact wire which dangled from her waist.

'Stop,' Lock said, the Sig trained on her.

She complied.

'OK, that hand there' — he nudged the centre

of the beam at her right hand — 'bring it up again.'

She began to raise it, away from the wire, her fist still bunched, hard enough that her knuckles showed white. Then, as her right hand came level with her shoulder, suddenly she whipped her arm back, and up. A sudden flash of steel as she launched the knife hidden in her hand at Lock.

The burst of light reflecting off the whirling blade proved enough to put him off as he took aim. His shot cannoned high and wide as the blade found its target, embedding itself high in his chest, a few inches in from his left shoulder.

Lock stumbled forward and fell, the knife thumping in an inch deeper as he hit the tracks, the Maglite rolling from his grasp.

He felt his grip on the Sig weaken. The pain in his chest was intense. Each pulse of agony stronger than the last.

The gunshot brought shouts from both ends of the tunnel. He picked out Ty first.

'Ryan?'

He could hear the fear in Ty's voice when the echo of the question met with no reply.

'Ryan!'

The cavalry was on its way. Lock felt it. But it was nowhere near close enough to save him now.

He heard Mareta step towards him, looked up just in time to catch her right foot square in his face. His neck juddered back.

'Why don't we escape together?' she said, her

right hand fumbling for the other metal contact wire.

'Ryan!'

Ty's voice again, one among many. Lock wondered why it sounded more distant when Ty had to be getting closer.

Lock tightened his grip around the butt of the Sig as Mareta's hand went lower, then suddenly reappeared with the other contact wire. Inches between the two wires now. The circuit almost complete.

He took a breath and tilted his gun wrist up as far as the joint would take it.

His finger forced the trigger.

The recoil jolted down his arm so hard that tears sprang in his eyes from the pain that spread across his chest.

The round caught Mareta square in the face, obliterating her nose, cartilage splintering across her cheeks. She rocked backwards on the balls of her feet, her arms splaying out to the side as she tried to regain her balance.

She fell on to her back and lay there. No flailing. No death throes. Arms outstretched, and legs together, in a curiously Christlike pose.

Ty was first to her. He took no chances, firing once into her forehead then once through the bottom of her throat, the angle of the bullet enough to sever the top of her spinal column but stay clear of any explosives. With grim satisfaction, he turned to Lock.

Lock pushed himself slowly to his feet. Ty did his best to push him back down.

'Help me up, you asshole,' Lock grunted.

'You're hurt.'

'Yeah, and you're ugly.'

Ty pulled Lock to a standing position as JTTF agents swarmed in all directions.

'Back the hell up, for Chrissakes! Let the bomb unit guys through!' Frisk shouted.

Ty regarded Mareta's corpse without a hint of emotion. 'Pretty smooth wet work.' Then he saw the colour dissolve from Lock's face. 'Dude, you need some attention. I can live with ugly, but you're gonna struggle with that shiv sticking out of you.'

Lock held on to his friend for support. 'One more thing to do.'

'They're both dead,' said Ty, exasperated. 'We're done.'

Lock fixed his gaze back down the tunnel, towards the light. 'One final thing.'

★ ★ ★

'You don't come all this way on New Year's Eve and miss this, do you?' Lock asked Ty as both men stood in the centre of the triangle that formed Times Square.

Two paramedics hovered close by. Their repeated attempts to give Lock all but the most basic attention had earned them only a snarl and a demand for some morphine to tide him over. 'And not that weak-ass shit I had before.'

The ball descended in silence from a pole mounted on the One Times Square building. Save for law enforcement and other emergency personnel, the place was empty. Everyone

394

stopped what they were doing to watch its progress. As the mass of crystal reached the end of its journey, signalling the passing of one year and the birth of another, Lock slumped against Ty's shoulder, barely able to keep himself upright.

'Happy New Year, brother.'

Epilogue

At the edge of the group of mourners who had gathered for Janice Stokes' funeral, Lock spotted Carrie. No microphone, no camera, here only to pay witness to a life lived and lost. Nearby stood John Frisk and a couple of other agents from the JTTF.

As Janice's coffin was lowered into the ground next to her parents, he reached out and touched Carrie's hand.

She half turned, and smiled at him. 'They finally let you out then.'

'Got the all clear this morning,' Lock reassured her.

In truth, he'd spent most of the time since it all went down being briefed and debriefed by an array of government agencies. He'd quickly worked out the reason it was taking so long: they wanted to be assured of his silence on certain matters.

They needn't have worried. Bio-terrorism was as much about inducing fear as death, and the way Lock saw it, fear wasn't something people were short on. Not these days, anyway.

Carrie leaned into him. 'Is it OK if I . . . ?'

'Hundred per cent safe.'

She nestled her head in between his neck and shoulders, breathed in his smell, then kissed him gently on the lips. It made his heart thump inside his chest. Her hand fell into his.

He gave it a little squeeze and leaned in even closer to her. 'I'm not sure people are supposed to make out at funerals. It may be considered inappropriate.'

They turned back round to face the graveside, still holding hands. On the other side of the grave, Lock caught sight of Don Stokes, sandwiched between two burly correctional officers. Don acknowledged Lock with a nod, handcuffs precluding a wave.

Don had pleaded guilty to his part in the exhumation of Eleanor Van Straten and was looking at two years. Cody Parker was staring down five and assured martyrdom status.

Nicholas Van Straten hadn't made it, but the entire board of Meditech were under federal investigation and looking at the business end of twenty years in prison, corporate buccaneering now seen by the great American public for what it had been all along, high seas robbery.

There had been worldwide outrage at the use of the detainees. Middle Eastern countries in particular had had a field day, although Russia remained strangely silent. China didn't chip in either, figuring, with typical neo-communist efficiency, that here, finally, was a productive use for dissidents. Congress and the President spun it as proof positive of the greater need for federal regulation over private enterprise, and no one on Wall Street dared contradict them, for fear that lights would be shone into other areas.

'I gotta go say hello to a few people. You wait for me,' Lock said, excusing himself.

'I've waited this long, haven't I?' Carrie said,

brushing away a stray strand of blonde hair from her face.

Lock approached Frisk and put out his hand. Frisk looked like he wasn't sure whether to thank Lock or strangle him, so they kept it brief.

Don Stokes was being led back to a Department of Corrections truck when Lock caught up with him.

Lock glanced back at the grave. 'I'm sorry about your sister.'

'She stayed true to her beliefs.'

Lock didn't have anything in reply that wouldn't spark an argument. He was done with people. And their beliefs.

'How you dealing with prison?' he asked.

'It ain't as bad as you painted it.'

'Oh yeah?'

'It's worse.'

Lock was watching Don being put back in the DOC van when Carrie joined him at the bottom of the hill.

'So what now?' she asked him.

He turned to look at her. 'You tell me.'

★ ★ ★

Her apartment still felt like a home. When Carrie went into the kitchen and closed the door behind her he scanned the photographs in the living room. Paul hadn't made a reappearance. It was about the only thing that had truly preyed on his mind when he was in isolation.

Carrie called through from the kitchen. 'There's someone else here who's missed you.'

'You missed me?' Lock asked, unable to keep the smile from his face.

'Maybe just a little.'

He stepped through into the kitchen. Angel greeted him at the door, her tail a blur. Lock scratched behind her ear. She thumped one of her back legs against the floor by way of appreciation.

'What you been feeding her? She's put on weight,' he said, stepping back and taking a better look.

Carrie laughed. 'She's pregnant.'

Lock studied the dog. 'Guess you're not so much of an angel after all.'

'I spoke to Richard Hulme. Asked him if Josh might want the pick of the litter.'

'What'd he say?'

'He said he'd love one. They're moving out to Washington, and he's going back to work for the CDC.'

'It'll never work. Richard's got way too developed a sense of morality to work for the government.'

'I think it'll be good for him. And Josh. There are too many bad memories in that apartment of theirs.'

'Some pretty good memories in this one,' Lock said, looking around.

'What you thinking about, cowboy?'

'Ah, nothing, forget it.'

She handed him a steaming mug of coffee.

'Thanks.'

'I've been doing some thinking too,' Carrie said.

He could feel his heart jump back into his throat. 'Oh yeah?'

'I was thinking that maybe you'd like to stay here for a while. Look after the new arrivals when they get here.'

'You're asking me to provide close protection to a bunch of mutts?'

'So, what do you say?'

Lock wrapped his arms around her waist, and frowned. 'Guess it might keep me out of trouble.'

Acknowledgements

My thanks to:

Luigi Bonomi, for leading the kick-ass security advance party at LBA. Luigi is to agenting what Tiger Woods is to golf.

Steely-eyed dealer of death, Selina Walker, and the rest of the counter-attack team at Transworld, for their hard work, passion and commitment.

Rienk Tychon for beating everyone else to the punch, and Holger Kappel for showing such great taste.

Through the entire process, I have been surrounded by a personal escort section worthy of an unpopular head of state. Special thanks must go to Gregg Hurwitz for being such an inspiration, Andy Carmichael for instructing me in the black arts of the grey man, and all our family and friends on both sides of the Atlantic.

During the writing, Diesel headed my canine support unit, ably assisted by Angel (the world's least appropriately named Labrador), Dfor, Magic and Silver.

Finally, to my two-woman residential security team, Marta and Caitlin. I love you both so much.

We do hope that you have enjoyed reading this large print book.

Did you know that all of our titles are available for purchase?

We publish a wide range of high quality large print books including:
**Romances, Mysteries, Classics
General Fiction
Non Fiction and Westerns**

Special interest titles available in large print are:
**The Little Oxford Dictionary
Music Book
Song Book
Hymn Book
Service Book**

Also available from us courtesy of Oxford University Press:
**Young Readers' Dictionary
(large print edition)
Young Readers' Thesaurus
(large print edition)**

For further information or a free brochure, please contact us at:
**Ulverscroft Large Print Books Ltd.,
The Green, Bradgate Road, Anstey,
Leicester, LE7 7FU, England.
Tel:** (00 44) 0116 236 4325
Fax: (00 44) 0116 234 0205

THE UNWANTED

Brett Battles

The meeting place was carefully chosen: an abandoned church in rural Ireland just after dark. For Jonathan Quinn — a freelance operative and professional 'cleaner' — the job was only to observe. If his clean-up skills were needed, it would mean things had gone horribly wrong. But an assassin hidden in a tree assured just that. Suddenly Quinn had four dead bodies to dispose of and one astounding clue — to a mystery that was about to spin wildly out of control . . .

BOOK OF SOULS

Glenn Cooper

A shocking truth lies within the pages of an ancient library, locked inside a high-security complex beneath the Nevada desert. The US government intends to keep it classified. But a group of ex-employees want the world to know. When a single volume, missing from the original collection, surfaces at a London auction house they persuade former FBI agent Will Piper to obtain it and unlock the ultimate secret of the library. Will finds that the text holds clues, revealing that the book has had a profound effect on the history of mankind. But he's being watched. As Will nears the final revelation, he becomes a direct target for a deadly group — guardians of the library's secret. However, the truth is too powerful to keep hidden . . .

EVEN

Andrew Grant

David Trevellyan takes a late-night walk between a restaurant and his New York City hotel when he sees a huddled shape in the mouth of an alley. A homeless man has been shot dead. As David steps forward, a police car arrives and he realizes — he's been set up. A survivor of Royal Navy Intelligence, Trevellyan's been in and out of trouble before. But as the FBI take the case, he's sucked deeper into the system. He penetrates a huge international conspiracy, which spans from war-torn Iraq to the heart of the USA. Failure will mean death, but success will bring redemption — for himself and for the huddled corpse from the alley. His motivation is his life-long belief: you don't get mad — you get *even*.

LOVERS, THE

John Connolly

When Charlie Parker was still a boy, his father, a NYPD cop, killed a young couple. A boy and a girl barely older than his son. Then took his own life. There was no explanation for his actions . . . Stripped of his private investigator's license, and watched by the police, Parker is working in a Portland bar and staying out of trouble. But in the background, he is working on his most personal case yet, an investigation into his own origins and the circumstances surrounding the death of his father, Will. It is an investigation that will reveal a life haunted by lies, his father's betrayal, and by two figures in the shadows, with only one purpose: to bring an end to Charlie Parker's existence.

EVIDENCE

Jonathan Kellerman

In a half-built mansion in one of LA's glamorous neighbourhoods, the bodies of a young couple are found, murdered in flagrante and left in a gruesome post-mortem embrace. A grisly crime for veteran homicide cop Milo Sturgis and psychologist Alex Delaware to solve. The male victim was eco-friendly architect Desmond Backer, who disdained the sort of grandiose superstructure he's found dead in. Mr Backer was notorious for his seductive powers — the exception being his ex-boss, Helga Gemein. Milo and Alex's list of suspects grows ever longer, as the homicidal mix includes conspiracy, and a vendetta that runs deep. But the investigation veers in a startling direction — Alex and Milo end up on the wrong end of a cornered predator's final fury.

WHERE THE DEAD LAY

David Levien

Frank Behr's friend and mentor Aurelio Santos is brutally murdered and Behr wants answers and revenge. But then his old boss, captain of the Indiana police, pressures him into accepting a case from a private investigation firm. Two of its operatives have gone missing. Behr complies: his acceptance is key to his return to the force. The search for the missing detectives takes him into Indianapolis' criminal underworld, a place rife with shocking brutality and vice. He tries to discover what the connection is between the gambling rings operating there and the detectives' disappearance. Then, as Behr uncovers a thread connecting the detectives to his friend's brutal murder, he is forced to confront an ominous, deadly new breed of organized crime . . .